THE WITCHES OF WANDSWORTH

The Reverend Bernard Paltoquet Mystery series: Book 4

by

Pat Herbert

PROLOGUE

If you were out and about at six o'clock on a particular brisk, bright April morning in the early nineteen-fifties, you might have seen a mangy black cat slink its way past St Stephen's Parish Church in the London Borough of Wandsworth and make its way through the bars of the vicarage gate next door. If you had stopped to watch, you would have seen the formidable shape of the vicarage housekeeper loom out of the front door with a broom in her hand, ready to strike the trespassing feline should it have the temerity to venture further up the path.

However, if you weren't in the vicinity at that time, but sauntering across the Common a few streets away instead, you might have seen a sight of a much more disturbing nature. The body of a young girl, partially hidden by foliage and piles of newly mown grass, is seeping blood from a deep wound in her stomach. She is very, very dead.

"That bloody cat's been 'ere again, Vicar."

Reverend Bernard Paltoquet is sitting down to his breakfast as Mrs Harper imparts this piece of information to him.

Although Bernard is more interested in putting golden syrup on his porridge than learning about the antics of some stray cat, he doesn't say so. When his doughty housekeeper is in full flow on one of her rants, he has long since given up trying to get a word in edgeways.

"Really, Mrs Aitch? What did he want this time?" he asks vaguely, stirring his porridge.

"'E wants kicking, that's what 'e wants."

"He's probably hungry, poor thing. You must be able to find him some scraps. Couldn't we adopt him? I've always liked cats."

"Over my dead body," exclaims Mrs Harper, the porridge spoon poised precariously over Bernard's head as she doles out the oats. "I 'ate bloody cats!"

"Dear, dear, Mrs Aitch. Well we won't make an international incident of it, will we?"

Mrs Harper sniffs. "'Urry up with your porridge, as the bacon and eggs'll get cold," is all she says.

&

If you had walked past the vicarage while this interchange was going on and carried on down to the corner of the road and turned left, you might have entered a pretty crescent called Hallows Mead. If you'd carried on walking along this crescent, you would have eventually found yourself outside a very odd-looking dwelling called Appleby Cottage.

Its strangeness is mainly due to its lop-sided appearance, as if the builder was very drunk when he erected it, or the cottage itself has been squashed on one side by a large object from outer space. The windows are poky but sparklingly clean, as are the white net curtains hanging in them. But the most notable thing about the structure is its virtual invisibility to the naked eye. Indeed, if you were standing right outside it, you would need to look more than once to see that it is there at all.

This humble dwelling belongs to two equally strange and lopsided females. Vesna and Elvira Rowan are somewhat advanced in years and, like their squat, almost hidden home, keep themselves very much to themselves. However, far from leaving them alone, the local gossips are intrigued by their unintentional air of mystery. What have they got to hide? It is obvious, of course: they are witches.

With names like Vesna and Elvira, coupled with the surname of Rowan, what else can they be?

So, the legend has grown up around them. It doesn't help their case that both women look like witches. As far as the locals are concerned, they only need pointy hats and warts to confirm their witch status. These they don't have, but they dispense herbal remedies to those people gullible enough to believe in their efficacy. They are harmless infusions for the most part, but to those who take them, they are magic potions, easing their rheumatism or headaches like no preparatory medicines can. Most people, therefore, conclude they are right in their assumption that they are witches, the only doubt being whether they are white ones or black ones.

The sisters have shared the funny little cottage in Hallows Mead since just after the Great War when, as two sprightly twenty-somethings, they moved into the district from, again according to more local gossip, 'somewhere foreign'. Mrs Harper has often complained to Lucy Carter, the woman who serves as housekeeper to the local doctor, Robbie MacTavish, that they shouldn't be bringing their arty-farty foreign ways to the neighbourhood. Where will it all end? she asks. Will they be eating snails and dancing the fandango before long? Lucy shares the older woman's reservations about dodgy foreign ways.

But let us leave them to their gossip now and continue along Hallows Mead Crescent to the corner, cross over into Balaclava Terrace and turn left at the junction with Crimea Terrace into Marlborough Street. Just along on the right you'll see a friendly-looking house with a brass plate on the gate announcing, 'Doctor's Surgery'. This is where the local GP, Robbie MacTavish, sees his patients and, on the floor above, has his living quarters.

Robbie is a close friend of Bernard Paltoquet, the vicar we have already met. They have known each other for about six years, when both parties first moved into

7

Wandsworth. Inseparable almost from day one, Robbie and Bernard can be found most evenings ensconced in the vicarage study, playing chess, smoking their pipes and imbibing whiskey, should you have need to contact them for anything during those hours.

So, we have come more or less full circle and are back on the Common. When we passed by a short while ago, the body of the unknown young girl had yet to be discovered, but now there is a mass of people, among them, no doubt, all the gossips already mentioned. They are eagerly watching events unfold behind the blue police tape.

A makeshift tent has been erected to conceal the body from the public gaze. Inspector Philip Craddock and his oppo, Sergeant Brian Rathbone, are standing inside. The older man, Craddock, is now bending down and looking closely at the congealing wound in the girl's stomach, but the weapon which had inflicted it is nowhere to be seen. It is a case of cold-blooded murder.

PART ONE

The First World War and After

Chapter One

Vesna Rowan stared out of the window. Her tiny garret room overlooked a pleasant, well laid-out park. It was a sight she usually found uplifting, but today she just sighed as she surveyed the scene, cupping her hand under her chin. It had been a hot and sunny summer, and she had enjoyed her stay in Rouen, but her heart wasn't in it anymore. She had just found out that her fiancé had been shot as a deserter, many months after she had tried to trace his whereabouts at the end of the War. When everyone else had come home, all those brave boys who had managed to climb out of the trenches still alive, Vesna had received no news of her fiancé, Private Rodney Purbright. Then the letter from the War Office had finally arrived.

Her older sister, Elvira, wasn't so upset by the news. In fact, she almost welcomed it. She had never liked the man, and she was sure he was a coward. After all, hadn't he deliberately shot himself in the foot at the beginning of the War, hoping not to be sent back after recuperation? Vesna had protested vehemently at this. How dare she presume he had shot himself on purpose? There was absolutely no foundation for saying such a thing. Plain-faced Elvira was only jealous because pretty Vesna had a fiancé and she hadn't. At least, that was how Vesna saw it.

The last Vesna had heard of him had been in France in 1917, and so she and her somewhat reluctant sister had spent the last eighteen months in that country trying to trace him. But now that the War Office telegram had reached them, there was no reason to stay. Vesna's dream of finding her poor young man in some French hospital, identity unknown, was dashed. Her sister had been right, after all. He had been a coward all along. But he was so handsome, so how could he be?

"Come on, Vessie, we can't stay here much longer, can we?" Elvira had said. "We need to work. Our money won't last more than another couple of weeks."

Vesna had had to agree. She turned from the window now and glared at her sister as she entered the room.

"I've been thinking, love. I like it here. Maybe I could stay. Get a job," she said. "You can go back, if you want."

"I don't want to go back without you," said Elvira sullenly. "Besides, what work could you do here? You hardly speak the language, as it is."

"I speak it better than you," declared Vesna. "That nice man at the hotel offered me a job as a chambermaid the other day."

Elvira smirked. "You? Work as a chambermaid? Clear up after other people? That's a laugh. I've cleared up after you all your life. Since Mum died, anyway. When did you ever lift a finger?"

"You're just a bloody bore," replied Vesna. "The times you tell me that. Why should I be grateful for doing what any loving sister would do? I can't go on being beholden to you forever."

"I don't expect you to. I just expect you to be kind and considerate to me sometimes, that's all."

Elvira tried not to let her vain sister see how she had upset her. Yet again. She bit her lip as she felt tears smarting behind her eyes. Vesna just stared at her with contempt.

"You hated me having a boyfriend, didn't you? You resented my good fortune from the beginning. You were just jealous, and you did everything you could to thwart us. He was handsome, and he loved me, and you couldn't stand that, could you?"

Elvira looked down at the well-worn carpet. She knew in her heart of hearts that what her sister was saying was all too true. After all, her vivacious younger sibling had all the advantages she hadn't. What would become of her if Vesna got married and left her alone? She wasn't pretty enough to find a man of her own. It was fear of being alone that was driving her. Jealousy came into it, of course, but being alone worried her much more

She cleared her throat. "Look, Vessie, I don't want to argue with you. I'm sorry you feel like that. I – I only want you to be happy. But I want to be happy too. Don't I have a right?"

"Of course, but making me unhappy isn't the way to do it."

"Of course it isn't. I just want us to be together, like always. I don't want you to – leave me." Elvira admitted it at last and watched the expression on her sister's face.

"So that's it!" she exclaimed. "I thought as much." Her tone softened a little. "But, Elvie, I can't always think about you, can I? If a man wants to marry me, should I turn him down because you don't want to be alone? After all, you could get married too."

"You know that's impossible," said Elvira, turning from her sister and walking towards the door. "I have as much chance of getting married as flying to the moon. Have you noticed the men beating a path to my door? Well, then. Anyway, what's this about a 'nice man at the hotel'? What man? What hotel?"

Vesna drummed her fingers nonchalantly on the window sill. The sky had clouded over, and a few drops of rain had begun to fall.

"Oh, didn't I mention him before? He's the manager of l'Hôtel Grande Illusion in Sainte Michel Boulevard. I bumped into him when I was walking past one day last week, which made me drop my shopping. He helped me pick it up."

"I'm sure he did," said Elvira with just a hint of sarcasm in her tone. "So, what happened then? He offered you a job on the spot, I suppose?"

"Of course not! He asked me to tea in the hotel and we got talking. He asked me what my plans were and whether I would be staying long in Rouen."

"I see. So, what are you going to do?"

Vesna sighed. "Come home with you, of course," she said finally.

Chapter Two

The Rowan sisters returned to England in September 1920. Vesna had wavered about remaining in Rouen right up until they got on the train but finally decided that England was probably best. However, she made it clear to Elvira that she wasn't going back home to Bootle. After their mother's death from breast cancer just after the war had started, their father had taken up with some floozie whom he'd met in the pub, probably even before she had died. Now, by all accounts, he had made it legal, and she was ensconced in the family home, and both sisters agreed it was no place for them anymore.

Vesna declared she could get a job anywhere and suggested that London would be the best place. Elvira was sceptical but didn't much care where they went as long as they stayed together. So, after a protracted search for somewhere they could afford to live, they finally managed to secure a small cottage in the borough of Wandsworth at a reasonable rent.

Vesna soon found work in the local grocery store where her pretty face and friendly manner were well received by shop owner and customers alike. Meanwhile, Elvira stayed at home making the cottage as comfortable as she could for herself and her sister. Vesna paid the rent, so Elvira did the housework and the cooking. It was an arrangement that suited Vesna very well, but her plain, older sibling wasn't so happy. She wanted to be out in the world earning a living just like her sister. Instead, she was doomed to be tied to the home doing the housework and waiting on Vesna hand and foot. Elvira was sick and tired of it all.

The death of her fiancé had been a blow to Vesna, but she had soon recovered from it. Her blonde vivaciousness had caused a stir among the local menfolk, and she found herself the centre of much attention from them. Not so poor Elvira, whose dark, gaunt and lowering looks put them off straightaway. And, as they only ever saw her when in the company of her much prettier sister, the contrast was more obvious. She had long since given up all hope of marriage and having a family. Her sister was her only family now, but it was a bitter pill for her to swallow.

"Look, dear," she said to her sister on one of the rare evenings when Vesna wasn't going out with one of her beaux, "I need to do something more than just stay at home cooking and cleaning for you."

Vesna looked at her sister's sulky face and shrugged. "It's not just for me, though, is it? You have to eat as well, and I provide the means to do that as well as give us a roof over our heads."

There was no denying that, of course. "I know, love, but I need to do something more. I need to get out and meet people too."

"Well, what do you suggest? If I get married, you won't have to worry about me anymore, and then you can do what you like."

"But I won't have any money coming in, will I?"

"Then you can get a job, can't you?"

"But I'm not fit for anything, Vessie, you know that. I'm not exactly popular, am I? And men don't like me."

"You should make more of an effort," said Vesna sharply, who had been reading the latest novel from Boots' lending library and was resenting the interruption. It was a lovely story about forbidden passion and a little risqué in places. Right up her street.

"How? What do you suggest? You got all the looks and personality."

"Oh, stop feeling sorry for yourself," said Vesna, putting down her book at last and getting up to pace the room. "You're not that bad looking if you'd only use a bit of rouge and some lipstick. You don't make the most of yourself."

"Perhaps I don't, but I can't compete with you."

"Well, no, I admit that I'm much better looking than you," said Vesna, giving her an appraising look. "But women much plainer than you get married all the time. After all, most men out there aren't oil paintings either."

Elvira smiled grimly at this. It had never ceased to annoy her that, no matter how unprepossessing a man was, he would always assume he could chat up the prettiest girls and ignore the plainer ones. And it often worked. There were a lot of ugly men walking about with beautiful women on their arms, and it wasn't always just because they were rich.

"Anyway, Vessie, I've been thinking. You know those old herbal remedies that Granny left us the receipts of?"

"Those old things? I've no idea where they are," said Vesna.

"*I* do. I was wondering if I could make them up and open a little shop to sell them. What do you think?"

"That sounds a bit bonkers to me, Elvie love."

"I don't see why. If you could lend me the rent on a little shop, I'd soon be able to pay you back once I start selling the remedies. You must remember how good they were. They always seemed to work on us. Whenever we had an ache or a pain, Granny had a cure. I'm sure I could make a living out of them."

Vesna came and sat down next to her sister on the sofa and took her hand. "Dear old Elvie, you're mad but I love you."

"So, you don't think it's a good idea then?"

Vesna looked serious for a moment. "No, I'm not saying that. I don't honestly know. But, if that's what you want to do, then you should do it. I'll give you the money to set it up and if you make any profit, perhaps we can share it?"

Elvira almost felt like crying, she was so grateful. She hugged her sister warmly. She had never expected Vesna to agree and certainly did not expect her to cough up the money. Sometimes, but only sometimes, her sister gave her a pleasant surprise.

Chapter Three

It was a chill December afternoon a few months later, when Rodney Purbright wandered down Hallows Mead Crescent, Wandsworth for the first time, searching for a cottage called 'Appleby'. He studied the hastily scrawled piece of paper that Mr Rowan had given him. Yes, definitely 'Appleby'. He glanced up and down the pretty row of cottages, all with individual names like 'Rose', 'Michaelmas', 'Honeysuckle'; but he couldn't see 'Appleby' anywhere.

Then he finally noticed a rather squashed-looking little building in between two smarter properties and went up to it to get a better view of the name plate on the front door. He hoped this dump wasn't what he was looking for. One of the bigger cottages would have suited him much better. But, no, he was to be disappointed, yet again. Life had kicked him in the teeth so many times, he could hardly expect his luck to change now. And he was right. Appleby Cottage looked like it had been added to the street very much as an afterthought. At least it was a roof over his head, he supposed.

Elvira's little enterprise, with her sister's financial backing, had taken off surprisingly well. They had easily found a little shop in which to start selling their grandmother's herbal remedies and, in the space of a couple of months, the people of Wandsworth were swearing by their healing powers. Whether it was a headache, earache, backache or any other ache, you name it, Elvira Rowan, the proprietress, had a solution for them all. Some even said that she had given them cures for more serious illnesses, like measles, mumps and whooping cough. One old lady even declared that her cancer had receded through taking a special concoction made up especially for her by that forbidding-looking Rowan woman. Word spread fast after that, and Elvira was kept very busy dispensing her 'miracle' cures.

Meanwhile, Vesna was happy to be a 'sleeping partner' in the business. She was still content with her job at the grocery store which had even diversified into selling items of clothing and some ironmongery, which made it even more interesting. Added to which, her life outside her work was one long whirl of parties and dances, being taken hither and thither by this boy and that. Recently, however, she had settled on one special young man: Harry Banks, the darkly handsome son of the local butcher. She had succumbed to his charms one evening as he knelt before her, declaring his entirely honourable intentions, and they became engaged on the spot.

Private Rodney Purbright, ignorant of how life had moved on for Vesna Rowan, stood outside Appleby Cottage savouring the moment. Even if he had known, it would have made no difference to him. As far as he was concerned, their engagement still held good. He had come back from the dead to claim her.

His handsome face betrayed no vestige of his past indiscretions as he stood there. He was still as prepossessing as he had always looked, maybe even more so. His war experiences (those he hadn't been able to duck out of) had left no visible scar. He was tall and straight as an arrow, blond and athletic, a young man most women would fall for on the spot. Vesna would be no different. She would run into his arms when she saw him again, of that he had no doubt.

He opened the gate and walked up the garden path. On the threshold of Appleby Cottage, he stood poised with his finger over the doorbell. He was about to meet his lovely Vesna again after an absence of nearly three years, but what if that sour-faced sister of hers answered the door? So what, he thought. His plans didn't include that bitch, so she could say what she liked. He knew his Vesna. She loved him, had always loved him. That was all that mattered.

He wasn't getting any warmer standing on the doorstep, the sun having already set even though it was only four o'clock. He hesitated no longer and pressed the bell. He heard a hollow clanging sound echo through the little cottage. It seemed much too loud for the size of the place, almost threatening to relieve it of some of its brickwork.

After a few moments, Elvira Rowan opened the door. He watched with detached amusement as she collapsed against the wall, holding her chest. Serve the silly cow right, he thought. Must have come as a bit of a shock, seeing him large as life when she obviously assumed he was dead.

"Who is it?" came a voice from down the passage. "Are we expecting anybody? Harry's not coming till six."

Rodney gave Elvira his most devastating smile, the one that usually melted the hardest of hearts at twenty paces. But it had no effect on Elvira. She remained propped against the passage wall, with one hand on the front door knob, trying to get her breath.

"Hello, *Miss* Rowan," he said snidely, with an emphasis on the 'miss'. "Long time no see, eh? How are you?"

"Elvie! Who is it?" came the persistent voice from inside. "Invite whoever it is in or send them packing. You're letting in all the cold air."

Finally, Elvira found her voice. "Rodney!" she breathed. "What – who – what…"

"I know," he said cheerfully. "I've been gone a long time, haven't I? War does that to people. But you knew I'd always turn up again, didn't you? Like a bad penny."

"But – but … You're supposed to be dead…"

Rodney Purbright continued to smirk. "Not exactly a corpse, am I? Look, can I come in? As your lovely sister said, you're letting all the cold air in."

She stood to one side and cringed as he brushed past her into the narrow passage. "Wait," she said, grabbing him by the arm. "Let me break the news to Vessie first. It might come as a bit of a shock."

"Very well, of course," acquiesced Rodney Purbright. After all, he had all the time in the world now, hadn't he?

✍

"But how on Earth?" Vesna stared at her sister in astonishment.

"Don't ask me, love," said Elvira, sitting down beside her on the sofa. "He's out there in the hall, or it's his double."

"But he's supposed to be dead!"

"I know that, and you know that, but someone's not told him that, it would seem."

Vesna sighed. "I suppose I'd better see him?" she said, trying to remember what he looked like.

She was about to marry 'Handsome Harry' Banks; he was the one she loved now. Why did Rodney have to come back from the dead? Now, of all times. How long had she been searching for him, praying he was still alive? Now she wished with all her heart that he was dead.

"I think you'd better see him, Vessie." Elvira broke her train of thought. "Even if it's only to find out from his own lips what happened and why he's alive after the War Office told us he wasn't."

Rodney Purbright presented himself to Vesna with a grin all over his arrogant, film star face. She shrank before his hard blue gaze. Whatever had she seen in him? she wondered. He was still as handsome as she remembered him, but there was something cold and calculating about his very Aryan looks, something she had never noticed before. Maybe that's what being dead does for you, she thought wryly. Whatever would Harry say?

"Haven't you got a kiss for your long-lost fiancé?" he asked, holding out his arms.

Vesna avoided his embrace and gave him a chaste peck on the cheek.

"Just that? After all this time? Me doing my bit for King and country?" He looked hurt, but there was mockery lurking in his eyes.

"It's – it's been a long time, Rodney," she said quietly. "Things have changed quite a bit since you've been gone. Besides, the War Office told me you were dead."

"Dead? I'm not dead. Why would they say that?" His feigned shock and surprise were very convincing.

"It must have been a case of mistaken identity," interrupted Elvira practically. "I suppose these things can happen in wartime. So much mayhem … it's a wonder anyone knew what happened to *anyone* during those years."

Rodney smiled. "Exactly. I'm sure I'm not the only one who was thought dead in all that. But, as you can see, I'm definitely not."

He searched their faces anxiously. He could see something akin to mistrust in their eyes, something he hadn't bargained for.

Vesna turned to her sister. "So, Elvie, he's not such a coward after all." She said this with some relish, enjoying her sister's discomfort.

"Me? A coward? I should say not," said Rodney with feeling. "I've killed a few Hun in my time, I can tell you. Risked the bayonet and the shelling. It was hell, but I got through it. Others weren't so lucky."

Elvira sniffed and looked askance at him. "So, someone, whom the War Office thought was you, was shot for cowardice in the face of the enemy. Have you got any idea how they would have made such a mistake?"

"God knows," said Rodney airily. "As you yourself said, just a case of mistaken identity, I suppose. Anyway, now I'm back, do you think you could put me up till Vessie and I are married?"

He looked around him, taking in what he obviously thought was to be his 'billet' for the time being, too full of himself to notice the look that passed between the sisters.

Chapter Four

Rodney Purbright stretched out his long, elegant legs in front of the parlour fire. Vesna sat in the chair opposite and stared morosely at him. They could hear Elvira clattering about in the kitchen, making tea.

Tea! thought Vesna. What was the point of tea, unless you could cause someone to disappear by drinking it? What was she going to do with this man, now slumped in the chair before her, with that smug leer on his face? It had once been a face she had loved, along with the rest of him. Why did he have to turn up now, now that she had Harry Banks where she wanted him?

But Rodney Purbright wasn't going to prevent her from marrying Harry. He could drag her through every court in the land, his accusation of breach of promise wouldn't make any difference. Vesna had been told officially by the War Office that her former fiancé was dead and, as far as she was concerned, he could stay that way. No judge would determine otherwise, of that she was sure.

She glared at him as he basked in the warmth of the hearth fire, seemingly a permanent fixture. What was she going to do? No matter how many times she asked herself that question, answer came there none. She wasn't strong enough to physically turn him out, and Elvira wasn't either. Even between the pair of them, they would be no match for this burly young man, the epitome of physical fitness as he obviously was.

While Vesna was thinking these thoughts, her tapestry neglected on her knee, Rodney had thoughts of his own. Naturally, they were in direct opposition to hers. Looking around the cosy room, he was revising his opinion of the place which, at first, he had dismissed as much too small. Its smallness, he now saw, had its advantages. The December cold was well and truly shut out in this little fortress. Larger rooms were a bugger to heat, he remembered from his childhood. He had been brought up in a mansion, more or less, but the inadequate heating had meant he was always cold from November through to March each year, a martyr to one illness after another. Vesna's little home was, in fact, a splendid billet. He approved of the way the sisters had obviously made the most of the place, its homely atmosphere seducing him like a sensuous woman.

There was, of course, one slight snag in all this. Elvira. He suspected she would take some shifting. He knew she despised him, and the feeling was entirely mutual. She had seen right through him from the start and now that he was back, she was likely to put obstacles in the way of his marriage to her sister. The sooner she was sent packing the better.

"So Vessie, darling," he said, breaking the silence between them at last. "Where do I sleep?"

Elvira was bringing in the tea tray as he said these words. She nearly dropped the lot. Vesna abruptly stood up.

"Where do you sleep? What do you mean?" she demanded querulously.

"Yes, what *do* you mean?" echoed Elvira, carefully putting the tray down on the occasional table next to him. Her hands were shaking as she did so, and the cups rattled noisily.

"Thought it was plain enough," he said with a shrug. "I presume you have a spare room? After all, it wouldn't be right to put me in with Vessie – not until we're married, now would it?" He said this with an unpleasant leer.

Elvira stared in horror at him and then at her sister, who was staring back at her in equal horror. Rodney

Purbright, seemingly impervious to their reaction, held out a languid arm to accept the tea from Elvira.

"Would you like a piece of cherry cake?" she asked him through gritted teeth.

"Very nice," he said, smacking his lips. "Homemade?"

"Yes, fresh this morning."

"Who's the cook?" he asked, as he realised the cake was the most delicious thing he had tasted in ages.

"I am," said Elvira. "Does it meet with your approval?"

"It certainly does," he declared. "Can I have another slice?"

He began to think that Elvira should stick around after all. She could do all the cooking and cleaning for them, as long as she wiped that disgusting scowl off her face.

Vesna gave her sister a secret sign, nodding her head in the direction of the kitchen. Their unwelcome guest was too busy demolishing his second slice of cake to notice them scurrying out of the room.

"What on Earth are we going to do with him?" asked Vesna, almost in tears.

"Search me," said her sister. "He's your problem, not mine."

"He's both our problem, Elvie, don't you see that? I mean, if he plans to stay here. You don't want him around any more than I do."

"No. I never liked him from the beginning, as you know." She gave her sister a stern look, then seemed to soften. She sat down at the kitchen table, wiping her hands on her apron. "But it looks like we're stuck with him."

"Please, Elvie, help me. We must be able to get rid of him somehow. We can't have him living here with us. The whole thing's unseemly."

"That's putting it mildly," grinned Elvira mirthlessly. "But he *does* have a claim on you. We can't just chuck him out."

"No. I was thinking that myself. Not even the two of us could manage that. He looks very strong. His time in the army must have added the muscle," observed Vesna, sitting down at the table opposite her sister. "But surely we can *persuade* him to leave? If I make out that I intend to marry him still, but that I don't want any gossip going around. He must see that his living here compromises my position."

"I don't think that'd wash," Elvira pointed out calmly. "Not while I'm living here as well."

Vesna's face fell. "I suppose not. Oh dear, then we're stuck."

As she said this, the subject of their discussion loomed through the kitchen door. "What's going on girls? Having a mothers' meeting?" he asked with a sardonic grin. "Forgot you had a guest, did you?"

But that was the one thing they couldn't forget, no matter how much they would have liked to.

Chapter Five

Rodney Purbright had absolutely no intention of leaving Appleby Cottage and the Rowan sisters were powerless to turn him out. They followed him as he leisurely climbed the stairs after demolishing the rest of the cherry cake and four cups of tea.

"I think I'll take *this* room, ladies," he said, opening the door of Elvira's bedroom. "This will suit me nicely – for the time being, anyway."

"But this is *my* room," protested Elvira. "You can't sleep in here."

He turned and stared at her. "Don't worry, I don't expect *you* to stay in here with me." He screwed up his fine, aquiline nose and looked down its length at her. "I hardly think you would make me a suitable sleeping companion. You're not my type."

Vesna butted in. "How dare you! Get out of my sister's room!"

He remained immovable. "No, I don't think so. I like it. The bed looks very comfortable too." He tested his theory by bouncing up and down on it.

The two women stood by helplessly as he walked across Elvira's room to the lace-curtained window. "These things will have to go, for a start," he said, fingering them in disgust. "No self-respecting man would put up with these. Haven't you got any plain ones? Or, better still, a blind?"

Vesna took her sister by the arm. "No, sorry," she told him. "You'll have to put up with them. Anyway, make yourself at home. Elvie and I have to prepare the supper."

Elvira looked at her, stunned. Vesna put a finger to her mouth. "Shhh!" she hissed. "Come downstairs."

She gently pushed her sister down the stairs and into the kitchen. Closing the door, she took her by the hand and sat her down at the table. "We've got to get rid of him, Elvie. I hate him."

Elvira glared at her. "How do you think *I* feel? He's taken over my bedroom. Where am I supposed to sleep?"

"Oh, don't fuss, love. You can bunk in with me for now. We have to form a plan of campaign."

"Oh, right," said her sister, somewhat placated. "Maybe we should get Harry round here to sort him out."

"That's exactly what I was thinking. You go and tell him what's happening. I'll stay here and clatter about so that he won't suspect anything."

Elvira immediately made her way up the hall and pulled on her thick coat. The snow was falling in large flakes now, and she didn't relish the thought of ploughing her way through it to the butcher's shop in the High Street where Harry worked with his father. But there was no help for it.

"Be careful, Vessie," she whispered, as she opened the front door. "I think he could be very dangerous if you get on the wrong side of him. Keep buttering him up."

"Oh, don't worry. I intend to. He mustn't get a whiff of what we're planning."

As Vesna stood on the front doorstep watching her sister pick her way gingerly down the slippery path, there came a booming voice behind her. "Where's that sister of yours going?" demanded Rodney Purbright.

"Er, we forgot the flour," said Vesna hastily. "For the steak pie," she added by way of further explanation.

"I see," he said. "Very well. I like a nice steak pie. Don't forget the kidney."

Elvira escaped out of the gate and headed off towards the High Street. Harry Banks will soon sort him out, she thought grimly.

ॐ

Vesna followed Rodney back into the parlour. She watched as he sat down in front of the fire once more and started to toast his stockinged feet.

"So, Rodney," she said, clearing her throat. "Why have you come back after all this time? Where have you been? Don't you think you owe me some kind of an explanation?"

"All in good time," he replied. "Anyway, I thought you'd be glad to see me back. Haven't you missed me? I thought I meant the world to you. You told me so often enough."

Careful not to arouse his suspicions, she replied, keeping her voice even, "Of course I missed you. But you've been gone a long time. Things change. *People* change."

She came and sat down in the armchair on the other side of the hearth. "My life's moved on. Er, I think you should do the same. Get yourself another girl. They must be queuing up. You'll soon forget me."

Rodney Purbright grinned at her lasciviously. He thought about another young woman, now faraway, whom he once thought could have made him happy. There had been others, too.

"How could I forget you and all we meant to each other?" he said, reaching out his hand to stroke her cheek. She flinched inwardly as he did so. "We made a vow, Vessie, and I intend to hold you to our bond." Then the grin disappeared as suddenly as it had come, and he fixed her with a flint-like stare. "No matter what."

Harry Banks was in the act of chopping up some pig's liver for a customer when Elvira rushed into the shop.

"Elvira!" he exclaimed. "Where's the fire, old girl?"

He wasn't nearly as handsome as Rodney Purbright, or as tall, or as muscle-bound, but there was something rather charming about his thin, sensitive face and soft hazel eyes. His gentle features suited him as he was as gentle as they were, and a kinder man than Harry Banks would have been hard to find, unless his father was nearby.

Elvira could see why her sister had fallen for him. She only wished she could find someone like Harry herself, but that was a mere pipe dream, of course. In fact, if she had been tempted to admit her feelings, she would have had to say she loved her sister's second fiancé as much as she loathed her first. Just because her eyes didn't match, and her nose was a little too large, she was still a woman with feelings like any other. But, like all men, Harry had eyes only for Vesna, so she kept any romantic thoughts about him strictly to herself. But, no matter how she tried, her heart always gave an involuntary lurch whenever she saw him. And today, despite the desperate circumstances she and Vesna found themselves in, was no exception.

"Sorry, Harry," she said, catching her breath. "I've come from Vesna. Her old fiancé, the one we thought was dead, has turned up and is making all kinds of threats."

Harry put down his lethal looking cleaver and came around the counter. Elvira secretly pictured this very cleaver sticking in Rodney Purbright's head, and it gave her a frisson of pleasure. He gently took her arm and led her through to the back room. Several shoppers were lining up to be served but, at that moment, he didn't care. His Vesna was in trouble and he had to help her and her sister, even if old Mrs Harding was demanding her week's ration of tripe at that moment.

"Dad," he called out. "Can you serve, please? I need to take a break for a minute."

A rotund, red-faced man of about fifty-five appeared from the cellar below. "I'm doing a stock take, Harry. Can't you deal with them? Oh, hello, Miss Rowan," he said, catching sight of Elvira as his son was leading her into the back room. "How are you?"

"She's fine, Dad," intercepted Harry. "Can you just serve?"

"Of course," said his father, sensing the urgency in his son's tone. "I'm on my way."

"Here," said Harry, seating Elvira by the rather inadequate radiator. "Now, when you feel calmer, please tell me what's going on."

"He just turned up out of the blue and said he was going to stay with us until he and Vesna got married. He's taken over my bedroom," she moaned. "I can't stand him. He's a nasty piece of work. Vessie sent me to fetch you. You must help us to get rid of him. Please, Harry."

While she was saying this, she looked at him with growing concern. He wasn't a match for Rodney Purbright on his own, she realised. "You'd better bring your dad along," she said. "He's a very big man, and I don't think you'll overpower him on your own."

Harry, who knew he was no Charles Atlas, smiled. He was a little hurt at Elvira's lack of confidence in his powers but didn't say so. "Okay. You go back now, and me and Dad'll come round as soon as we close. You're not in any immediate physical danger, are you?"

"No, I don't think so," she said, getting up and buttoning her coat. "We'll keep him happy till you come. We're going to cook him a steak pie. I hope he chokes on it."

So saying, she made her way back through the snow, praying that Rodney Purbright had been behaving himself in her absence.

"I don't think you should get involved, son."

Harry Banks stared at his father in amazement. "Not get involved? What do you mean? I *am* involved! She's my fiancée. We're getting married, Dad, or had you forgotten?"

Arnold Banks sighed. "Of course I haven't forgotten. I think you know your mother and I aren't very happy about it. After all, you hardly know the girl. You've only been walking out with her for a fortnight. And she's two years older than you."

"So what? What's her age got to do with it? I only know that two weeks is long enough to know I want to spend the rest of my life with her." He paused and gave his father a forlorn look. "I love her, Dad."

The old butcher paused in the act of returning some unsold lamb chops to the freezer and turned to face his anxious son. "You tell me that, but don't you remember you were just as keen on Milly Wynyard not so long ago. Said you couldn't live without her."

"That was different. Are you going to put those chops in the freezer or are you going to let the blood drip all over the floor?"

"How was it different?" asked the older man, putting the chops away carefully. They would be snapped up tomorrow first thing, he knew.

Now that meat was coming off the ration, he was able to buy in more and offer a wider selection than he had been able to recently. He had to make sure there was enough to go round, even though there wasn't the money about like before the War. People were just about managing now, but they would always find the money for a good piece of meat to fill their bellies. They'd had enough of going without, thought Arnold.

He sighed and faced his son. "I still don't know what happened there. You never explained properly. You'll drive your mother mad, son. Now this Vesna … I mean, what sort of a name is that, anyway?"

"Look, Dad. Milly was a nice kid, but she was so immature! Vesna's a *woman*. She understands me completely. We have a laugh when we go out. She and I share the same sense of humour. Do you see what I mean?"

"Certainly, I do, lad. Have fun, by all means. But wait a bit till you're sure she's the right one for you. You're only nineteen. You've got your whole life ahead of you. Why tie yourself down with a wife and maybe kids too? Time enough for that when you've lived a bit more."

Harry tried to interrupt but his father was in full flow. He raised his hand. "Anyway, even if you are daft enough to marry this girl, it doesn't seem right that we should go interfering with this chap who's turned up. He's just come back from the War, and he was her fiancé long before you. He must have the prior claim."

"Maybe. But Vessie's sister says he's behaving in a very threatening manner towards them both and it can't be right to do that. If Vessie's changed her mind about marrying him, he should respect that and leave her alone. That's what any decent man would do."

"Whatever the situation, my boy, you shouldn't get involved. If she's serious about you and doesn't want anything to do with her former fiancé, then all well and good. But you need to wait and see what happens. After all, if she can dismiss him that easily, what does it mean for you? Maybe she'll meet someone else who'll take her fancy and throw *you* over. Don't you see? Look son, I'm not trying to put the mockers on anything. All I ask is that you keep out of it and wait and see how the land lies once the dust has settled."

Harry followed his father up the cellar steps into the shop. He turned the sign to 'closed' and smiled at his father. He was a dear man, but he didn't understand. He didn't understand at all.

35

Chapter Six

"So," said Rodney Purbright, "where *is* this so-called fiancé of yours? I thought you said he was coming to sort me out."

Elvira answered on her sister's behalf. "He said he was coming and bringing his dad. So, make it easy on yourself and leave now before you end up with a black eye or worse."

"Ooh, dear!" he exclaimed in mock horror. "I'm scared! See – I'm quaking in my boots."

Vesna was watching out of the front window for a sign of Harry or his father. "They're taking their time," she said nervously. "The butcher's has been closed for over half an hour."

"Don't worry," said her sister. "They'll be here. Harry said."

"Well, where is he?" Vesna demanded, panic rising in her voice as she turned to look at Rodney. "I don't like him sitting there, looking at us like that."

"And you think *I* do?" Elvira rejoined. "Don't worry. Calm down. They'll be here soon."

As if in answer, the doorbell rang. Vesna rushed to the front door and admitted Harry Banks, who was unaccompanied. She brought him into the parlour to confront her former lover.

"I thought you were bringing your dad," said Elvira, arching her eyebrows at him. They were the most elegant things about her, as she painfully plucked them night after night for want of anything better to do.

Harry looked down at his feet, as if ashamed. "I – I'm sorry, he didn't feel it was his place to interfere."

"Quite right!" Rodney piped up. "It's something we need to settle, man to man. How about a drink? What's the beer like at the Bricklayer's? I passed it on the way here."

Harry shuffled his feet and coughed. "Good – the beer's good," he said, eyeing Vesna slyly, while she stared at him open-mouthed.

She couldn't believe he was kowtowing to this horrible man. He was about to take his fiancée from him, and all he could do was chat about the quality of the local beer.

"Right!" declared Rodney, standing up at once. "Let's you and me pay a visit and have a pint or three. I'm sure we can sort out this little difficulty." With that, he put a languid arm around Harry's shoulders and hustled him out of the room. "See you later, ladies."

"Little difficulty!" screamed Vesna when they had gone. "So, I'm just a 'little difficulty', am I?" She was fuming.

"Well, I didn't expect that," observed Elvira. "So much for your precious boyfriend. I thought he'd be a man and stand up to him. Punch him on the nose, at least. I can't think what's come over him. He was all for sorting him out good and proper when I left him. "

"Must have been his dad, I suppose. It's very annoying," said Vesna. "If Harry won't do anything, I don't know what we'll do."

Elvira shrugged helplessly. "I really thought Harry wouldn't let you down."

"Well, I want nothing more to do with him after this. What a wimp!"

"Maybe you should marry Rodney, after all?"

Although Elvira had meant it as a joke, it didn't go down well with her sister.

"You're not serious?" she yelled at her. "The man's a scoundrel! We don't know what went on with him in the War, for a start. He was supposed to have been shot as a coward, remember?"

"I was only kidding," said Elvira with a sigh. "Besides, you were the one to insist that he *wasn't* a coward, remember?"

Vesna snorted back her rage. "Well, I admit I could've been wrong. But I tell you this, I'd sooner kill him than have him hanging round our necks indefinitely."

Elvira had a sneaking suspicion her sister wasn't altogether joking. "Get a grip, Vessie," she said calmly. "He won't stay once he knows it's a waste of time."

"You think so?" asked Vesna, her voice at least an octave higher than her usual range. "Then you're more of a fool than I took you for." She slumped down in the chair recently vacated by Rodney Purbright.

"Well, you never know..." Elvira tried again. "Maybe Harry will convince him to go. We needn't despair just yet."

Rodney and Harry found a table near the window of the Bricklayer's Arms on Maple Street, the nearest pub to Hallows Mead. It was a popular meeting place for the locals and was already packed, even though it had only been open half an hour. Harry caught sight of his father at the bar but didn't approach him. He knew he wasn't happy that his son had defied him and gone to see Vesna, but Harry's sense of honour hadn't allowed him to just ignore the situation. He also had to make sure his fiancée wasn't in any real danger.

But, far from being a danger to Vesna and her sister, this Rodney Purbright seemed a very decent sort. He had paid for their first pints which showed he wasn't mean with his money. A man who stood you a pint couldn't be all bad, or so thought Harry Banks.

"Well, Harry, old chap, this is a bit of a rum do, isn't it?" said Rodney jokily. "Cheers!" He clinked his beer glass against Harry's. "Good to meet you – even if it is in these rather unusual circumstances."

"Cheers," responded Harry, taking a long swig of his beer.

It was cold and smooth, and he felt good once the liquid reached the pit of his stomach. Nothing like a cool pint of beer to sort out the troubles of the world.

"The way I see it," said Harry, wiping the froth from his mouth, "is that you have the prior claim and I don't want any trouble about it."

The older man stared at his companion in surprise. His plan had been to get his young rival drunk and tip him in the canal on the way home. Now it looked like such extreme measures wouldn't be called for. He would still have liked to thrash this upstart just for taking what was rightfully his, but he supposed there really wasn't any point.

"That's very big of you, young sir," he said cheerfully. "But I didn't expect such an easy victory. Surely you aren't prepared to give up the young lady without a *bit* of a fight?"

Harry smiled, still a little nervous of him, despite the man's outward air of amiability. "I don't want to fight you, sir," he said with some deference. "I understand you fought in the War. I was just a bit too young. You have every right to come back and claim Vesna as your bride."

"Well, you would have thought so, wouldn't you?" said Rodney, finishing his pint and already on his feet to fetch another. "But it seems she prefers you now."

"My round," insisted Harry, ignoring Rodney's observation. Only an hour ago, he would have said that was true, but now he wasn't so sure. Vesna no doubt saw this friendly man-to-man talk as a betrayal.

"Put your money away, boy," he heard Rodney say. "This is my treat."

The man went up a few more notches in Harry's estimation at this. There was no doubt of it; he was a decent bloke and he had no right to come between him and Vesna. The more he thought about what his father had said, the more he began to see the wisdom of his words. He was right. He *was* too young to settle down. Even with someone as lovely as Vesna Rowan. He felt a qualm when he pictured her in his mind's eye, her face turned up to his for a kiss. He pushed the image away as he saw Rodney returning with the beers.

He might have thought differently if he had known what the older man was thinking. As it was, he was unaware of how Rodney liked to get the upper hand of any man, and that his giving in so easily had only riled him. But, not knowing this, Harry was quite happy to accompany him along the canal path on the way home.

Chapter Seven

Rodney Purbright loomed up the path of Appleby Cottage sometime after midnight. The Rowan sisters had put off going to bed, dreading his return. It had been too much to hope that Harry Banks would have talked him round and persuaded him to leave them in peace. Elvira had suggested that Vesna should go to bed as she needed to be up early the next morning for work, but she wouldn't hear of it. So, the two sisters, united for once in their anxiety, sat waiting.

They heard him fumbling at the front door, followed shortly after by a loud thumping. They were even more scared of him now that he was obviously the worse for drink.

"Don't let him in," whispered Vesna, holding onto her sister as she made to get up from the sofa. "Perhaps he'll go away!"

"And perhaps he'll wake up the whole neighbourhood," said Elvira sensibly. "We'll have to let him in anyway, all his stuff's here. He'll need to take it with him when he finally goes."

"But he *isn't* going, is he?" wailed Vesna. "I think he's going to kill me."

"Kill you? Why on Earth should you think that? He said he was going to marry you, you silly woman."

The thumping was growing louder and was now accompanied by a thick, guttural, drunken voice. "Let me in! It's cold out here!"

Elvira opened the door just as he was about to thump on it again, narrowly missing his fist in her face.

"About time!" he slurred, falling into the passage, burping as he did so. "Oops! Pardon me," he giggled. "Where's the sunshine of my life?"

Vesna came out of the parlour as he said this. "You're drunk!" she observed unnecessarily. "Have you no shame?"

"None at all, my pretty one," he grinned, insinuating his long arm around her cringing shoulders. "Now, what about a goodnight kiss, then?"

Vesna pushed him away in disgust. "No! You stink of beer. Go to bed. We want you out of here tomorrow morning." She said this last as firmly as she could.

Rodney Purbright seemed to sober up suddenly. "I thought I'd made my position clear," he said. "Here I am and here I stay. We shall be married next week. Do you understand me?"

Elvira came and stood by her sister's side. "Where's Harry? Did you get him drunk? I presume you talked him round, got rid of him?"

Rodney Purbright started to giggle again. "Got rid of him? You could say that. He was very drunk – much drunker than me. He fell in the canal."

Vesna and Elvira caught their breath as he said this. "Fell in the canal?" they exclaimed in unison. "What – and you left him there?"

Rodney waved an airy hand. "Oh, it's all right. He can swim. The most he'll get is a chill – or possibly double pneumonia. But I think I've persuaded him to relinquish all rights where you're concerned, my pretty one."

He tried once again to put his arm around the object of his affection, but Vesna managed to duck in time. He collapsed, laughing, against the wall.

"You bastard!" she spat at him. "How could you leave him in there? He might have drowned."

"Oh, no. He was swimming quite happily when I left him. Well, not happily, exactly. Must have been freezing in there as he broke the ice when he fell in. But I just wanted to make it clear where he stood, that's all. Now, if you ladies will excuse me, I need to go to my bed."

"*My* bed, you mean," muttered Elvira under her breath.

Rodney Purbright turned as he started up the stairs. "Not anymore, my dear," he sneered. "And, by the way, if either of you get any ideas about disturbing me in the night – to have your wicked way with me," he paused and giggled again, "I think it only fair to tell you that I shall defend myself – with this, if necessary." So saying, he pulled out an army issue pistol from inside his snow-covered jacket.

The two sisters gasped. "You shouldn't still have that, surely?" said Vesna, horrified.

"What I should or shouldn't have doesn't signify, my sweet. I've got it and I think you should be careful in future." He waved it at her nonchalantly, then continued his unsteady way up the stairs.

Vesna stared at Elvira, then burst into tears. They stood together in the hall waiting for the sounds above them to cease. It dawned on them, as they stood there, that now they knew that Rodney Purbright had a gun, they were, to all intents and purposes, being held hostage in their own home.

Rodney awoke to a bright December morning in Appleby cottage. He recalled the previous day's events with satisfaction and grinned sleepily. This is a comfortable bed, he thought; too comfortable for the likes of Elvira Rowan. Someone who looked like her deserved only an iron bedstead without any mattress.

But Vesna Rowan was a different story. Although he had met better looking women, she suited him. Her blonde earthiness appealed to his baser instincts; he could visualise her in his bed in the throes of lovemaking and enjoying every minute. No lying back and thinking of England for the likes of her. So, he had firmly decided, he would make her his wife come hell or high water. If she didn't want to marry

43

him, that was *her* problem. She would be having no say in the matter. And, now that Harry Banks was out of the way, she had no excuse.

He slowly eased himself out of the warm bed and sauntered over to the window which was wet with condensation. He gave an involuntary shiver as he opened it and breathed in the cold morning air. Yes, he thought, this feels like home at last. After all the ducking and diving he'd done over the last few years, he deserved it. Vesna and her sister would see to all his needs, one way or another. He had to admit that Elvira could certainly cook, so she could stay around. In fact, he would insist upon it. No sense in booting her out, as Vesna couldn't even boil an egg.

He looked back on the last few years and thought about the decisions and actions he had taken, regretting nothing. If he had his time over again, he decided, he wouldn't change a thing. He'd had an adventure or two, but now it was time for him to settle down, get a job and raise a family.

Continuing to take in gulps of air, he made a desultory attempt at some knee bending exercises until he was out of breath. Returning to the bed, he thought all that was missing was a bell by his bedside to summon the sisters to attend to his needs. What he needed right now, he decided, was a cup of tea and a large fried breakfast, but he supposed he would have to go downstairs for it. He would have to put that right and sharpish.

"I can hear him moving about up there," said Vesna, who was putting on her coat to go to work.

"He must be thinking about breakfast," said Elvira, frowning up at the ceiling which looked in danger of collapsing under the weight of the man's heavy army boots. "I wish you weren't going to work."

"I've got no choice, love," said Vesna, looking in the hall mirror to straighten her hat and touch up her lipstick. "I can't let Bert down, can I? He's only got one pair of hands, and Saturday's our busiest day."

"I know, but still, this is an emergency. Surely, he'd understand? Maybe he'd even come and sort him out for us?" Elvira looked at her sister hopefully.

"Look, Elvie, let's get one thing straight right now. I don't want anyone else to know our business. I don't want Bert involved. I'll come back as soon as I can tonight, and we'll think of something to get rid of him. And, in the meantime, why not open the shop today for a change? I know you don't on Saturdays as a rule, but it'd give you a chance to get away from him."

"Yes, I'll do that. I've got quite a few remedies to make up from yesterday anyway."

Vesna, now ready to face the cold snow outside, smiled grimly at her anxious sister. "That's good. And don't worry. I'll think of something to get rid of him. There's more than one way to skin a cat…"

As Vesna closed the front door behind her, Rodney Purbright appeared on the landing above. He called down to Elvira, who remained standing in the hall.

"Any chance of a cup of tea and some breakfast?"

She straightened up at once and spun round to look up at him as he tramped down the stairs, making the flimsy banisters shake.

"Get your own," she spat at him. "We've had ours. I think there's an egg left."

Rodney Purbright's face took on a hard stare. He reached out and grasped Elvira by the throat, making her almost choke.

"Now then, sunshine," he said through gritted teeth. "That's no way to talk to your future brother-in-law, now, is it?" He shook her, making her choke even more.

All Elvira could do was gurgle. Finally, he relaxed his grip, allowing her to splutter and get her breath back. She tried not to show how scared she was, and remained facing him in the hall, barring his way to the warm kitchen.

"I'll talk to you any way I like," she gasped, rubbing her throat. "If you want breakfast, you're out of luck. There isn't any food in the house at the moment. Saturday's our big shop day, and as we weren't expecting any 'guests', we haven't stocked up yet."

"Don't you take that tone with me," he said in his most threatening manner. "I suggest that, if that's the case, you amend the situation by going to the shops right now."

Elvira was so angry, she had no emotion left to feel afraid of him. "And how do you suggest I pay for all this extra food? We only just manage as it is."

He laughed suddenly. "Is that all that's bothering you?" He fished in his trousers pocket and pulled out a large, white, five-pound note. "Would one of these help?"

Elvira snatched it from him eagerly. "It certainly would. I haven't seen one of these for years."

She folded it up and put it in her apron pocket. If they were to be stuck with this man, at least he didn't seem to be mean with his money. They could afford to eat very well on his fiver for a fortnight.

Chapter Eight

"It'll be a piece of cake, Elvie."

"Don't be so ridiculous," said Elvira Rowan. "You must be completely off your head. What you're suggesting is – well, it's plain wrong!"

The two women had spent a long and uncomfortable week under the same roof as Rodney Purbright and were at the end of their tether. Producing his gun whenever one or other of them tried to challenge his authority, he had them completely under his thumb, attending to his every whim, and now the last straw: he had produced the dreaded marriage licence. It was all fixed, he told them, for a week on Friday. With that, he had tramped up to bed, leaving them to digest this as best they could.

"And don't forget my cocoa, Vessie," he had called out as they heard him slam the bedroom door.

It was after midnight as they sat by the dying fire, holding each other's hands. As sisters, they had been chalk and cheese all their lives. Now, in their adversity, they were united as one. They had to, somehow, get rid of Rodney Purbright before he dragged Vesna up the aisle. It would be, literally, a shotgun wedding, as Elvira pointed out, not without some irony. The poor women were in fear of their very lives.

"I know where he keeps it – the gun," said Vesna. "In your bedside table. You said the lock was broken, so that won't prove a difficulty."

"But it's murder what you're planning. Besides he's bound to wake up as you open the drawer. It always creaked, remember?"

"Haven't you forgotten, sis?"

"Forgotten? Forgotten what?"

"Granny's special receipt for insomnia?"

47

"Oh, that. Yes, well, we always tell people it works, but does it really? It's only herbal. Probably a good relaxant, but I don't think it's as good as a pill you'd get from a doctor."

"Maybe not. But if we crush up a few in his cocoa – that should do the trick." She didn't say that she'd already done that and given it to him only half an hour ago.

"God, Vessie, you're really serious about doing this, aren't you?"

"Do you have any better ideas? We'll be quite safe. Once we've done it, we'll just tell anyone who asks that he's gone home, and that he and I aren't getting married after all."

"Well, obviously we'll have to do that, seeing as how he's probably told all his cronies down at the pub about his plans," said Elvira. "It'll look odd if he just suddenly disappears. Somebody might start asking awkward questions."

"Oh, come off it," said Vesna crossly. "No one'll be that bothered about him. He's only been here five minutes. Those so-called buddies down at the pub won't remember him in a week. They only get drunk together, and they're only his mates until the money runs out."

"I wonder where he gets it all from," said Elvira, changing tack. "I've often wondered. He doesn't work, as far as we know."

"I remember he had some rich relatives in Malmesbury he was always telling me about," said Vesna. "When we were first engaged, he told me that they were getting on and he was expecting them to die any minute. He said that they were going to leave their money to him."

Elvira looked grim. "So, they must have died, then," she said. "Unless he bumped them off. I wouldn't put it past him."

Vesna giggled nervously. "I know he's a bad egg and all that, but do you really think he'd have killed them?"

"Why not? Isn't that what we're planning to do to him?" Elvira pointed out. "And we're nice people – not like him. I believe anyone's capable of murder, given the circumstances."

"I suppose you're right," said Vesna. "Although I don't think he'd really harm us."

"Well, if you think that, then why don't you just stand up to him and tell him you won't marry him?"

Vesna glared at her. "I've tried. What more can I do? He won't take no for an answer. But, whatever happens, I'm not marrying him. So, as I see it, we've got no alternative."

"But if we get discovered – we'll hang."

Vesna smirked. "We won't get discovered," she said firmly. "I've got it all worked out. I'll get the gun while he's asleep and shoot him in the head through the pillow so it won't make too much noise. Then we'll bury him under those blasted rose bushes. They don't produce any flowers, anyway, so maybe he'll prove useful as fertiliser, if nothing else."

"I've never seen you like this," said Elvira, standing up and taking the clock from the mantelpiece to wind it up. "I think you should think again. Let's go to bed and, in the morning, we'll put our heads together and devise a plan to get rid of him that won't involve actual murder."

Vesna shrugged and stood up, smoothing her velvet dress carefully. "I think you've forgotten just one tiny detail, sis," she said.

"And what is that, pray?"

"They can't hang you for murdering someone who's already dead."

Elvira stopped halfway up the stairs and turned round. She hadn't thought of that. Vesna gave her a friendly push and they continued their way up to bed.

Lying in bed later, Vesna's thoughts turned to young Harry Banks. Although she was still angry with him for not helping her get rid of Rodney, she still missed him. He couldn't have loved her, after all, she realized. He was avoiding her now whenever she saw him in the street and Elvira said that he'd got his dad to serve her whenever she went in the butcher's.

What toads men were, she thought sadly. She had thought the world of Rodney; the sun had shone out of every orifice of him. Then she had found out his true character. She had thought the same of Harry, but now she knew he was just the same. She almost wished he'd drowned in the canal. She had heard through various sources that he'd even taken up with someone else. How fickle he was. Professing undying love to her one minute, the next walking out with another girl.

She turned fitfully in the bed. She could quite happily kill Harry Banks for his betrayal. And, as for Rodney Purbright, she was determined to dispatch him out of her life and nobody, not even her sister, was going to stop her. She sat up and threw back the covers, feeling for her slippers under the bed.

She paused outside her sister's bedroom door, the room usurped by Rodney Purbright. She listened to the sounds of snoring through the wood panelling and smiled grimly to herself. She heard the clock in the parlour strike two o'clock; he would be well away by now.

She had shaken ten of her grandmother's powder cures for insomnia into his cocoa and he had complained that it was very bitter. She had made the excuse that it was a new brand she was trying and said she wouldn't give it to him again. And that was a promise she would gladly keep.

Screwing up her courage, she turned the door knob as quietly as she could, praying that it wouldn't creak or, worse still, that he hadn't locked it from the inside. Her luck was holding so far, and she managed to creep into the room without disturbing his slumbering form. Now, all she had to do was retrieve the gun from the bedside cabinet, which, unfortunately, was on the far side of the bed. She sneaked around it which, although only a single, seemed to take ten years to navigate. The sweat popped out on her forehead, and her hands felt decidedly clammy.

She was about to kill this man in cold blood but, as she kept reminding herself, he was dead already. That much was a fact, documented in writing by the War Office. Who was going to look for him now?

She remembered, as she reached the bedside table, that the knob on its one drawer had come off, and the only way to get inside it was to get a purchase on the edges that jutted out at the front and yank it hard. She also knew that it creaked violently as it opened. How she was going to manage that without waking him, heaven only knew. She fervently hoped that her granny's sleeping powders were strong enough; by her calculation he must have swallowed at least half the amount she put in his bedtime beverage before he refused to drink anymore. She waited and watched for a moment as he snored blissfully on. Rodney Purbright might have had two lives, but she was determined he wasn't going to have three.

Chapter Nine

He slept on, dreaming of his audacious past. He had been a clever sod, even if he said so himself. He hunkered down into Elvira's cosy blankets as his dream began to evolve to show his slightly younger self at the start of the War.

Private Rodney Purbright had been discharged as fit, his self-inflicted gunshot wound well and truly healed. In fact, the bullet had only grazed the skin of his big toe, because his hand had been shaking so much as he fired the shot. In his dream now, he was much braver and shot his whole foot off. He felt no pain as the scene dissolved to find him on a train trundling back to the front, his foot now intact.

He tossed in his sleep as the dream found him on a train bound for the Somme. He was standing in the crowded corridor as it chugged its way through the south of England, just as it had done in reality. Voices singing *It's a Long Way to Tipperary* resounded around him. All those stupid sods, they were just cannon fodder. They wouldn't be singing soon. They'd be whimpering and calling for their mummies.

But Rodney Purbright had never intended to be one of those cheery 'Tommy Atkinses'. He threw the blankets off as his dream began turning into a nightmare, a nightmare he had, along with millions of other poor buggers, already lived through over and over again.

His dream still held him in its grip and suddenly he was holed up in a filthy trench dug out of French soil, along with some fresh-faced lads who weren't singing *It's a Long Way to Tipperary* anymore. Looking around him, he could feel his insides turn to water. Not again. He couldn't go through all this again. He had had this nightmare many times before; the bullets and grenades falling thick and fast into his trench. He could hear his commanding officer yelling at him and all the others to go 'over the top'.

Suddenly it was all too much for him, just like it had been in reality. He let out a yell, clambered out of the trench and made a desperate dash for it. He didn't know where he was going and made no attempt to fire his rifle at the enemy. He just ran and ran, dodging missiles, until he stumbled over the bodies of some dead soldiers. He couldn't tell if they were German or English as it was pitch dark. Then his hand came into contact with something metal hard and he knew they were Germans. He closed his eyes as he pulled the helmet off one of the dead men's head.

"Right, Purbright. On your feet."

He struggled to open his eyes, wishing the nightmare would end. It had always ended here before, but the sun was streaming down on the dead bodies around him as it relentlessly continued. He blinked and rubbed his eyes, staring at the boots of an English officer. His own commanding officer had found him. He lost the contents of his bladder as he stumbled to his feet and found himself being manhandled by two other soldiers.

"That's right, men. Truss him up like a chicken and don't leave his side for an instant. Be like a mother to him."

The two young privates tied his hands behind his back and pushed him towards a waiting wagon.

"Get him out of here," yelled the commanding officer. "I only hope we don't waste time on his court martial – if you get my meaning."

So, they were going to shoot him like a dog, were they? They had tried that once before. But it took more than two mere bits of boys to get the better of Rodney Purbright. He almost purred in his sleep. He was enjoying his dream now.

He was in the back of the wagon, sitting between the two men who had been told, in no uncertain terms, to dispose of him. It would be a cold day in hell before he'd let them do that. He weighed them up physically. One of them was thin but wiry; the other was well over six feet tall and broad shouldered with it. He would be difficult to overpower, that was certain. Then there was the man in charge of the wagon. He looked the toughest of them all.

As he sized him up, the man looked over his shoulder at him. "You're a bastard, aren't you?" he said, not expecting a reply. "Here we are, up to our necks in muck and bullets, and you decide to bugger off and leave us to it. I hope you don't expect any mercy from us, Purbright. By rights, we should be taking you back to HQ to stand trial but, quite frankly, we can't be arsed."

One of his two escorts, the thin and wiry one, fumbled in his tunic and pulled out a squashed packet of cigarettes. Rodney was surprised when he pulled out a dog end and, lighting it with a match struck on the heel of his boot, handed it to him.

"Here," he said quietly. "Not much left, I'm afraid, but you're welcome to it."

He accepted the fag eagerly, calculating how he could get this man to help him escape. By this kind gesture, it looked as if he was on his side. If he could persuade him to release his hands, between the two of them they could overpower the other men.

The kind young soldier now addressed the driver. "Just shut your mouth, Dick," he said. "This man's just scared – like all of us."

The driver grimaced and then spat, whipping the poor mule pulling the wagon within an inch of its wretched life. "Yeah, but we don't all run away, do we?"

Rodney remembered feeling humiliated throughout that drive. He tried to wake up, but his eyelids wouldn't move. Back in the hell he was forced to relive, there had come the turning point. Just as it had that day.

"I need a piss," he said suddenly.

"Well, you'll just have to tie a knot in it. Or go in your trousers," came the reply from the driver. "Although you've probably done that already, anyway."

"Don't be such a heartless beast," protested Rodney's young protector. "Stop the truck."

The older man raised his bushy eyebrows heavenwards. "For God's sake, you a fool or what?" He pulled on the mule's reins and the beast came to a grinding halt, snorting with relief.

"Let the man have a bit of dignity," insisted the young soldier, his companion now agreeing with him. "We'll both take him, if you like. Make sure he doesn't get away."

"You'll have to untie his hands, so watch it," grumbled the wagon driver. "I don't suppose either of you want to hold it for him."

Rodney was helped down out of the wagon by his escorts. When his hands were untied, he rubbed his wrists gratefully, feeling the circulation slowly returning. He stumbled between the two men, thinking furiously. It was now or never.

Then it had been a matter of seconds for Rodney to shoot one of his escorts.

"What have you done?" The young soldier who had been so kind to him was glaring at him now. "How did you do that? One minute he was standing there with the gun, the next you had it in your hands and shot him with it. I can't understand how you did that."

"No?" smirked Rodney. "The quickness of the hand deceives the eye. Now, hand over your rifle."

Meekly, the young man obeyed, and Rodney pointed the weapon at the driver's head. He died instantly as a bullet seared his brain.

With two of them dead, Rodney turned to the young Tommy who had shown him such compassion. He felt no answering compassion as he finished him off. After all, he had been ordered to kill him and he was obliged to carry out that order, fag or no fag. He knelt down and fumbled through his tunic for his identity papers. He removed his own papers and placed them in the dead man's pocket. He checked his other pockets for anything else that might suggest he wasn't who the papers now said he was, but the only thing he found was a small, creased photograph of a pretty blonde holding a baby. He screwed it up and threw it on the ground.

Quickly shovelling some earth over the bodies, he took one of the soldiers' rifles and headed back to the waiting wagon. He stroked the poor mule gently and climbed up onto the driving seat. At the click of Rodney's tongue, the mule at once started trotting slowly towards the nearest town. The sun was rising over the sparse, war-torn fields. It was going to be a warm day.

The sweat poured off him as the image faded. He slumped back on his pillow, slowly becoming aware that the gun digging into his brain was no longer part of his dream.

Chapter Ten

Vesna Rowan stared at the slumbering form of Rodney Purbright illuminated by the full moon through the small lattice window, now stripped of its lace curtains.

The gun was heavier than she expected, and her hand trembled as she held it. She turned it over, studying it carefully by the moon's rays, hoping the safety catch was on. Her knowledge of modern weaponry was practically non-existent.

She forced herself to concentrate on what she had to do, and the fear her intended target could wake up at any minute spurred her on. She prayed the gun was loaded, not wanting to hesitate longer than necessary by checking the chamber. Just point the thing, she told herself.

She looked around for something soft to put over his face. She didn't dare risk waking him by removing one of the pillows under his head and didn't want to lose any more time by retrieving a pillow from her own bed. Cursing herself for not having the foresight to bring a pillow with her, she was relieved to see he hadn't discarded the lacy cushion on the club chair in the corner.

Clasping the cushion to her breast, she eased herself up to the bed again and very gently placed it over his sleeping face. Shaking with fear and adrenalin, she pointed the gun at the cushion and squeezed the trigger. There was a muffled explosion and it was all over. The smashed and bloody face of her former fiancé was revealed as she removed the pillow. His cold, staring eyes looked accusingly at her through a pile of feathers.

∾

The following morning, the snow was falling thick and fast, battering the windows of the tiny, lopsided cottage. Vesna, who hadn't been able to sleep all night, was at the kitchen table when Elvira strode into the room to make the breakfast.

"Vesna!" she exclaimed, filling the kettle. "You're not usually up this early. I wondered where you were when I woke. Couldn't you sleep? Perhaps you need one of Gran's receipts."

"I don't think so," said Vesna, eyeing her nervously. "I couldn't sleep for a very good reason."

"Oh?" said Elvira, not really interested. "Well, now you're up, you can help me set the table. I suppose we'll have to take 'his majesty' his breakfast as usual."

"No, Elvie. Not today," said Vesna, looking sheepish. "Nor any other day, either."

"What do you mean?" Elvira dried her hands on a tea towel and took some eggs from the larder. "I suppose I'll have to do them sunny side up. He always complains if I don't." Turning from the larder, eggs in hand, she studied her pretty sister's somewhat flushed face gravely. "What's going on, Vessie? What are you trying to say?"

Elvira came and sat down at the table beside her sister, who was now shaking like a leaf. Suddenly she burst into tears, tears she had stored up for the past two weeks, ever since Rodney Purbright's unwelcome return.

"Oh my God, Vessie – you haven't? Please tell me you haven't done anything silly."

"I have," she wailed. "I couldn't stand it any longer. I won't get you involved, I promise. Except I've got a body to get rid of, and you're the only one I can trust to help me and not shop me to the police."

Elvira tried to take in what her sister was saying. "But how? How on earth did you manage to do it?"

"I – I shot him when he was asleep. With his own gun. I put several of those herbal sleeping powders into his cocoa, like I said, and, well, he didn't wake up, and I – I shot him."

"Are you sure he's dead?" was Elvira's next question. If the deed was done, there was no point in holding a post mortem now. Dead was dead in anyone's language.

"Of course I'm sure. I blew half his face off. It was horrible."

Elvira shuddered. "Oh Vessie, you poor, brave, stupid fool."

"You *are* going to help me, aren't you?" Vesna was scared now, her sister looked so disapproving and fierce.

"Don't be silly, Vessie, of course I am. We're blood, we're family. I'm going to help you. Just let me think for a moment."

She returned to the larder and put the eggs back in the hideous china hen-shaped container. Sitting down again, she took her hand in an uncustomary gesture of love and solidarity. "We could put him under the rose bushes like you suggested…" she began.

"Yes, we could, couldn't we?" Vesna's face brightened through her tears.

و

A solitary owl hooted as a cold, pale moon stared down into the little front garden of Appleby cottage. It was two o'clock in the morning and, apart from the owl who flapped its wings occasionally, nothing stirred. The frost glinted on the grass as the Rowan sisters carried a large and extremely heavy roll of carpet out of the front door.

They looked up and down the crescent as they put down their burden and straightened their aching backs. It had been a mammoth task for the small-boned women to lift the dead weight of Rodney Purbright off the bed and roll him up in the carpet. It had taken them the best part of two hours to do it, and a further half-an-hour to manoeuvre him down the stairs.

They stood in the front garden, waiting and listening. Not a sound. Not a single noise disturbed the still night. The leaves had long since fallen from the trees, so not even the rustle of foliage could be heard. Even the owl was quiet now. They looked at each other and then embraced for a few brief seconds. No words passed their lips. No words were necessary. This night would be one they would never forget.

The ground was rock hard as Elvira started to dig vigorously beneath the rose bushes. Vesna, meanwhile, put on the kettle in preparation for the warming cups of tea that would inevitably be needed as the night progressed. It had been agreed that Elvira, being the taller and stronger of the two, should do most of the spadework, with Vesna taking over when she was too exhausted to continue.

So, the weary hours passed, and it wasn't until nearly five o'clock before there was a hole deep enough to put the body in. Vesna remembered how she had loved the fact her fiancé was such a fine, tall, strapping young man; now she wished with all her heart he had been a midget.

But the work was done at last, and all that remained was to shovel the earth back over the body. Just in time, they remembered to bury the gun with it. Soon all was as before, the ground just looking well dug beneath the rose bushes. Nothing untoward could be seen and it was, thankfully, still pitch dark. Soon, they knew, the first stragglers of the morning would start to wander down the crescent. For them it would be just another working day.

Exhausted, they climbed the stairs to their shared bedroom. Although Elvira's room was now unoccupied, she had no intention of sleeping in there again until she had changed the sheets and fumigated the room thoroughly. And, she thought with grim satisfaction, put back the lace curtains.

Both sisters were soon plunged into a deep sleep, until the noise of the paper boy whistling, the clatter of milk bottles and the rattle of the letterbox two hours later brought Elvira to alert wakefulness. Vesna stirred but didn't wake.

Elvira, lying beside her, tried to get back to sleep but it eluded her now. Every bone in her body was crying out for some soothing liniment so, giving up the struggle, and careful not to disturb her sister, she rose and went to the window. She stared down at the newly dug earth beneath the rose bushes and gave an involuntary shudder. Only they knew what was buried under them, thank goodness. Wrapping her candlewick dressing gown around her thin frame, she crept down to the kitchen to make some breakfast. The physical energy she had expended had made her ravenous.

Frying some eggs and bread, she relived in her mind the events of the night before. She reflected that, despite the horror of the enterprise they had just undertaken, it had brought about a kind of rapprochement between her and Vesna. They had never been particularly close but helping to dispose of Rodney Purbright's remains had given her an advantage she had never had before. Vesna needed her on side; needed to ensure her continued loyalty.

She turned over the eggs with an expert flick of the spatula. Their relationship would be on a completely different footing from now on. Vesna would no longer have the upper hand. She would have to treat her with respect instead of doing her down like she usually did. Elvira smiled as she dished out the eggs and fried bread. There would be some changes made around here now.

As she sat on at the kitchen table, eating her well-earned breakfast, she noticed that the room had grown markedly colder, even though the fire in the range was burning fiercely. She hugged the shawl around her shoulders and shivered. It was going to be a hard winter.

Chapter Eleven

It had been nearly eight months since the Rowan sisters had been bothered by the presence of the living Rodney Purbright. The dead version had been under the rose bushes in the front garden of little Appleby Cottage for all that time, and the blooms which had resulted were the talk of the neighbourhood. Their scent had not only filled the cottage's garden, but most of the crescent as well. Clevedon Powell, a retired colonel who had recently moved into Hallows Mead Crescent a few doors down from the Rowans, was envious of those roses. He leaned over the front gate at Elvira one evening, demanding to know "how the hell she did it". Of course, Elvira didn't tell him the real reason for the splendid blooms, but simply smiled enigmatically and echoed a comment she had heard on a recent gardening programme on the wireless. "The answer, Colonel, lies in the soil." This had sent him into a fuming rage as he trudged back to his home and glared at his own poor specimens. Their soil must be the same as his, so why weren't they benefiting from it, too?

But, although the Appleby Cottage roses continued to bloom and make the garden look and smell glorious, inside the cottage it was a different story altogether. Elvira couldn't account for the constant coldness in the place and, even in the middle of one of the hottest Augusts on record, she was forced to wear thick cardigans and woolly socks when indoors.

For Vesna, it was even worse. She felt the cold just as much as her sister, but she also felt a 'presence' she couldn't quite describe. One evening in late September she couldn't stand it any longer. There was something preying on her mind and now, she decided, was as good a time as any to get it out in the open. She looked across at her sister who was busily writing up herbal receipts on a new card index system. After watching her for several minutes, she finally let out a scream.

"Can't you stop that pen from scratching?" she cried. "It's putting my teeth on edge."

Elvira looked up in surprise. She blotted the card she had been writing so diligently and gently blew on it.

"Sorry, Vessie," she said mildly, "I'll go into the kitchen to finish these off if it bothers you that much."

"Oh, stop being so *reasonable*, Elvie," snapped Vesna. "Stay where you are. I've got something to tell you, anyhow."

"Oh?" Elvira took another card from the pack and dipped her pen into the inkpot.

"I can't stand living here any longer," she said. "I'm going away…"

This made Elvira drop her pen, spilling the ink from the nib onto her white blouse. "Going away?" The thought of her lively sister not being there made her suddenly panic.

"You know we haven't been happy since …"

"Since *you* killed Rodney Purbright, you mean?" said Elvira with venom, rubbing at the ink stain, making it spread further. "Blast it!" she muttered under her breath.

"You helped me bury him, don't forget," spat back her sister. "And it's no good rubbing your blouse like that. You need to put sugar on it."

"And I've been regretting it ever since," muttered Elvira, leaving Vesna to guess whether her regret was for helping her bury Purbright's body or for rubbing the ink into her delicate silk blouse. "I should never have agreed to do it. I should have shopped you to the police."

"But you *did* help me," Vesna pointed out. "You wouldn't have seen me hang, would you?" Not waiting for an answer, she carried on. "The point is, I've met this bloke …"

"Bloke? What bloke?"

63

"Oh, just some bloke that came into the shop. He comes from Cromer."

"Cromer? What's he doing here, then? It's a long way to come for spuds, isn't it?"

"Oh, he was just passing through. Called in for some oranges and a packet of cigarettes, that's all. He's a travelling salesman."

"Okay, so what are you saying? You're planning to go off to Cromer with a man you hardly know and leave me here with … with …"

"With what exactly?"

"You know full well. It's something to do with *him*. Why it's so cold in here all the time."

"You don't really believe he's haunting us, do you?"

"Yes, I do," said Elvira. "And so do you. Anyway, you can't just go off with this man. Are you going to marry him?"

"He's asked me," said Vesna, looking down at her slippered feet in embarrassment. "I've been meaning to tell you all week."

"I suppose I should congratulate you," sniffed Elvira, standing up and going to the window.

It had just started to rain and the sound of spattering against the panes made the room feel even colder. She hugged her shawl around her shoulders.

"Look, Elvie, love. I'm sorry. But it's a chance I have to take. He seems very keen on me, and he's got a nice little semi, he tells me. Just waiting for the right little wife, he said."

"All very cosy. I must say I don't like the way you've fixed this all up behind my back."

"I'm sorry," repeated Vesna. "But I really have to take this chance, don't you see? I wouldn't go if it wasn't for this place."

"What do you mean? You just said it's not haunted, so what about this place that you have to up and marry a man you hardly know?"

"No, I just meant …" Vesna paused.

"What? What precisely did you mean?"

The younger woman looked sheepish. "Oh, just that it's the memories. Of what – what happened."

"And you're planning to leave me here to face them alone? I wasn't the one who murdered him and now you're abandoning me, even after I helped you and shouldn't have done."

"Look, Elvie, it'd be better all-round if I wasn't here, really it would. Anyway, you've got your shop and the business is doing well. It would be silly to leave all that now. I'll write to you – often."

"Do I get an invitation to the wedding?"

Vesna flushed at her sister's sarcastic tone. "Er, it's just going to be a registry do. In Cromer. I don't think it's worth your while coming all that way."

"You *are* going to get married, aren't you?" Elvira began to pace the room.

"Of course. What makes you think I'm not?"

"It all seems a bit sudden, that's all."

"Well, sudden or not, that's the way it is. I'm going to start packing now. Derek and I are leaving on the one o'clock train tomorrow."

Elvira ran out of the room and up to her bedroom, slamming the door. She flung herself on the bed, clutching the newly cleaned eiderdown as dry sobs vomited out of her mouth. It seemed she was doomed to remain in this fridge of a cottage alone while her sister played fast and loose with Derek in Cromer.

After a while, she lay quietly, breathing fast. She felt utterly exhausted. What a miserable existence it was. The cottage held no attractions for her anymore. With Vesna gone, what was she to do? She had the shop, it was true, and people were popping by all the time with their worries, aches and pains. She was getting quite a reputation among the locals and even further afield. Maybe, given time, she wouldn't miss Vesna so much. But somehow, she knew she'd never get over losing her. Although Cromer wasn't so far on the train, to Elvira, Vesna might as well have died.

She knew, in her heart of hearts, that her sister wasn't going to marry this Derek. He was probably married already. What was she thinking of? Vesna had already broken all the rules by committing murder, and now she was about to ruin her life yet again by going off to live over the brush with a married man. It seemed to Elvira that once you started on the slippery slope, there was only one way to go – and that was down.

Chapter Twelve

Elvira still missed her sister, even though she had been gone for almost a year. When she first left, Vesna wrote at least twice a week, telling her all her news. Derek was a charming man, she said, and they were very happy together. They only had a couple of rooms, but they were clean and bright. (What happened to that semi? Elvira had wondered.) Once Derek became a retail manager, and no longer needed to travel up and down the country, things would be much better all-round. But, for the time being, they were very happy. She wasn't in love with Derek, but he treated her well, gave her lots of little treats, and they had lots of fun together.

Elvira had written back just as regularly with her own news which wasn't nearly as exciting as Vesna's. There was no man in her life to talk about, but she had been able to tell her that Harry Banks had become engaged. She had taken a vicarious pleasure in passing this on, although she supposed it was water off a duck's back now that her sister had Derek and seemed to be very happy with him, married or not.

The correspondence between them had gone on all through the months leading up to Christmas but, by then, Vesna's letters had tailed off, reducing to a mere trickle by January. By April, Elvira stopped waiting for the postman to bring a letter with a Cromer postmark; she knew there wouldn't be one.

One morning in early May, she was in the front garden doing some weeding when she stood up to give her aching back a rest. As she stood there, shielding her eyes from the bright sun, she thought she was seeing things. She rubbed her eyes and inwardly screamed as she realised she'd managed to get some dirt in them. As they watered, the figure she thought she had seen advanced further towards her. When she could focus once more, she knew it hadn't been a mirage. Her sister stood before her, a weak smile on her pale, thin face.

Elvira took her in her arms while Vesna stood there, arms limply at her sides, not returning the hug. Not noticing or caring, however, Elvira continued to hug her, full of joy at seeing her again. Maybe it was just a visit, but the heavy suitcase she was carrying belied a fleeting one. Eventually, she relaxed her hold and took the suitcase from her.

"It's so good to see you, love," she gushed. "I was beginning to wonder what had happened to you. You stopped answering my letters."

Vesna stared at her tall, dark sister and saw someone she hardly recognised. Flushed as she was with happiness at seeing her sister again, Elvira looked almost handsome, and she felt a sudden pang of affection for her. She grabbed her hand.

"It's good to see you too, Elvie," she said. "I – I missed you."

Elvira led her into the cottage but, as she did so, noticed her wince at the sudden coldness. She, herself, had grown so used to it, she hardly noticed it anymore. Vesna, hugging her coat around her, walked into the parlour and sat down on the battered, old sofa. Elvira could see she was far from happy.

"I'll put the kettle on," she said brightly, "then you can tell me all your news."

Vesna looked around the room. "The place hasn't changed much," she observed.

"What did you expect? You haven't been gone *that* long."

"No, I suppose not."

A few minutes later, they were sitting side by side, drinking hot mugs of tea. Elvira had managed to dig out a couple of chocolate digestive biscuits, which Vesna devoured greedily.

"Have you eaten lately?" asked Elvira.

"Not since last night," she replied, through a mouthful of crumbs.

"You must be hungry. I'll cook some eggs and bacon."

"Lovely."

Elvira got up at once, but Vesna pulled her down again. "There's no hurry," she said. "I want to talk to you first."

Elvira studied her young sister's face closely. She was looking very tired. There were dark circles under her round blue eyes. Her cheeks were pale and much thinner than she remembered.

"No, love, you must eat first," insisted Elvira, standing up again. "It will only take a few minutes to rustle up a decent meal. Once you've eaten, then you can tell me all about it."

"You're a brick, Elvie," muttered her sister, as a tear began to trickle down her dry cheek. "You're not one to judge, are you? Whatever I've done, you won't mind, will you?"

Elvira almost laughed. Considering she'd covered up a murder for her, it was all too true.

⁂

Half an hour later, the two women were sitting at the kitchen table, the remains of Vesna's meal still waiting to be washed up.

"That was delicious, Elvie. Just what the doctor ordered. Any more toast, by the way?"

Elvira stood up directly and fetched the toasting fork. "Let's go into the parlour and we'll toast some bread by the fire."

Although it was a fairly warm day, the parlour fire was kept going all the year round in an effort to fend off the unnatural cold inside the cottage. It had little effect, however, and the sisters shivered as they huddled around the hearth, toasting thick slices of homemade bread.

"Do you feel up to telling me what happened, Vessie?" asked Elvira, buttering a slice of toast for her. "I mean, are you back to stay?" She looked at her expectantly, her lower lip quivering slightly.

"That all depends ..." Vesna bit into the hot toast, and butter trickled down her chin.

"On what, love? I really don't want you to leave again. Is Derek – I mean has your husband ..."

"Oh, come off it, Elvie, you knew I wasn't going to marry him, didn't you?"

Elvira looked away in embarrassment. "I – I didn't know for sure, but I suppose..."

"It's all right, dear, you were quite right. He was already married. What a complete fool you must have thought me."

Elvira sighed, shaking her head. "I know it was hard for you – staying here. You thought you had a way of escape. I understand."

"You're too good to live, Elvie. You should've found a good man to marry. You deserve it – much more than me. It wasn't fair that I got the looks. I'm a selfish so-and-so."

"Don't say that," ordered Elvira firmly. "You've been good to me – I wouldn't have the shop if it wasn't for you."

"Anyway, I intend to make it up to you now," said Vesna. "I've learnt my lesson. Derek was just having fun. When he was fed up with me, he went back to his wife. It's an old story."

"You poor love," said Elvira, studying her sister's face.

She seemed closed in on herself and didn't invite the hug Elvira wanted to give her. They had never been demonstrative in their affection for each other and now, when Vesna needed comfort, Elvira didn't know how to give it.

"Never mind, Vessie. No one need ever know. You're just the same as before you went away. People won't be any the wiser…"

Vesna gave her an ironic smile, as she wiped away her tears. "I think they might, you know. You see… I'm going to have a baby."

PART TWO

The Mid-Nineteen-Fifties

Chapter Thirteen

Bernard Paltoquet stared at himself in the full-length hall mirror. Today was his thirtieth birthday, but he was feeling and, in his own opinion, looking at least ten years older. He still retained all his hair, which was a plus point but, on closer examination, he noticed some grey at the temple and forehead. Oh dear, he thought, tempus is definitely starting to fugit.

He didn't consider himself a vain man, but he had a dread of getting old. He also had a dread of putting on weight. Turning sideways, he continued to stare at himself, holding in his stomach, not daring to breathe out. What he saw reflected back at him gave him cause to feel even more concerned. He was getting a pot. Most men got pot bellies through drinking too much; his worst enemy couldn't accuse him of that. But wolfing down all the delicious meals Mrs Harper dished out to him, and demanding second and third helpings, was proving his downfall.

He sighed and turned away from the offending mirror. It was probably designed to make you look fatter and older than you really were, he thought hopefully. Like those in fairgrounds.

Entering the dining room, he found the table spread with the usual accoutrements for breakfast. He heard Mrs Harper singing away in the kitchen, and the wonderful aroma of sizzling bacon wafted towards him as he sat down at the table. Should he just have a piece of toast and a cup of tea? Hang it all, he then thought, it *was* his birthday, after all. If he didn't deserve a good breakfast on his birthday, when did he deserve it? The dieting and exercise would have to wait for at least another twenty-four hours. He and his friend, Robbie MacTavish, had planned to celebrate with a meal in the West End that evening; he couldn't be on a diet for that, could he?

Mrs Harper brought his breakfast through from the kitchen and plonked the plate down in front of him. "'Appy birthday, Vicar," she greeted him, and placed a white envelope next to his food.

He was touched. A birthday card from his devoted, but unsentimental, housekeeper: that had never happened before. He opened it with pleasure, but his face fell when he saw it wasn't a card at all. It was two small photographs of Mrs Harper, instead. They weren't even nice photos, as she was scowling.

"What's up?" she asked, as he stared at the photos.

"Er, well, Mrs Aitch. These pictures – they're – like you," he finished lamely.

"'Course they're like me," she said. "They *are* me."

"Well, thank – thank you."

"You don't 'ave to thank me, Vicar. Just sign the back of them, saying they look like me."

Bernard was beginning to understand. Could it be that Mrs Harper was applying for a passport or some such other legal document? He dutifully signed where requested wondering, as he did so, where his birthday card was.

"In case you're wondering," she said, as if reading his thoughts, "I'm getting a passport done." She puffed herself up with pride.

"Oh, right," said Bernard, handing the photos back to her, secretly glad he wasn't meant to put them in his wallet next to his bosom. "Are – are you planning a trip abroad then?"

"You could say that," she grinned, as she poured out more tea for him. "You know old Mrs Selfridge at number forty-four?"

"Mrs Selfridge? Yes, of course, a nice old body. Doesn't come to church very often, though."

"Well, no. She's 'ad a lot to contend with lately. 'Er 'usband 'as just popped 'is clogs."

"Pardon? Oh, I see. I'm sorry to hear that. Should I go and visit her to offer my condolences and what comfort I can, do you think?"

"You can if you like, but you won't find 'er shedding no tears over that layabout. Geoff Selfridge was a waste of space, in my opinion – and in 'ers. Dying's the best thing 'e ever did, 'cos 'e's left 'er a nice little nest egg. She 'ad 'im well insured, she weren't daft. She's going on a cruise round the Mediterranean and 'as asked me to go with 'er, all expenses paid. So, like, I could 'ardly turn it down." She eyed Bernard cautiously. "I know it means you'll 'ave to do without me for a couple of weeks, but I'll find someone to look after you, don't worry."

Bernard's heart sank at the thought of doing without Mrs Harper's stew and dumplings, not to mention cakes and apple pies, for two whole weeks, but realised he was being selfish. He cleared his throat gallantly.

"I'm very pleased for you, Mrs Aitch. You deserve a nice holiday. When – when is this trip of yours?"

"Oh, not until June," she said, scraping some crumbs off the table cloth. "But I need to get my passport form and photos in the post soon. I don't know 'ow long it'll take."

"Well, I hope you have a lovely time."

"Thank you, Vicar. Oh, by the way …"

"Yes?" said Bernard, as he munched his toast.

"Did you 'ear about the body they found on the Common yesterday?"

"Body? Oh, dear me, no. Was it a heart attack victim or something?"

"No. It was murder, they're saying. A young girl, apparently, in 'er teens. All 'acked about. 'Er 'ead 'ad been severed from 'er body. Is it in the paper?"

Bernard shrugged. "It hasn't arrived yet. I'll give that paperboy a thick ear when I see him. He's always late these days. Can't get out of bed, I suppose."

"Well, there you are. Ain't it terrible though?"

"Terrible, indeed. Do they know who the poor girl is?"

"No, I ain't 'eard nothing about that."

Mrs Harper started to return to the kitchen but, as she did so, he called after her. "Has the post been yet?"

Surely there would be a card from Robbie, at the very least. He realised, as he thought this, the poor dead girl on the Common wouldn't be celebrating any more birthdays, with or without cards. He felt humbled as he tucked into his eggs and bacon.

As Bernard was finishing his breakfast, his friend Robbie was in his surgery, going through his list of patients which, that early April morning, mainly consisted of cold and flu sufferers. Nothing out of the ordinary, he noted, disappointed as on most mornings. What he wouldn't give for something a little more out of the ordinary, like a ruptured spleen or a champagne bottle leg.

Robbie studied his first patient with concern. At first glance, this seemed a more interesting case than he was expecting. She was a middle-aged, careworn-looking woman with a very pale complexion, dark circles around the eyes and a general air of 'unwellness' about her.

"Ah, Mrs Carstairs, please do sit down. What can I do for you?"

"Well, Doctor, I've not been sleeping very well, and I've got this dreadful headache. I wouldn't normally have bothered you, but it's been days now and I really can't stand it much longer."

"I see," said Robbie, writing something on his pad. "Perhaps I should take your blood pressure first of all."

He wrapped a thick black band around the woman's arm and started pumping.

"I don't think it's anything physical, Doctor," said Mrs Carstairs as she felt the pressure on her arm build. "It's just the worry, you see…"

Robbie raised a quizzical eyebrow. "Worry?"

"It's our daughter – Helen. I think she's got in with a bad crowd."

"Oh, dear," said Robbie, removing the arm band. "Well, your BP is a little high, but not abnormally so."

"I don't really know who to turn to. She's been staying out to all hours and not saying where she goes or who with. I've been away for the last couple of nights, staying with my sister who's not well." She paused, as if considering what to say next. Then she continued. "When I got home this morning, her bed hadn't been slept in. That was the last straw. I don't know where she is. She's only seventeen."

"I know Helen – Helen," said Robbie, writing something more on his pad. "She came to see me – er, a few weeks ago." He stopped. He realised too late that he probably shouldn't have said that.

"She did? She never told me. What about?" The look on Mrs Carstairs' face was enough to break his heart.

"Oh dear, Mrs Carstairs, you know I can't tell you," he said. "But she isn't unwell or anything like that, so don't concern yourself on that account."

"Oh, well, that's something I suppose."

"Look, take this prescription for painkillers for your headache and try not to worry too much about your daughter. Teenagers are often difficult. Growing up's a painful business sometimes. If you still have the headache after a few days, come back and I'll organise some tests for you." He rose to show his patient to the door.

As he opened it for her, she hesitated. "What is it, Mrs Carstairs?" he asked kindly.

"Er – well, it's my hubby, Henry," she said falteringly. "He – he gets headaches too. Not like mine, though. They're much worse – or so he says. He's always holding his head. I'm very worried about *him* as well as Helen."

"I'm so sorry," said Robbie. "But you know I can't do anything for him until he comes to see me, don't you?"

"Yes, of course," said Ivy Carstairs, looking resigned. "But he won't go near doctors – doesn't believe in them, he says. Can't you give me something for him too? Or will these pills you've prescribed for me be all right to give him?"

"No, you can't give your husband these pills. I haven't prescribed them for him, and I won't prescribe anything until I have examined him." Robbie spoke very firmly.

"I see," she said. "I suppose I knew you were going to say that. It's just that he doesn't seem the same person since he's had these headaches. He never used to be so miserable. Not that he was ever the life and soul, like. But he gets angry at the least little thing these days and takes his pain out on me and Helen."

"I'm sorry, Mrs Carstairs, but you must try and persuade him to come and see me. Until he does, I can do nothing."

After she had left, he sat back down at his desk, taking a breather before his next patient who he could hear coughing in the waiting room. He recalled Helen Carstairs' visit only too vividly. She was a pretty blonde, but her prettiness had been dimmed by the strain she was under. He hadn't helped ease her worry by confirming her pregnancy and advising her to confide in her parents. She had told him she was afraid of their reaction and thought it very likely they would throw her out of the house. He couldn't see the mild-mannered Ivy Carstairs doing that, but he couldn't answer for her father, as he had never met him. He just hoped, for all their sakes, Helen would tell them the truth before it became obvious and they could see for themselves what was happening to their daughter.

∾

Contrary to the intelligence put about by Mrs Selfridge and spread with glee by Mrs Harper, the body on the Common wasn't as mutilated as it was supposed. The stomach had been ripped open, which was bad enough, but at least the head was still attached to the body.

"Who found her, do we know?" asked Inspector Phil Craddock of his young subordinate.

He idly swung around on his office swivel chair while he waited for Rathbone's response. The chair creaked under his excessive weight, causing the younger (and slimmer) man to worry that it was about to collapse under him.

"Some old chap walking his dog, sir," he replied. "A statement's already been taken."

"Hmm," said Craddock, deep in thought. "If it weren't for the dog walkers, half the bodies would remain undiscovered, I reckon."

"Just as well," observed Rathbone wryly. "We've got enough on our plates with the ones that *are* discovered."

"That's true. Has Bucket come up with a cause of death?"

"His initial finding suggests by a deep stab wound to the abdomen, but he isn't ruling anything out until he's got her on the slab."

Craddock winced. He hated the way the bow-tied, goatee-bearded Graydon Smythe-Bucket wallowed in his work. He could hear him using that very term, 'got her on the slab', and he didn't like it one bit. Didn't the man realise these bodies had once been human beings, with families and friends who cared very much about their deaths? The man was an arrogant, stuck-up bastard and they were some of his better points.

"Do we know how long she's been dead?"

Rathbone studied his notebook. "Er, between about seventeen and twenty-four hours according to Mr Smythe-Bucket. But he thought it was possibly even longer."

"Vague, isn't he?" Craddock sniffed.

Brian Rathbone smiled. "I don't think he wants to commit himself at this stage." He knew only too well what his boss thought of that particular pathologist.

"No, of course he doesn't. Anyway, the first thing we need to do is find out who she is and inform the next of kin. Get on to it, Rathbone."

"Yes, sir."

Sergeant Brian Rathbone was relieved to be dismissed by the inspector as he was still having trouble keeping his breakfast down, even after a gap of several hours since seeing the body. He had never got used to viewing dead bodies, especially first thing in the morning. Inspector Craddock, he knew, felt exactly the same, but he'd been longer in the job and knew how to hide it better. Now, he thought, all he had to do was identify the corpse and then break it to the next of kin.

A piece of bloody cake.

Chapter Fourteen

Bernard had been looking forward for over a week to the posh West End meal he and Robbie were to share that evening. He was looking forward to it all the more as it was Robbie's treat. Mrs Harper had sniffed when Bernard told her he would be 'dining out'. She prided herself she could compete with the best chefs in the West End, but if they wanted to waste their money, that was up to them. It was no skin off her nose.

Robbie had booked a table at Simpson's in the Strand and Bernard hoped it would be a night to remember, as his birthday, so far, had been a washout. He hadn't received a single card, not even from his dear friend Dorothy Plunkett, but at least Robbie would bring one round to him that evening. He knew the good doctor wasn't one to waste money on a postage stamp.

Robbie arrived at the vicarage at seven-fifteen complete with the expected card and a carefully wrapped parcel. Bernard suspected that Robbie's housekeeper, Lucy Carter, had wrapped it because it looked far too neat for Robbie's handiwork. Bernard also suspected that Lucy had bought the present on his behalf but dismissed this thought as unworthy and uncharitable.

"Hello, Bernie old chap," Robbie greeted him. "Happy birthday." He handed his friend the card and gift. "Hope you like aftershave," he added, spoiling the surprise. "Lucy chose it – I'm no good at that sort of thing."

Bernard smiled, hiding his disappointment as best he could. "Thanks," he said.

"Come on, old boy, taxi's waiting. You can open it later," as he watched Bernard struggle with the wrapping paper. "It's Old Spice," he informed him, thus spoiling any element of surprise that was still left.

"Oh, very nice," said Bernard with all the enthusiasm he could muster.

"Leave the card," said Robbie. "I think I forgot to sign it, by the way. I'll do it later. Come on."

Bernard left the card and aftershave on the hall table and followed his friend out to the waiting taxi.

"This is very good of you, Robbie," he said, stepping into the vehicle. "You shouldn't have spent all this money on little old me, you know."

As the cab moved off, Robbie laughed. "Well, I'm getting some pleasure out of it too. We don't do this every day of the week. You can reciprocate on my birthday, if you like."

Bernard gave an inward sigh. If he could afford it, he thought. A vicar's stipend didn't stretch to many extravagant nights out.

అ

When they were seated at their table in the sumptuous surroundings of Simpson's studying its ornate menu, Robbie asked Bernard if he knew the Carstairs family. Ivy Carstairs' visit that morning had been preying on his mind all day.

Bernard, however, was too busy studying the menu to pay much attention. "Hmm?" was all he managed, his mind concentrating on the all-important question of what to have for a starter.

Robbie looked at his friend in disgruntlement. It was taking him ages to choose his food. "Come on, old chap," he said, "the chef will have gone home by the time you're ready to order."

Bernard looked up from behind the large menu card which practically hid him from view. "Sorry. It all looks so delicious…"

The waiter hovered over them impatiently as Bernard continued to waver between the Welsh rarebit and the

French onion soup. Finally, he plumped for the soup and the waiter whisked the menus away before he could change his mind again.

"Sorry about that," said Bernard, "but I want to enjoy every mouthful, and I don't want to make a mistake by ordering something I'm not going to like."

Robbie smiled. "Of course you don't, but the food's all good here. I'm sure whatever we have will be first rate," he said.

"Yes, thanks again, Robbie. This is a real treat." Now that the all-important decision on starters had been made, Bernard remembered what his friend had just asked him. "Why do you ask about the Carstairs?"

"Ivy Carstairs came to see me today and she told me she was getting headaches because she's worried about her daughter, Helen. And she's also worried about her husband's health."

"Oh dear," said Bernard. "I know the Carstairs quite well. They come regularly to the Sunday morning services, although I fear that young Helen is dragged there by force."

"Anyway, let's enjoy our meal and talk about them later," said Robbie as the first course arrived.

No more was said on the subject of the Carstairs while the roast duck, sherry trifle and cheese board were in progress. When all the food had been dispatched, they sat back, lit cigars and sipped their postprandial brandies.

They looked around, taking in their elegant surroundings, feeling happy and relaxed. A band was playing *The Very Thought of You* and couples were smooching around the dance floor.

"Well, Robbie," smiled Bernard after a few minutes of contented cigar puffing and brandy sipping. "That was a meal to remember. Thank you so much."

"Don't mention it," said Robbie, swirling the brandy around his glass, watching the gold liquid making waves up to its rim. "This is the life, eh? You'd hardly know there'd been a World War, would you?"

"No, it feels good to be alive. Anyway, what were we talking about earlier? Mrs Carstairs' daughter, I think you said?"

"Yes. I was wondering if you had spoken to her recently?"

"Er, no," said Bernard thoughtfully. "She never bothers to speak to me. Even when we part at the church door, she just hides behind her parents. Doesn't even shake my hand. Can't wait to get away."

"Hmm," said Robbie, "I see."

"Why do you ask?" Bernard was suddenly interested.

"I really shouldn't say anything," said Robbie, puffing on his cigar with relish. "But, you're a man of the cloth, so I suppose it's all right…"

"Well…?"

"The poor girl's pregnant," he said at last, "and she dreads telling her parents. I'm sure her mother will be all right about it, but I'm not so sure about her father. He's a bit of a tyrant, by all accounts."

"Oh dear," sighed Bernard. "But I'm sure you're wrong about Henry Carstairs. He always strikes me as a decent sort, although he's been a bit miserable lately. We used to have a brief chat after the service, but recently he's only shaken my hand without speaking. Still, it must be a worry for his daughter – to have to tell a God-fearing cove like Carstairs that she's going to have a baby. She's only seventeen, isn't she? What will she do?"

"I don't know. I wish I did," said Robbie. "Anyway, let's have one for the road, shall we? Toast your birthday one more time. I booked the taxi for ten-thirty, so we've got time."

"I really shouldn't, you know," giggled Bernard, now more relaxed than ever. Some unkind people might have said he was as relaxed as a newt, but he wasn't going to apologize for being happy on his birthday. "One isn't thirty every day," he asserted. "So, why not?"

"Good! Waiter!"

When the second glass of brandy had been brought, Robbie grew thoughtful again. "You know, Bernie, do you think it's right we should be dining alone? I sometimes wish you and I had ladies to escort. Some nice, pretty women to take around to the pictures and meals and so on."

It was Bernard's turn to become thoughtful. The image of Dorothy Plunkett came to his mind, the woman he had met some six years ago. No one could say it had been a whirlwind romance, however. But there had been a spark between them, even so. It had been unfortunate that, before any romance between them could get off the ground, she had to return home to Devon to look after her ailing parents.

As if reading his thoughts, Robbie said, "Have you heard from Dorothy recently?"

"I got a letter from her last week. Her father's still being difficult. I think she'll be relieved when he finally goes. He's never very well, and she says life is becoming a trial to him."

"Dead, but won't lie down, eh?"

"That's a horrible thing to say, Robbie," he admonished him. "But, in a way, yes…. I suppose you're right."

Both men sat on, sipping their brandy, lost in their own thoughts, until the waiter announced their taxi was waiting outside to take them home.

Chapter Fifteen

"There's a Mrs Carstairs waiting to see you, guv. Says her daughter's missing."

Sergeant Brian Rathbone waited while his harassed boss searched for his pen. Inspector Craddock's wife had given it to him two Christmases ago, and ever since then he lost it, on average, about once every two weeks.

"You can never find a bloody thing in this place," he grumbled. "I put it down over there. Someone's walked off with it again. My wife'll skin me alive if I lose it."

"I'm sure it'll turn up, sir," said Rathbone soothingly. "I'm always losing pens, but they usually turn up in the end."

He stood patiently in his superior's office, waiting for him to stop blowing off steam.

"Blasted nuisance!" Craddock continued to rummage under a pile of papers on his desk. "It's got to be somewhere. Have you seen it?"

"Is it royal blue with a gold nib, sir?"

"That's it! Have you seen it?"

"Only when you last had it – yesterday."

"Ha ha, very helpful." He sighed and slumped into his chair. "I suppose it'll turn up, like you say. Anyway, what d'you want? It'd better be important."

"I think it's possible we may have found the identity of the murdered girl," said Rathbone, unfazed by the inspector's gruff manner. He had worked with him too long for that.

"Ah, right, good. Well done. Tell me more."

"Well, like I said, there's a Mrs Ivy Carstairs waiting to see you. She's come in to report her daughter Helen missing. From an initial description, the body could be her."

"Right, then. What are we waiting for? We'd better go and see her. We'll need to get her to make a formal I.D. Once Bucket has finished carving her up, of course."

❧

Mrs Carstairs paced up and down the room into which she had been shown by the desk sergeant. She hadn't much liked the look on his face when she had described her daughter to him. What did they know? What were they keeping from her? A kind policewoman had brought her a cup of tea which she hadn't been able to drink. She was much too nervous to swallow anything. Why didn't someone come and tell her what was going on?

After what seemed like a lifetime, two men entered the room, both with the same look on their faces as the desk sergeant. She felt she was going to faint.

"What's going on?" she cried. "Please tell me. Do you know where my daughter is?"

Inspector Craddock smiled at her. "Please, Mrs – er Carstairs, isn't it? Please sit down. Calm yourself. We just need to confirm a few details."

"Then why are you all looking so serious?" she asked, refusing to sit down.

Sergeant Rathbone took her gently by the arm and led her to a chair. "Try not to worry, Mrs Carstairs. We don't know anything about your daughter as yet. We just need a few more details."

"What do you mean? Do you know where she is?" she asked, finally sitting down.

"We know nothing for sure at this stage," said Craddock.

Ivy Carstairs felt cold, practically numb. Would they never come to the point?

"First of all, Mrs Carstairs, can you give us a detailed description of your daughter? Or, better still, do you have a recent photograph?"

"Yes – yes, of course."

She fished in her handbag and pulled out her purse. In the front flap was a black and white photo of a charming young girl, long hair framing a heart-shaped, Madonna-like face.

"Charming, charming," muttered Craddock.

His heart sank. There wasn't any doubt. The photograph he was holding was that of the dead girl on the Common. This poor woman's daughter had been brutally murdered, and he had to break the news to her. But he never chickened out of this unpleasant task, feeling it was the least he could do for the bereaved.

Craddock handed back the picture with a trembling hand and cleared his throat. "I'm afraid I've got some bad news, Mrs Carstairs," he said.

Dr Smythe-Bucket looked down his aquiline nose at the plump middle-aged woman being escorted by Sergeant Rathbone into his cold mortuary domain. He had finished his post mortem on the body of the unfortunate young girl found dead on Wandsworth Common and had come to the conclusion that she had been murdered by person or persons unknown. Inspector Craddock could have told him that without the benefit of cutting her up or spending a fortune on employing high-minded pathologists like Smythe-Bucket in the first place. But then that was only his opinion. No one else seemed to share it.

"This is Mrs Ivy Carstairs, sir," Rathbone informed him. "We have reason to believe that the – er – body is her daughter." What was left of her, he thought sadly.

"Ah, I see," said Smythe-Bucket, wiping his wet, scrubbed hands. "Follow me."

Rathbone could feel the woman tremble as they followed him along a dark corridor. He opened a door at the far end. It was a small room, the space almost entirely taken up by a long table on which reposed the body of the young murder victim. She was covered by a sheet, her face the only part of her visible. She looked peaceful, almost serene, as if she was merely sleeping.

"Is this your daughter, Mrs Carstairs?" Rathbone asked her softly.

He could see by the sudden pallor in her cheeks that it was. If he needed any further corroborative proof, she fainted in his arms.

≈

"So, we now have a positive I.D.," said Craddock with satisfaction. "We haven't lost too much time, but we must hit the ground running if we're to nail the bastard who did it. We have to interview anyone and everyone who knew her and try and establish a motive for her murder."

The inspector, his team of detectives surrounding him, was in his element now. "We need to speak to her parents, of course, and any friends, particularly boyfriends."

He paused to let this sink in. He hadn't been surprised to learn Helen Carstairs had been pregnant, although he had been disappointed. There were too many teenage pregnancies these days. She had looked like an angel from heaven with that innocently beautiful face. But you never could tell. He just hoped she hadn't been taken against her will.

"Now," he continued, once he had put everyone in the picture about the pregnancy, "it would appear the murder took place sometime between ten o'clock last Tuesday evening and five o'clock Wednesday morning. We can't – or rather Bucket can't – pinpoint it any more accurately than that. So, anyone who saw or talked to her before ten o'clock on Tuesday needs to be eliminated from our enquiries."

After the team had dispersed, Craddock turned to his oppo. "This never gets any easier, does it? She was so young."

"I know, guv," said Rathbone. "Can I get you a coffee?"

"Not that stuff from the canteen, thanks. Here, take half a crown and go and get some from Fred's café, and a couple of bacon butties while you're about it."

"Right you are," said Rathbone. "Oh, by the way, your wife called. Wondered if you were coming home this evening."

Craddock glared at the younger man. "I wish she'd get off my case. Doesn't she know I'm investigating a murder? She never gets her priorities right. Don't get me wrong, Rathbone, I worship the ground on which she walks, but she does get on my threepennies sometimes."

Rathbone grinned. He knew of old the ups and downs in the lives of his senior colleague and his demanding wife, Doreen. She called him at least three times a day to find out what he was up to. He was sure she led him a dog's life.

"Did you find your pen, by the way?"

"Oh, yes thanks," muttered Craddock, already immersed in a pile of papers on his desk. "It was on the floor over by the radiator. Don't know how it got there."

"Oh, well, never mind. Glad you found it. Perhaps you should call your wife, sir? She sounded pretty agitated."

Craddock gave him a withering look as if to say would you call her if you were in my shoes? Rathbone took the hint and went in search of the coffee.

Chapter Sixteen

"What are you doing to that poor beast, Mrs Aitch?"

Mrs Harper was poised with broom in hand, ready to strike a mangy-looking black cat who was climbing in through the kitchen window as Bernard entered the room. It was the morning after his birthday outing and he was in search of aspirin to ease his aching head. It wasn't a hangover, he told himself. Just too much rich food, that's all.

"I'm just showing it it's not welcome, Vicar. It keeps trying to get in 'ere and I'm not 'aving it. It's covered in fleas!"

Bernard bent down to try and entice the cat to come to him, but the poor creature was too scared to move.

"Here, puss," he said gently. "Take no notice of the frightening lady. Her bark's worse than her bite."

This cut no ice with the feline, however, who continued to cower by the stove. The mention of the word 'bark' probably didn't help either.

"Don't encourage it," she ordered. "I've got enough to contend with without chasing cats all over the place."

"Do you know if it belongs to anyone, Mrs Aitch?"

"I think it belongs to those weird sisters in Hallows Mead Crescent. It wouldn't surprise me. After all, people say they're witches. D'you know what Mrs Selfridge said to me the other day?"

Bernard sighed. "No, Mrs Aitch. What did she say?"

"That that body they found on the Common was sacrificed in one of their rituals. They're a strange pair, they are. They say they put curses on people. Especially the older one. There's an evil-looking woman, if you like. 'Ave you seen 'er?"

"That's not a nice thing to say," said Bernard. "No one can help what they look like. And I don't pay any attention to that sort of gossip, you know that. Now, let's give this poor creature some milk, shall we?"

"Hmmph!" muttered Mrs Harper with a world of meaning in it. "Shall I cook it a piece of steak while I'm at it?"

"Don't be silly, Mrs Aitch. A tin of Kit-e-Kat or a cod's head will be all that's required. Can you put them on your shopping list today, please?"

"Are you seriously going to keep this wretched thing?"

"I am. At least I'm going to see it's fed properly and then, if it doesn't belong to anyone, I'm going to adopt it. I've always liked cats."

❧

So, despite Nancy Harper's objections, it seemed the vicarage had acquired a pet. Bernard had already decided to call it Beelzebub, and the housekeeper agreed the name was apt. As she observed, it looked like the very devil with its wild orange eyes staring out of its black face. The feline, himself, wasn't objecting to his new name or his new home, both of which he had obviously decided would do for him. At least until a better prospect came along.

Mrs Harper, although still unsure of it, had given in to Bernard's wishes on the matter. Black cats were supposed to be lucky, she remembered. Anyway, she had more to concern herself with than stray moggies. The mystery of the body on the Common, for example.

Rumours were circulating at a rate of knots and many people had their own pet theories about the person responsible for the murder. Top of the list were the two 'witches' in Hallows Mead Crescent, whom both Nancy and her friend, Gladys Selfridge, insisted were responsible. As the two women went about their daily chores, in and out of butcher's, baker's and greengrocers, they imparted to all

94

those waiting to be served the benefit of their wisdom on the subject.

Robbie was disgusted when he first heard of the rumour from his housekeeper, Lucy Carter.

"That's a wicked lie," he declared. "To accuse those two poor old women of such a thing! Where do people get these ideas from? Reading too many trashy horror stories, I shouldn't wonder. Not to mention the flicks."

"Well, you say that," said Lucy, much put out by Robbie's reaction to her news. She had been all agog to tell him and now he had put her firmly in her place. It didn't deter her for long, however. "There's no smoke without fire, you know," she said huffily. "I bet those two are up to something. Only the other day young Wilf Frobisher's wart dropped off, and it was because they'd given him some concoction to take."

"With all due respect, Lucy," said Robbie, "Wilf Frobisher's wart is neither here nor there."

"Not to Wilf it's not…"

"Please, listen. I want you to stop spreading these rumours about the Rowan sisters. By all accounts, they've had a hard life and I won't have you adding to their troubles. I'm not in favour of them giving these so-called herbal remedies to people, but they're not doing any real harm. They're certainly not capable of murdering anybody."

"How do you know?"

Robbie was losing his patience. "Just stop spreading this gossip. If you catch anybody saying these things, just you refer them to me."

"All right, keep your hair on," said Lucy resignedly. "Did you know that the vicar's taken in their cat, by the way?"

"What are you talking about now?"

"Those two old witch… er, women, had a cat but it now seems to be living at the vicarage. According to Nancy, anyway."

"It wouldn't surprise me. Nancy Harper may be a bit gruff on the outside, but she's as soft as butter inside," he grinned.

"No, it wasn't Nancy's idea to keep the cat. It was the vicar's. She says it's a nasty thing, covered in fleas."

"Bernie's idea? I never knew he liked cats. Well I never."

"I don't know whether the Rowans know about it yet. They'll probably have something to say about it when they do."

"I don't think Bernie would actually *steal* it from them. There must be some reason he's taken it in. Maybe I'll pay him a visit after lunch. Talking of lunch, is it ready yet?"

Chapter Seventeen

Inspector Craddock was seated in the front room of one of the many terraced houses proliferating in Wandsworth, and indeed in many London boroughs, in the early 1950s. Number 58 Flamingo Drive was similar in size and design to hundreds of others, but the owners had stamped their own individual mark on it. The Larkin family had lived there for nearly twenty years and, during that time, it had been renovated three times. This was due to Gilbert Larkin's keen interest in do-it-yourself, something in which he excelled. His son, Tyrone, was also keen so, as soon as he was old enough, he took on the role of 'builder's mate' and much of the house's newly painted façade was down to him.

All this Inspector Craddock didn't know and cared about even less. He was here on a very serious matter which had nothing to do with interior or exterior design. Mrs Alma Larkin had made him a cup of tea on his arrival and was now awaiting the purpose of his visit with some anxiety.

"So, Mrs Larkin," he said, after he had slurped down most of his tea in one go, "your son is at work, you say?"

"That's right. He's got an important job in the city in a shipping company," she announced with pride.

"I see. I need to contact him. Do you have a phone number for his office?"

Mrs Larkin went to the sideboard and picked up the address book by the big black Bakelite phone, which was a recent, and much heralded, addition to the household. After shuffling through the pages for a few moments, she finally arrived at the information Craddock was after.

"Here you are," she said. "It's Museum 6401. I'll write it down for you."

"Thank you, Mrs Larkin. Could you also put the address?"

"I'm not too sure of the *exact* address. I think it's in Fish Street Hill, near to the Monument."

"That'll do. Do you know the company name?"

"James Lane Shipping Lines." She said this without hesitation and wrote the details down.

"Thank you, Mrs Larkin," he said, taking the piece of paper from her. "You have been most helpful."

"Can't you tell me why you want to talk to my son?" she asked, pouring him a fresh cup of tea. "Is it – is it about Helen?"

"We need to speak to him, Mrs Larkin, as I understand he was – er – walking out with her. Is that right?"

"Well, he's been seeing a couple of girls, as far as I'm aware. Nothing serious," she stressed.

"We just need to eliminate him from our enquiries," Craddock explained as he rose to leave. "Thank you for the tea."

"Be kind to him," she said as she opened the front door. "It's been a bit of a shock – for us all, of course, but especially for him."

Craddock guessed the doting mother knew nothing about poor Helen's pregnancy and, if she did, would probably never believe her son responsible for her predicament. Mothers and sons! There had been many cases in his own experience of such unswerving devotion. It didn't matter how heinous the crime, the guilty man's mother would defend him to the last. He was a parent himself, but he never let sentiment blind him to his son's faults. Terry Craddock was proving a handful now that he had entered his young teenage years. He sighed.

He never liked to prejudge anybody, but he had to admit that he was already prejudiced towards young Tyrone Larkin. If, as he supposed, the young man had got Helen in the family way, then he had every reason to dislike him. However, despite this, he didn't think he was her murderer, even though he had yet to meet him. The photograph on the sideboard had showed a fresh-faced youth with a sunny smile and an innocence almost as palpable as that of Helen Carstairs.

He climbed into his battered Ford and pointed it towards the City.

❧

Half-an-hour later, he sat impatiently in the lavish reception area of James Lane Shipping Lines, waiting to speak to his number one suspect. The blonde receptionist (why were they always blonde, he wondered) had stared at his warrant card in awe and immediately buzzed through to the post room. He smiled as he overheard her say: "When you've finished dishing out the teas, Ty, there's a police inspector here to see you. What have you been up to eh?"

Important job? He supposed so. Tea was always important, but Mrs Larkin had led him to believe her son was something more than just a mere tea boy. He got up and paced the room, beginning to think that Tyrone Larkin was never going to make an appearance. Had the receptionist frightened him? Had he made a quick getaway through a rear exit? Was he sitting, quaking in his boots, in the toilet?

As he was wondering this, however, a rather attractive, dark-haired young man appeared meekly before him. The inspector's instincts rarely let him down and they hadn't let him down now. He had doubted Larkin was a murderer just by looking at his photo and, now that he saw him in the flesh, he was even more convinced of his innocence.

"Hello, sir," said the young man pleasantly, holding out his hand. "I'm sorry to have kept you waiting."

"Not at all," said Craddock, shaking his hand. The young man's grip was firm and reassuring. "Is there somewhere private we can talk? Where we won't be disturbed?"

"Is the boardroom free, Sally?" Tyrone called across to the receptionist.

"For the moment. There's a meeting due to start after lunch, so you've got about three-quarters of an hour."

Once settled in the pleasant, sun-filled boardroom, Craddock studied the young man carefully.

Tyrone Larkin smiled at him, showing no trace of nerves.

"Would you like a tea or coffee, Inspector?" he asked.

"No, thanks," he replied. He cleared his throat and adopted the formal manner he always used when interviewing suspects. He found it kept them on their toes. "You know why I'm here, I suppose?"

"Yes. My mother called me and said you were on your way. Poor Helen. She was a sweet kid. I wonder who would do such a wicked thing? She wouldn't have harmed a fly."

"Did you know she was pregnant?" Craddock asked bluntly.

The young man blanched. "Pregnant? But how?"

Phil Craddock eyed him quizzically. "My dear young man," he began, "surely you know…"

"Yes, of course," said Tyrone impatiently. "However, I'm definitely *not* the father. We never had – er – relations. I had too much respect for her and she was much too young. Not just in years, she was – *innocent* somehow, do you know what I mean?"

The chief inspector smiled. Yes, he knew exactly. Both young people were barely out of nappies in his eyes. Babes in the wood.

"I had no intention of taking advantage of her in that way," Tyrone pressed his point. "She always seemed so innocent and unworldly. I never dreamed that … I must say this news has shocked me very much. Whenever I tried to touch her – you know – in a more intimate way, she always recoiled. Maybe she just didn't fancy me. I always thought it was just because she was afraid I would go too far. But I would never have done that, honestly, Inspector."

"Very well," said Craddock, putting the cap back on his fountain pen which, for once, he hadn't managed to lose. "Thank you."

"Is that all, then?" Larkin watched Craddock carefully, as if trying to gauge his reaction. "I'd like to help, I really would," he continued. "You see, Helen was the first girl who really meant anything to me. I can't believe she was seeing someone else behind my back."

"So, you had no idea?"

"No, of course not. I wouldn't have thought her capable of deceit. Still, you live and learn, I suppose."

"Yes, I suppose you do," agreed the inspector.

Visibly relaxing, he put his pen and notepad back in his jacket pocket. He often found he got more out of his suspects if he chatted to them in an informal way.

"By the way, when did you last see Miss Carstairs?"

"Er, Saturday night. We went to the pictures."

"What did you see?"

"*The Big Heat* with Glenn Ford. Brilliant! I don't think Helen liked it much, though. Too violent for her taste."

The Inspector smiled. "I saw that film," he said. "I tend to agree with Miss Carstairs. Too violent."

"But you must see things like that every day of the week." Tyrone smiled sardonically.

"Not as often as you might think," he replied. "So, what time did you leave her on Saturday night?"

Tyrone thought for a moment. "Let me see. The film finished at ten-thirty and I walked her straight home. Her parents don't – er, didn't – like her to be out after eleven."

"Did she seem preoccupied, nervous, upset?"

"Not especially. She seemed her normal self to me. She was always moaning about her parents keeping such strict tabs on her, though. Oh, wait a minute, I've just remembered something."

"Yes?" Craddock leaned forward.

"She said she was going to an all-night party the next evening, but she wasn't going to tell her parents."

"I see. Did you advise her not to go, or to tell her parents at least?"

"Of course I did. I didn't like the idea of her staying out all night. She'd never done anything like that before. And she didn't even ask me to go with her."

"Did you ask her why she didn't want you to go, too?"

"Yes, but she just laughed. Said she thought I was a bit too prim and proper for such things. That really upset me."

Craddock was beginning to see a side to Helen Carstairs he hadn't suspected. Perhaps she wasn't as lilywhite as she had at first seemed. If young Larkin's testimony was to be believed, of course. And, like all good policemen, the Inspector was keeping an open mind.

Chapter Eighteen

"What's this I hear about you having got yourself a cat, Bernie?"

Robbie was sitting in the vicarage study, enjoying a cup of Earl Grey and one of Mrs Harper's delicious rock cakes, while Bernard was adding the final touches to his next sermon before joining him by the fire. Although it was April, there was still a chill in the air, and the roaring flames added a cosy glow to the vicar's eyrie which Robbie never failed to appreciate on his many visits.

"Yes, a little black moggy," Bernard smiled. "He's taken quite a fancy to me."

"Where is it now?"

"I think Mrs Aitch's feeding him. She makes out she doesn't like him, but she's always giving him tit bits. Beelzebub's got round her, all right, although she'd never admit it."

"Beelzebub? You call the cat Beelzebub?" asked Robbie in astonishment.

"Yes. I think it suits him."

"Hardly a suitable name for the inhabitant of a vicarage, old boy," laughed Robbie.

"No," agreed Bernard, laughing. "But it was Mrs Aitch's idea, really. She said he looked like the 'very devil', so the name's stuck."

"I see." Robbie finished his rock cake, and wiped the crumbs from his waistcoat. "Er, Bernie, are you sure you should be keeping him? I mean, I understand he doesn't actually belong to you."

"Oh, you've heard the talk going around that I've stolen him from those Rowan sisters, I suppose."

"Well, yes. I mean, did you bother to check if it belonged to anyone before you took it in?"

"The state he was in, I thought it very unlikely it had a home," said Bernard. "The poor thing looked half-starved. He was always coming round for scraps anyway, so I decided to feed him up and keep him. He's free to go whenever he wants to, but he doesn't want to."

"I'm sure it doesn't. It knows where he's well off. Cats are like that. But what if it does belong to the Rowans? It wouldn't look very good, would it? The headline in the local rag, I mean. 'Local vicar steals cat from lonely old women."

"Oh, shut up, Robbie. The cat's been here a few days now and they've not come round yet. If he was theirs, they're probably glad I've taken him off their hands."

"You're probably right," smiled Robbie. "These cakes are smashing. Mrs Aitch has excelled herself. I wish Lucy could cook as well."

Bernard gave him a wry smile. "I'm sure she's got other compensations," he said knowingly. His friend's relationship with his housekeeper wasn't purely platonic, he was sure.

"Have you heard about that dreadful murder, Bernie?" asked Robbie, quickly changing the subject.

"Yes, isn't it terrible? Poor Mrs Carstairs! She's completely distraught.

"And Mr Carstairs has taken to drink. According to Mrs Aitch, that is. But from what I know of Henry Carstairs, I find that very hard to believe."

"Well the shock of his daughter's murder could have tipped him over the edge."

"I'm planning to pay the grieving parents a visit later," said Bernard. "I'm not looking forward to it."

"Did you know that Helen was pregnant?"

"No!"

"Yes. I suppose I shouldn't be telling you but, as the poor child is dead, I don't see it will do her any harm now. She came to see me a while ago and I advised her to tell her parents, but she was afraid of their reaction. I think she was more worried about her father than her mother."

"That wouldn't surprise me," said Bernard seriously. "Although I respect Henry for being such a staunch attendee at my services, he comes across as a bit like a Victorian father to me. I don't know how he'd react to his precious daughter getting pregnant out of wedlock. Poor Helen. She was a sweet, pretty girl. I wonder who would want to kill her?"

"Haven't you heard the rumour going round?"

"What rumour?"

"Apparently people are saying the Rowan sisters sacrificed her in one of their rituals. They think they're witches."

"Balderdash!" exploded Bernard. "I've told Mrs Aitch in no uncertain terms to stop spreading this tittle tattle. Some people have nothing better to do than listen to it. They're just two unfortunate, lonely women who should be pitied, not vilified."

"I agree," said Robbie thoughtfully. "I told Lucy not to be taken in by such rubbish, but you know how these women like to gossip."

Just then, the door of the study creaked open a fraction and then it creaked open a little more. They looked up as a small black paw appeared, gradually followed by the rest of the animal. Beelzebub crept over to Bernard and jumped onto his lap, mewing softly.

"You're a pushover," observed Robbie, smiling.

Not blessed with a natural charm, Mrs Harper was nothing if not blunt and to the point. If she liked you, she might let you know eventually by giving you an extra biscuit with your tea. For the likes of Mrs Harper, this was tantamount to a declaration of undying love. Bernard had been blessed many times over with extra biscuits, both real and metaphorical. If, on the other hand, the vicarage housekeeper didn't like you, then she had no compunction in making it clear from the outset. However, it was sometimes difficult to distinguish the two reactions, and people had often been under the impression, perhaps for many years, that Nancy Harper harboured a deep dislike of them when, in fact, the opposite was true.

In the case of Miss Elvira Rowan, there was certainly no love lost. Bernard's housekeeper had heard many strange stories about her and her equally dotty sister, Vesna. She had no concrete proof that the stories were true, however, only the word of such founts of knowledge as Mrs Gladys Selfridge; word which she took as gospel.

"I've come about my cat," Elvira Rowan stood on the vicarage front doorstep, looking daggers. Her tall, dark, looming figure overshadowed the shorter, dumpier Mrs Harper who was determined not to be intimidated.

"Your cat?" she queried, all innocence.

"Yes, don't look as if you don't know what I'm talking about," said Elvira, folding her arms in a threatening manner. "Is the vicar in?"

"'E's busy. I don't know nothing about no cat. Now buzz off!"

"Not until I've seen the vicar," said Elvira doggedly. "I must speak to him."

Mrs Harper sniffed. People who knew her of old, knew what one of those sniffs implied, and they didn't relish being the cause of it. But Elvira Rowan was in ignorance on this point and continued to stand her ground.

"Well?" queried Elvira impatiently. "I haven't got all day. Are you going to let me in? I just want a word. I won't keep him long."

"You want to ask 'im about the cat?"

"The cat?" Elvira hesitated. "Well, yes, that and … other things. I need his advice."

The housekeeper seemed to relent slightly. "You want 'is advice, you say?"

"Yes. I've not just come about the cat. To tell you the truth I can't stand the mangy thing. But my sister is upset at losing it, so I said I'd come and ask for it back."

"For someone who likes cats, she didn't look after it like she should 'ave," observed Mrs Harper, not without justification. "The poor thing was always on the ear'ole for food until 'is nibs took pity on it. She should 'ave cared for it better, then it wouldn't be round 'ere all the time."

"Vessie's a bit absent-minded these days," said Elvira, a faraway look in her eyes. "I know she always means to feed it, but she sometimes forgets."

"Only sometimes? It didn't look as if it'd been fed for a month. Look," said Mrs Harper finally, heaving a sigh. "All right. I'll see if 'e'll see you. You'd better come in."

Elvira squeezed around the housekeeper's bulky frame and stood waiting obediently inside the hallway.

If Nancy's welcome hadn't been all it should be, Bernard made up for it by his friendly greeting and offer of afternoon tea.

"Now, Miss – er – Rowan, isn't it? What can I do for you?"

Bernard smiled at the plain-faced old lady who stood stiffly before him, her back as straight as a ramrod.

"I've come about the cat," she said bluntly.

"Do sit down," said Bernard affably. "No need to stand on ceremony. I'll just remove Beelzebub..."

As he lifted the protesting feline out of the chair, he realised this was the cat that Elvira Rowan had come about.

"Oh, I see ... *this* cat?"

The cat wasn't happy at being manhandled. It had been having a lovely dream about a fully stocked fish pond and an overcrowded bird table.

"Yes. I must say it looks much healthier since the last time I saw him. I wouldn't have recognised it."

"Well, he was in a bit of a state when he came to us. I thought he was a stray."

"Yes, well, as I explained to your housekeeper, he's my sister's cat, really. I don't like him, myself. I'm not a cat person. They make me sneeze."

"Well, I'm sorry, Miss Rowan, but she can't have him back if she can't look after him properly."

"No, well, I see that. I'll tell her… Actually, I really came to see you on an entirely different matter …"

At that moment Mrs Harper barged in with the tea tray and made an opera out of putting it down, pouring out and handing round plates and cups. Bernard and Elvira waited in silence while she clattered about. Finally, she left the room when it was obvious her duties had been thoroughly discharged and she was no longer required.

But, eaten up with curiosity as to why they had both fallen silent on her entrance, she remained outside the study door with her ear pressed up close to the wood panelling. However, the solid oak panelling prevented her hearing anything clearly. What could that batty old woman have to say to Bernard that was so private? She couldn't wait to tell Gladys about Elvira's visit. Something was up, and she was sure it wasn't anything to do with the cat.

"I was just wondering if you knew anything about this awful murder, Vicar," said Elvira when she was sure they were quite alone. "I don't know whether you have seen the bereaved family or anything?"

"Not as yet, Miss Rowan," said Bernard, eyeing her suspiciously. "I will, of course, offer what comfort I can in due course."

"And I'm sure they'd be grateful," she replied. "Er – " She hesitated.

"Yes? What is it?"

Bernard didn't like this woman very much, but he knew a little about her past and how she and her sister had been generally viewed with suspicion by the locals. Unjustifiably, in his opinion, although he supposed he couldn't really blame them. The Rowans didn't go out of their way to be sociable.

"It's just that – er, do you know what they're saying, Vicar?"

"Saying? Who?"

"People. Around here."

"No, I don't listen to idle gossip."

"Well, of course. I know that. But I believe lots of people are blaming us for the murder. They're saying we sacrificed the girl on the Common in some sort of Black Mass ritual."

"Take no notice," advised Bernard. "People can be very unthinking and ignorant at times. It'll soon blow over."

"Well, I hope so as it's affecting our business."

"Your business?"

"Yes, our ancient herbal cures. People aren't buying them at the moment and it's our only source of income these days. We've got some savings, but they won't last long at this rate."

"Don't worry. I'll say something in my sermon on Sunday. I'll tell them it's unchristian to make insinuations without any proof. They'll listen to me."

Elvira seemed to relax as she listened to his words. Bernard could see a slight bend in her spine now. "Thanks so much, Vicar. You're very kind."

"Not at all. That's what I'm here for," he said, giving her a reassuring smile. "But, if you want to show your gratitude in a more tangible way, you can do something for me."

Elvira looked at him, a nervous smile playing on her lips. "Do something for you? Er, well, if I can …"

"Let me keep the cat?"

Chapter Nineteen

"One thing's certain, Rathbone, Tyrone Larkin is no murderer."

"What makes you so sure, sir?"

"Instinct, my lad. My copper's nose. When you've been in this business as long as I have, you'll know. I've not got it wrong yet. I think we need to look even closer to home."

Sergeant Rathbone stared at him. "Closer to home? The family, you mean?"

"Yep. It's a well-known fact that most murders are committed by people closest to the victims. Husbands, lovers, er, parents…"

"Parents!" Sergeant Rathbone scratched his head in astonishment. "You're not suggesting that that sweet little Mrs Carstairs killed her own daughter, are you?"

Craddock gave him an old-fashioned look. "Helen did have a father, too, Rathbone," he pointed out.

Brian Rathbone, who had a small daughter himself, couldn't even conceive of such a possibility. "I think you're barking up the wrong tree, there, guv," he said. "He must be as heartbroken as his wife."

"Come on, Rathbone. It happens. Unfortunately." Craddock rummaged through his in-tray. "Okay, someone's nicked my pen again," he grumbled.

"Why don't you attach it on a bit of string round your neck?" suggested Rathbone, not entirely joking.

"Get out! Go and make yourself useful. Those door-to-door interviews need going through again. Go and help with that."

"Okay, okay." Rathbone hated paperwork, but knew it was no use protesting when Craddock was in this mood.

Returning ten minutes later with several fat files under his arm, he found his boss scribbling furiously. He saw he was using that elusive fountain pen.

"Found it then, guv?" He placed the files on his desk with a heavy thump.

"No thanks to you," Craddock muttered. "It was on the floor, under the desk. Didn't you see it?"

"No. You sent me for these files, remember?"

"Hmmph!" was the only response.

"Anyway, sir, what did you make of this Tyrone Larkin, then? You didn't think he's the murderer, you said."

"We need to question Mr and Mrs Carstairs pronto. Like that mean's yesterday. Get your skates on. That's where we're headed next."

"But what about these files?"

Craddock glanced over at the toppling pile. "What are you doing with all that? We've got a job to do. Come on."

Rathbone sighed with impatience. "But you told me to go through the door-to-door interviews, sir – just a moment ago. Remember?"

Craddock tutted crossly. "Oh, pass them to that twit Jenkins, for God's sake. Keep him out of mischief. Now, let's get going."

There was no stopping Craddock now. He had the bit between his teeth and needed to find out if his instinct was right. He had heard varying reports from witnesses that Henry Carstairs wasn't the most likeable of men. A rather stiff, formal, unbending kind of person, by all accounts. Very strict with his daughter which, on the face of it, wasn't necessarily a bad thing. But then, he could have been *too* strict. Even if he had been strict for her own good, that hadn't worked, seeing as she was now dead. There was something fishy about Henry Carstairs, he was sure.

Rathbone, grabbing his coat, suggested with some temerity that maybe it was too soon to interrogate the grief-stricken parents.

"Strike while the iron's hot – that's my motto," said Craddock, pushing his subordinate out of the door. "We can't afford sympathy in this job."

In the car, driving to the Carstairs' home in Cherry Lane, Rathbone, who still couldn't believe that Henry Carstairs could have murdered his daughter, tried a different tack. "Have you heard what people are saying about those Rowan sisters, Guv?" he asked.

"Mrs Carstairs did mention it," muttered the Inspector. "Something about them being witches and sacrificing her daughter in one of their rituals. Bollocks!"

"Very probably, sir. But don't you think we should at least make some enquiries? Go and talk to them, at least?"

"All in good time," said Craddock. "They'll keep."

He didn't believe in witches. He swung the steering wheel as the car screeched to a stop outside number fifteen Cherry Lane.

But, unknown to Craddock and Rathbone, Bernard had got there a little before them. He had been putting off his visit to the Carstairs, unsure if it would be seen as a mere intrusion. His intention was to bring them comfort in his capacity as parish vicar, but how could he do that when he found it almost impossible to explain why God had let such an awful thing happen to their daughter in the first place?

Ivy Carstairs came to the door, accompanied by the sound of a yapping dog, and gave him a weak smile. "Hello, Vicar," she said. "Thank you for coming. Please, do come in."

He entered the stuffy parlour, closely followed by the little Jack Russell who was still yapping furiously at his heels, to find Henry Carstairs standing in front of the fire, rocking to and fro on the balls of his feet. His long face was

113

pale and drawn, and he looked much older than his forty-five years.

Now that he was here, Bernard found himself at a loss what to say to them. He shook Henry Carstairs by the hand and muttered his condolences. The older man mumbled his thanks as he gently nudged the little dog out of the way.

"Shhh, Charlie," he scolded, and Bernard could see tears standing in his eyes. He looked away in embarrassment.

Ivy Carstairs busied herself in the kitchen making the tea that nobody really wanted. Bernard coughed politely as he sat in the chair proffered to him by the bereaved father.

"I cannot say how sorry I am," Bernard burbled on, realising that the bereaved father had no more words in him. The silence between them was broken only by the clatter of cups and saucers in the kitchen.

"Wife's making some tea," Carstairs said at last, unnecessarily.

"Please," said Bernard, raising his hand gently. "Not on my account. I don't want to outstay my welcome. I just came to say that my thoughts are with you both, and if I can be of any help or …"

"Thank you," Carstairs broke into Bernard's speech abruptly, whether it was to save him from further embarrassment or simply to shut him up wasn't clear. "Kind of you."

Suddenly, he put his hand on the side of his head. Bernard could see him wince in pain. "It's not easy … as you can imagine."

"I cannot conceive how hard it must be for you," said Bernard softly.

"Not your fault."

Henry Carstairs' monosyllabic replies were getting on Bernard's nerves now. "I – I just wanted to – to – come and tell you that you're not alone … the church is always open to you, if you can find some comfort there …"

"Hardly there," said Carstairs, staring into space. Suddenly he became more animated. "Why should God want to take away my little girl? You answer me that."

Bernard didn't know what to say. His throat had started to constrict, and he now very much needed the tea which Mrs Carstairs was taking an inordinately long time in making. He coughed in an effort to find his voice, and fidgeted in his seat.

"It is indeed beyond any human understanding," said Bernard carefully. "Sometimes we just have to accept that things happen for a reason – that there is a more powerful force at work than we mere mortals…"

"Don't give me that claptrap." Carstairs' pent-up grief and anger were getting the better of him. "All my life I've gone to church – attended every Sunday – rain or shine. And where has it got me? My poor, darling Helen is dead and she never did a wrong thing in her life. I want no more of your god – you shan't see me in church ever again, I can tell you that!"

"I completely understand," said Bernard. "I probably wouldn't want to come to church, myself, if what has happened to you happened to me."

"What would you know about it? You haven't got any children, you can't know how it feels – it's like a pain deep – in here." Carstairs thumped his chest violently.

Before Bernard could think of something adequate to say in response, Ivy Carstairs returned with the tea tray. The atmosphere lightened a little as she busied herself pouring out and handing round.

"How can you bother with tea, Ivy? Your daughter has just been murdered in cold blood!" Henry Carstairs' earlier polite monosyllables had deserted him now as he gave full vent to his passion.

Bernard felt the cruelty of the man's remarks and could only imagine what they were doing to Ivy. He watched her hand shake as she handed him his tea.

"Don't, Henry. There's nothing'll bring her back."

Her husband watched her with a steely eye as her face crumpled and tears started to flow. She rushed from the room, her apron up to her streaming eyes. Bernard felt he had to say something.

"Look, Mr Carstairs – I know you're suffering – deeply – but did you have to say that? Your wife is suffering just as much as you."

The man just stared at him. "I think, Reverend, once you have finished your tea, you should leave."

Bernard thought so too and swallowed the scalding brew as quickly as he could. As he was leaving, he passed Craddock and Rathbone, who were just coming up the path to the front door. They tipped their hats to him and he responded in the same way. He secretly wished them luck as he closed the gate behind him.

Chapter Twenty

Craddock stared at Henry Carstairs, who was seated by the empty fireplace, a small Jack Russell at his feet, trying to get the measure of the man. He looked ill, which could mean he was heartbroken at losing his daughter or that he was consumed with guilt. He watched him rub his temples as if in pain. The strain was proving too much for his health, one way or another, he thought. Inspector Craddock decided he didn't much like him, or his dog.

Rathbone, who was particularly fond of Jack Russells, bent down and tickled the dog's ear, causing the little creature to run round in excited circles until his master told him in no uncertain terms to 'sit'.

"First of all, may we say how sorry we are?" Craddock began, after more tea had been served by Ivy. "We know this is painful for you both, but we do need to ask you some questions."

"Get on with it, Inspector," said Henry Carstairs abruptly. "The sooner you start, the sooner we can get rid of you. Don't mean to be rude, but…"

"I understand," said Craddock, secretly annoyed. No matter how hard he tried to sympathise with the man, he found he couldn't. He almost relished the bombshell he was about to drop. He cleared his throat.

"There's no easy way of saying this, but did you know that your daughter was pregnant?"

Both parents stared at him in horror. "Pregnant?" squeaked Ivy. "My little Helen was going to have a baby? It can't be true!"

"I'm sorry, but, I'm afraid it is."

"Oh, dear. That wicked boy!"

Craddock assumed she meant Larkin. "Yes, I understand your daughter was seeing this young man, Tyrone Larkin. Can you confirm that?"

"That's right. Such a nice, polite boy. I can't believe it."

"There is no way on God's earth that my daughter could have been pregnant," stated Henry Carstairs. He faced Craddock with a challenge in his hard grey eyes.

"I'm afraid there's no doubt about it," Craddock said as smoothly as he could. "Young people today have more freedom than we did when we were growing up. We can't watch them every minute, can we?"

"You're not saying my daughter was promiscuous, are you? She has only just died – she's not even been buried yet!"

Carstairs balled his fists but kept them at his side. Craddock glanced at Rathbone and raised his eyes heavenwards.

"I've spoken to young Larkin," said Craddock, keeping his gaze on Mrs Carstairs, not daring to challenge her husband further. "He assured me he wasn't the father."

"That's what *he* says!" Ivy was almost hysterical. Tears rolled unchecked down her sallow cheeks.

"I'm sorry to add to your troubles with this distressing information," Craddock said, pausing while she collected herself a little. "But we do need to ask if you know of any other boys who were interested in Helen. Anyone she went out with apart from Larkin?"

"She didn't have a string of them, if that's what you're implying," said Carstairs, rubbing his forehead ferociously. "You'll be accusing her of being a prostitute next!"

He sat slumped in his chair, holding his head as if it was too heavy for his shoulders. "My poor girl!" he muttered. "She never would have done anything like that willingly. She knew right from wrong. I'll kill the blighter when I find out who's responsible."

For the first time, Craddock began to feel sorry for him. He couldn't blame the man for his anger. He'd be exactly the same in his shoes.

Ivy sat down on the arm of her husband's chair and stretched out her hand to stroke his hair. He flinched as she did so.

"Henry suffers from blinding headaches, you know," she said. "I keep telling him to go to the doctor about them."

"Maybe he should," said Rathbone, not unkindly. "Maybe you both should. I think, in the circumstances, he would prescribe sedatives for you while you're going through this."

"Doctors! Bah! What do *they* know?" spat Henry, ignoring the seven or so years of study needed to become one. "Now, if you've nothing else to say, no more *'good'* news to tell us, would you mind leaving?"

It was a relief to get out into the warm spring evening and breathe in the fresh, blossom-scented air.

"Well, Rathbone, what do you make of Henry Carstairs now?"

"Rather unpleasant, I must say. But the man's not himself. How could he be? You have to feel sorry for him."

Craddock unlocked the door of his ancient Ford. "Against my better judgement," he agreed grudgingly. "But I still don't like him. He's not an easy man, is he?"

"No. I wonder how Mrs Carstairs puts up with him. Still, whatever the man's faults, I don't think he murdered his daughter. He seemed genuinely devoted to her. I think he was even more upset than his wife."

Rathbone seated himself as comfortably as he could in the rickety, broken passenger seat and fidgeted uncomfortably as something sharp dug into his back.

"When are you going to trade in this pile of junk?" he asked irritably.

"For what?"

"A car, for example?"

Craddock let that pass and revved up his protesting engine.

Chapter Twenty-One

"There's a Colonel Powell downstairs wanting to see you, Vicar," announced Mrs Harper one bright spring morning, not many days after the murder of Helen Carstairs.

Bernard was, as usual, struggling with the wording of his next sermon, made especially difficult because he had to find a way to introduce the subject of false accusations of witchery and devil worship. He had no doubt the Rowan sisters would be in church to ensure he made some sort of reference to what they saw as persecution. He just didn't know how to frame the words so they wouldn't offend his entire congregation, so it was a relief to be interrupted by this unexpected visit.

"Bring up another cup with my elevenses, please, Mrs Aitch," he said, as he shook the colonel by the hand.

He didn't recognise him as one of his parishioners. The man had definitely never appeared in his congregation before. He would certainly have remembered someone so distinctive-looking, with that large handlebar moustache obscuring most of the bottom half of his face.

Colonel Clevedon Powell was a man in his middle seventies, in rude health apart from a tendency to gout brought on by too much port, something he was well-known for in the neighbourhood. However, he was generally liked, and Bernard decided, as he shook the man's hand, that he liked him too.

"Now, Colonel," said Bernard, "what can I do for you? I don't think you're one of my flock, are you?"

"What are you talking about, man?" demanded the bluff old man. "I'm not a ruddy sheep."

Bernard laughed. "No offence intended. Just a pastoral term. Is the tea to your liking?"

Mrs Harper's refreshments were obviously going down well, as the colonel had finished his first cup and was holding it out for a second. Meanwhile, he had polished off two scones and was buttering his third. Bernard began to wonder if he got enough to eat at home.

"It's all right," mumbled the colonel between mouthfuls. "To answer your question, no, I'm not one of your 'flock', as you call it. I don't believe in any of that mumbo jumbo. Seen too much of life for that. I remember when I was in Peking at the time of the Boxer Rebellion – saw it all then. No caring God would have put up with what went on then, I can tell you."

Bernard began to fear the old soldier was about to drift off into a series of bloodthirsty reminiscences, so he coughed politely. "Er, Colonel?"

"Oh, yes, sorry," said the Colonel, coming back to the present. "Where was I?"

"In Peking," smiled Bernard.

"I know people say I'm an old soak and I'll say and do anything when I'm in my cups, but what I'm about to tell you is the absolute truth. I might have had a glass or two that night, but I was far from drunk."

"I see," said Bernard after a moment. "I have no idea about your reputation, having only just met you and I always speak as I find. So, please tell me what you came to tell me."

The colonel leaned forward, and Bernard detected a strong smell of alcohol on his breath.

"The night of the murder of that poor, unfortunate child," said the colonel, "I saw something that I still, to this day, can't quite believe. I mean, I always thought the Rowans were a bit dotty, but really! It was a bit much, even for them. But it wasn't even what they were up to that was the strangest thing ..."

"Colonel," said Bernard, an unaccustomed note of authority in his tone, "I would appreciate it if you would come to the point. Firstly, you say you do not believe in all that 'mumbo jumbo', as you put it. Yet to come to me, as a minister of God, obviously concerned about the recent tragic events. I would have thought that, if you saw anything that could assist the police in their enquiries, you should go to them and not to me."

Colonel Powell seemed thrown for a moment, then he coughed and collected himself. "Point taken, good man," he said. "Except, I don't know if what I saw will be believed by the police. I'm not sure I believe it myself. And, if I imagined it, the last thing I want to do is get those poor women into trouble."

"So, what you're saying – not that you've said *anything* yet – is you're not sure what you saw, but you want to run it past me before you go to the police?"

"Something like that. You see, they were young women when they first moved into the Crescent – I only live a few doors from them. They were – well, not to put too fine a point on it, attractive then. Well, Vesna was. A right bobby dazzler, if you get my drift. If I hadn't been happily married at the time, I'd have been after her like a shot." He coughed again.

"This is all very interesting, Colonel," sighed Bernard, his patience wearing thin. "But if you have something to tell me about what happened to that poor girl, then, please, tell me."

"Of course. Apologies. Not so young as I was and all that. Go off on tangents all the time."

"I understand," smiled Bernard,

"Good man," repeated the colonel. "Now, this is what I saw that night. I could have been drunk or half asleep, but I swear to you, I believe I saw what I saw…"

"And that was?"

❧

"Mrs Aitch …?"

123

Mrs Harper looked up from rolling out some pastry as Bernard entered the kitchen.

"Yes, Vicar?" She rubbed her nose with a floury hand, leaving a white spot on the end of it. "Can you be quick? I've got the dinner to get. This mutton pie won't jump in the oven and cook itself."

"Er, what time will it be ready? I promised Robbie I'd meet him for a drink at one o'clock."

"Oh, you did, did you?" Mrs Harper stopped rolling the pastry and put her floury hands on her hips.

"Look here, Mrs Aitch, as much as I appreciate what you do for me and your lovely cooking, it's *me* who employs *you*, not the other way about. I'll expect dinner at two o'clock. All right?"

Nancy Harper stared at him. He had never spoken to her in that way before. However, she only shrugged. Whether or not that meant she would obey his wish, Bernard could only hope so.

He turned to stalk out of the kitchen, a little shaken after his uncharacteristic outburst. Then he remembered why he had come to see her in the first place.

"Oh, by the way," he said, turning back. "I've just shown that old colonel out. Do you know anything about him, Mrs Aitch?"

"That old boozer? Gladys – Mrs Selfridge – was talking about 'im to me only the other day."

"Indeed? Is he – er, quite sane, do you think?"

"Don't know about that. Bats in the belfry, I shouldn't wonder. Gladys told me 'e'd asked 'er to marry 'im. Before 'er 'ubby was even cold in the ground and all. Bloomin' cheek. Anyway, she gave 'im short shrift, that's all *I* know."

"Right. Yes, I see. But do you think that what he says can be relied upon? Is he known for telling untruths? Does he incline to fantasize? Make things up?"

"What are you driving at, Vicar?"

"Oh, it's just something he told me just now. I wondered if – well, if he was just a little bit – er, you know…."

"Not the full shilling, you mean?"

"Yes. I don't mean to be disrespectful, but he told me himself he was a drinker, so I just needed to be sure he wasn't just – you know – "

"'Aving a laugh?"

"Exactly."

"Well, all I can say is, 'e may be a bit of a drunk, but I never 'eard of 'im telling fibs or anything like that. Why? What did 'e tell you?" Mrs Harper was consumed with curiosity.

"Oh, nothing much. Nothing you need concern yourself with, Mrs Aitch."

Chapter Twenty-Two

"Jenkins has come up with something interesting, guv."

Inspector Craddock was sitting in the police canteen, wading through a plateful of sausage, eggs and bacon as Brian Rathbone joined him at his table, carrying a tray on which were a modest cheese salad and an apple.

Craddock looked at the meagre meal in disgust. "You don't eat enough to keep a sparrow alive, Rathbone," he commented.

"Marion always has a hot meal waiting for me when I get home," said Rathbone, generously lacing his food with salad cream. "Anyway, the stuff you're eating will fur up your arteries and give you a heart attack before you're fifty."

Already forty-seven, Craddock didn't entirely welcome his subordinate's observation, but decided to ignore it.

"Never mind all that," he said, munching on a particularly large and juicy chunk of sausage. "What's this 'interesting' thing that Jenkins has come up with?"

"Well, Jenkins was speaking to young Percy Banks – you know, the butcher's in the High Street…"

"Hmm," said Craddock, dipping a fried slice into his egg. "Well?"

"Well, this Percy said he saw Helen enter the Rowans' cottage on the afternoon of her murder. It was about five o'clock, he said."

Craddock slammed the table, causing the salad cream bottle to leap onto the floor. "At last!" he exclaimed. "A breakthrough!"

"Yes, so it would seem," agreed Rathbone, retrieving the bottle which was, thankfully, unbroken. "It means the Rowan sisters could be involved, doesn't it? We were quick to dismiss the rumours about them, but it looks like we were wrong, doesn't it?"

"Possibly. We need to get round to them pronto." With that, Craddock cleaned his plate with the rest of his fried slice and stood up. "Come on, lad. We've work to do."

"But I've only just sat down," sighed Rathbone. "I haven't eaten all day."

"That's your lookout," muttered Craddock unsympathetically. "You can eat that apple on the way. The salad looks revolting anyway. I wouldn't feed it to a rabbit."

Grabbing his apple, Rathbone followed his boss out to the old Ford, and hopped in beside him. They were outside the door of Appleby Cottage ten minutes later. "Now," said Craddock, grinding the gears as he skidded to a halt. "Let's see what these two old biddies have to say for themselves.

Craddock rang the rusty bell hanging by the front door of Appleby Cottage. It clanged hollowly as he and Rathbone waited. The place looked neglected, half hidden between two larger, more prepossessing properties. The rose bushes that had once bloomed so spectacularly in the front garden had long since died. Hallows Mead Crescent was a much sought-after location, and the residents themselves were proud of their little community. They kept their houses and gardens in immaculate condition, so it was fortunate that the Rowans' cottage could hardly be seen from the road.

After a few moments, the door creaked open about two inches. "Who is it?" came a high-pitched, squeaky voice.

"Police, madam. Please open up."

"Can I see your warrant card?"

Craddock shoved it through the tiny gap. "Here," he said gruffly. "Come on now. We haven't got all day."

"Why are you here?"

Craddock raised his eyes to heaven in his exasperation. "We will tell you that when we are inside."

"Is it about the murder?"

Rathbone spoke, aware his boss was losing his patience already. "Yes, madam. We are talking to everyone in the neighbourhood about it."

"Well *I* didn't do it," came the reply.

"We aren't saying you did, madam," said Rathbone, looking at Craddock in amusement. "This is just a routine call."

"My sister's not home," said the voice, as the door began to close.

Rathbone stuck his size ten shoe in between it and the door jamb. "We'll only keep you a minute," he said.

He felt the door press against his foot and was about to remove it when Craddock gave the door a push inwards and both men tumbled into the tiny passage. Vesna Rowan ran into the parlour and slammed the door.

"Go away!" she called out from behind it. "My sister's not at home!"

The two policemen exchanged glances. There seemed no point in remaining as the woman was obviously frightened of them. They would get nowhere with her while she was in that state.

"Very well, madam," said Craddock. "We don't want to alarm you. We'll come back when your sister is present. Can you tell us when she will return?"

"Don't know," came the unhelpful reply.

As they stood in the passage, they began to notice a cold draught of air coming from above them. They looked up and saw that the window on the landing was firmly shut.

"Come on, Rathbone," said Craddock. "Let's get out of here. It's freezing."

They beat a hasty retreat and sat in the car. "That was one strange lady," observed the sergeant.

"That was one strange house," echoed Craddock. "It was much colder in there than it is outside. It's quite mild today. I wonder why it was so cold? The window wasn't open."

"I wondered that, too," said Rathbone. "It was almost like …"

"Like what?"

Brian Rathbone fiddled with the glove compartment, opening it to reveal several empty crisp and cigarette packets which proceeded to scatter onto the none-too-clean floor of the car.

"Watch what you're doing," grumbled the inspector.

"Sorry, sir," said Rathbone, gathering up the litter and shoving it all back into the glove compartment, which now wouldn't shut properly.

"Leave it alone," instructed Craddock crossly, as he turned the key in the ignition. "Like what?" he then repeated, as the car moved off.

"Like it was – I don't know," said Rathbone at last, watching the chief inspector's reaction closely.

"Like it was haunted?"

"Well, no, not quite that. But there was definitely something not quite right in there."

"You can say that again," agreed Craddock. "Those two bear a great deal more investigation, that's for sure. I only hope we can get more sense out her sister."

Chapter Twenty-Three

The Feathers was full of lunchtime drinkers when Bernard arrived just after one o'clock. He spied his friend seated in a booth near to the fire and made his way through the cheery crowd to join him.

"I've got you a sherry, Bernie," said Robbie, passing it to him. "Medium dry. Busy in here today, what?"

"Thanks, Robbie. Cheers!" Bernard looked around. "Well it *is* Friday," he observed, after his first sip. "We don't usually come in here on a Friday. Bound to be more crowded, I suppose. They all seem very happy, don't they?"

"Yes," smiled Robbie, swigging his beer. "Nearly the end of the working week. How are you? Anything interesting to report?"

"Well, I've had a couple of rather interesting visits lately," confided Bernard, taking another delicate sip of his sherry.

"You have? Do tell, old boy."

"Well, first of all, one of the Rowan sisters – Elvira – called on me. She said it was because of the cat ..."

"The cat?"

"Yes. You remember – you said you thought it might belong to them?"

"Ah, yes. So – was she very cross with you? Did she tear you off a strip and walk away with the moggy?"

"No, she didn't. In fact, she wasn't really bothered about the cat at all. It belongs to her sister, anyway. She said she didn't like it herself."

"So why did she come and see you then?"

"Ah, well, that's just it. I think it was just an excuse. I think she wanted to ask me what I thought about the murder."

"Hmm. I suppose it's only natural, you being a vicar and all that."

"Well, that's what I thought at first, but I think it was more than that. She's very worried about these ridiculous rumours going around."

"What – about them being witches who'd sacrificed Helen in some sort of sick ritual, do you mean?"

Bernard looked down at his empty glass and twiddled with the stem. "Yes. She said it was affecting their livelihood."

"Livelihood? How do you mean?"

"You know they sell herbal remedies?"

"Hmmph! Don't hold with all that. Dangerous, in my opinion."

Bernard shrugged. "Some people swear by them, Robbie."

"Hmmph!"

"Yes, I can see it from your point of view – as a doctor. But – anyway. I told her I'd say something in Sunday's sermon about rumour-mongering and the harm it can do. Nothing specific, you know."

"Better not, Bernie. Your congregation would desert you in droves." He laughed. "How about another?"

Robbie indicated his empty glass. Bernard consulted his watch, remembering that Mrs Harper would have his dinner on the table "promptly at two o'clock" as he had instructed.

"Yes, why not? My round. Could you do the honours, though? Don't fancy forcing my way through that crowd. You're bigger than me. Besides, they tend to feel obliged to pipe down when they see my collar, and I don't want to spoil their fun."

"No problem," grinned Robbie, taking Bernard's proffered ten shilling note. "Haven't you got anything smaller, old chap?"

"Er, no, sorry."

It took Robbie no time at all to grab the barmaid's attention, who had taken a fancy to him the first time she served him. He was delighted to stay and chat, which meant Bernard had to wait nearly ten minutes for his second sherry.

"Pretty girl," he observed as Robbie put the drinks down on the table. "You didn't lose any time chatting her up."

"Actually, she was the one doing the chatting up," smiled Robbie, flicking back a lock of thick sandy hair from his forehead. "But she's a fair piece, I have to say."

"Yes. She is rather comely. I haven't seen her before."

"She only started last week. Her name's Babs. Nicer to look at than Sid with his permanent scowl."

Bernard could only agree.

"It's about time we got a decent-looking barmaid. Sid's been losing customers hand over fist lately. Anyway," said Robbie, after taking a long draught of his beer, "you said you had had *two* interesting visits? You've only told me about the first one which, I have to say, wasn't all that interesting."

"If you say so," said Bernard testily, reaching in his top pocket for his pipe. "Have you got a light?"

"Well?" Robbie handed him a box of matches. "What about this other visit?"

"I've got a good mind not to tell you now." Bernard was almost sulking.

"Oh, come on, tell me if you're going to." Robbie was almost sulking too.

"Very well," said Bernard, sucking on his pipe. The fragrant tobacco soon helped to smooth his ruffled feathers and he relaxed. "You know old Colonel Powell?"

"That old buzzard," laughed Robbie. "What did he want with you? Never goes to church, as far as I'm aware. Likes a drop or two, so I believe."

"Yes, that's him. Mrs Aitch said he was a boozer. So, what he told me we can probably take with a large pinch of salt."

"Right." It was Robbie's turn to light his pipe now. "Go on."

"Well, I can't really say anything as he told me in strict confidence. But, well, I'm sure he didn't mean I couldn't tell you…"

Chapter Twenty-Four

Craddock and Rathbone were feeling decidedly uneasy after their visit to Appleby Cottage, although neither of them could exactly say why. The cold air pervading the Rowan sisters' little home had been inexplicable.

"Here we are," announced Craddock as he screeched to a standstill outside Banks', the butchers. "Let's see what Percy has to say for himself, shall we?"

Percy Banks was the spitting image of his father, Harry. He was now in full charge of the family butchery business since his dad had retired due to ill health. He smiled at the two policemen as they entered the shop. Although they were in plain clothes, it was obvious they weren't there to buy a leg of lamb or a pork chop. He had been expecting their visit and showed them into the back, leaving a youngster with a dripping nose to serve the next customer.

"He's a bit slow, but willing," smiled Percy, referring to his young shop assistant. "Now, I suppose you want me to tell you what I saw on Tuesday evening."

"That's right, Mr Banks. If you would," said Craddock.

They were sitting in a small room surrounded by packing crates, the sunset just visible through the pocket-sized window.

"Well, all I know is I saw Helen Carstairs go into the Rowans' cottage at about five o'clock that evening. Why she was there or how long she stayed, I've no idea. I was just passing the place on my way home."

"Right," said Craddock. "You're certain this was the evening of the girl's murder?"

Percy Banks scratched his head as if thinking deeply. "Absolutely," he said after a moment. "It was last week, I remember, because I had shut the shop a little early to get home to get ready for my date with my girlfriend. We were going to see that new flick at the Roxy, with Glenn Ford."

"*The Big Heat*?" asked Craddock. "Good film."

"Yep," agreed Percy. "But it was a bit gruesome, wasn't it? When that horrible gangster threw acid in that pretty woman's face, I had to look away. She was so attractive before that happened."

"Yes, a stunning actress," said Craddock. He had always been fond of Gloria Grahame, who seemed to be able to speak without moving her lips.

Rathbone thought it was about time he interrupted the film critics. "Aren't we straying from the point a bit?"

Percy laughed. "Yes, we are, aren't we? Anyway, that was definitely last Tuesday we saw the film and that was why I was early going home. I know it was the same evening I saw Helen go into the Rowans' as I remember thinking about the film as I watched her go in."

"I'm not sure I follow you," said Craddock, looking puzzled.

"Sorry, it's just that I had seen the stills of the film outside the picture house and Helen reminded me a bit of the actress I'd seen in those stills."

"Ah, Gloria Grahame, you mean?"

"Is that her name? Well, then. Yes."

"Right," said Craddock. "Let me get this right. Have you got your notebook, Rathbone?"

Rathbone had opened it to a clean page and licked the nib of his pencil, waiting to write down anything useful.

"You saw Helen Carstairs enter Appleby Cottage in Hallows Mead Crescent at about five o'clock last Tuesday evening. That would be the 20th."

"That's right."

"Do you know these Rowan sisters at all? Have you ever had any dealings with them?"

Percy looked serious for a moment. "Do I know the Rowans?" He seemed to be hedging.

"Yes," sighed the chief inspector impatiently. "Do you?"

"Well, not very well myself. But my dad used to go out with the younger one – Vesna – about thirty years ago. The older one, Elvira, is a customer of ours. That's all I know about her."

Craddock was interested now. "Ah, your father knew Vesna Rowan? Obviously, fairly well if he was dating her."

"Well, yes. They were engaged at one time."

"Engaged? So, what happened? I will probably need to speak to your father about her."

Percy looked worried now. "I'd rather you didn't bother him, Inspector. You see, he's not in the best of health, ever since …"

"Ever since what?"

"Ever since he fell in the canal that time. It was all Vesna Rowan's fault."

"What? Do you mean she pushed him in?"

"Not herself, no. But her fiancé did, although Dad says he was very drunk at the time and didn't remember exactly what happened."

"Just a minute," broke in Rathbone, going over his notes. "Can we backtrack a bit? Didn't you say your father was engaged to Vesna Rowan?"

"Yes, that's right."

"So – who was this 'fiancé' that was supposed to have pushed him into the canal, then?"

"Oh, right. I see the confusion. That was it, you see. This fiancé had come back two years after the First World War, after they all thought he was dead. He was a bit of a bully, from what Dad told me, but he was all right, really. Dad always thought anyone was all right if they bought the drinks, and apparently this bloke had bought the drinks all night."

"Go on," said Rathbone, scribbling furiously.

136

"Well, that's it, really. Dad was in the canal in the middle of winter, and he wasn't a good swimmer. Being drunk as well didn't help. He developed pneumonia as a result and since then he's had a weak chest."

"So Vesna Rowan's fiancé pushed your dad into the canal because he was jealous and wanted to marry Vesna himself?"

"I suppose so. Although the man seemed to disappear shortly after that, and as far as I'm aware Vesna Rowan never married anybody. Which is just as well as she's completely doolally these days."

Craddock grinned. "We paid her a visit just now and I must say she didn't seem quite the ticket."

Percy grinned back. "You could say that. Elvira has her hands full with her, I shouldn't wonder."

"Do you know where these rumours started about them being witches?" asked Rathbone.

"Oh that," said Percy dismissively. "It was all because they dispense these herbal remedies, I think. Although I suppose it's also because they're two spinsters living together, and people are suspicious of that sort of thing, aren't they? And then it's the way they look. I mean, Elvira looks like that witch in *Snow White*. Vesna's all right, though. Apparently, she was very pretty when she was young, according to Dad. You know how these rumours can grow out of all proportion. Anyway, I think that's all I can tell you. As you can imagine, there's no love lost between me and that Vesna woman after what she did to Dad."

"It was hardly her fault her fiancé pushed him in the canal," Rathbone pointed out.

Percy shrugged. "Well, if that's all, gentleman, I'd better see what that lad of mine is up to. He's probably chopped his hand off by now."

☙

"Well that was interesting, wasn't it?" observed Craddock.

Both men were back at the station comparing notes.

"Very," said Rathbone thoughtfully. "What do you make of it?"

"I think we need to take what that young man says with a pinch of salt. About him seeing Helen going into Appleby Cottage, I mean. He obviously bears them a grudge, so I wouldn't put it past him to try and add fuel to this witch sacrifice fire."

"I don't think he was trying to do that, guv," objected Rathbone. "I mean, he seemed like a decent, level-headed young man to me."

"Yes, so it would seem. But you must bear in mind that he feels bad about what happened to his father and could see this as an opportunity to get his revenge. When you pointed out that it wasn't Vesna Rowan's fault about what happened to his father, he didn't answer you, did he?"

"Hmm," said Rathbone thoughtfully. "That's true. I suppose you could be right."

"Anyway, the sooner we speak to that other Rowan sister, the better. We should get more sense out of her, anyhow. We'll also need to speak to Harry Banks at some point."

"Yes, guv," said Rathbone. "Do you want a bacon sandwich from the canteen?"

Chapter Twenty-Five

It was a bright morning in late April when Bernard and Robbie turned into Hallows Mead Crescent. As they approached the gate which bore the name 'Rosewood Cottage', they saw the subject of their visit bending over a rose bush, secateurs in hand. Bernard coughed politely to gain his attention.

Colonel Powell straightened up and turned to his unexpected visitors, wielding the secateurs in a somewhat dangerous manner.

"Sorry if we startled you, Colonel," smiled Robbie, reaching out to shake his hand. "I'm Dr MacTavish. And I believe you know our vicar, Reverend Paltoquet."

"Ah, yes, of course. Well, this is a surprise. To what do I owe the pleasure?" The colonel looked flustered but otherwise quite pleased. He didn't get many callers these days, not since his wife died, anyway. "You caught me pruning my roses. It's a bit late in the year, but we've had so much frost lately."

"Indeed," said Bernard. "They look fine rose bushes. I bet you get some excellent blooms in the summer."

"Not bad, not bad," said the Colonel proudly. "Once upon a time the Rowans had better blooms than me, you know. I used to ask them their secret, but they never would tell me. They've died off lately, though."

Bernard and Robbie had passed Appleby Cottage on their way to see the colonel, almost missing it. They had been a little surprised by its dilapidated condition but supposed the two women weren't as young as they used to be and were finding it all a bit much these days.

"Anyway, what can I do for you gentlemen?" he asked. "I'll get my char to make us some tea, shall I? I usually have a cuppa about this time."

"Splendid," said Robbie. "Shall we go inside?"

When the order for morning tea had been given to the colonel's charwoman, he showed them into the parlour which was very tidy and spotlessly clean, no doubt thanks to the obliging char.

"Do take a seat," invited Colonel Powell. "I'll just remove Brumus." So saying, he lifted a fat white cat off one of the chairs and made an attempt at brushing its fur from the cushion. "She always leaves her calling cards on the furniture, I'm afraid. Hilda – that's my char – is always complaining about it."

Once the tea had been brought, Bernard cleared his throat and began. "Er, it's about your visit to me the other day, Colonel..."

"Thought it might be," grinned the Colonel, stirring three large spoonfuls of sugar into his tea. "You must have thought I'd had a skinful, eh?"

"Well, what you told me took a lot of swallowing," Bernard admitted.

"I know it sounds fantastic, but it's the gospel truth. That's what I saw. Have you told the doc about it?"

Robbie nodded. "Colonel, actually I do believe you. So does Bernard here. We – er, we've had experience of these kinds of – er – things before. The reason we're here is to try and persuade you to tell the police about it."

The colonel gave a hollow laugh. "Well *they* certainly wouldn't believe me, would they? They'll just show me to a cell and tell me to sleep it off. I told *you*, Vicar, because I thought *someone* should know about what I saw. What you choose to do with that information's entirely up to you."

Bernard looked at Robbie, who tried again. "Now, look," he said. "We know it won't be easy to convince the constabulary. They only go on hard facts. But at least you will have informed them and then it will be off your mind. You would have done your civic duty."

The colonel looked unconvinced. "I don't know," he said slowly. "I really don't know. I've already got a reputation as a drunken old fool. If I tell them this, then I'll be even more ridiculed. I like a drink, same as the next man, but I don't really deserve my reputation, you know. I'm fond of my port – hence, my gammy foot." He gave it a vigorous rub. "But I haven't got the DT's or anything like that."

Robbie smiled. "I'm sure you're fine, Colonel. But maybe you need to get checked over to make sure." He had his GP's hat on now. "Have you got a regular doctor? You're not one of my patients, are you?"

"What's this? Touting for business, eh?" There was a quizzical look on the colonel's rubicund face.

"Not at all," laughed Robbie. "But it won't do you any harm to have a check-up. We don't want you keeling over with a heart attack, now, do we?"

The colonel drained his teacup before replying. "You're right, I know, Doc. But, to be honest, I've always been afraid of doctors – or rather, what they're likely to tell me I've got."

"Do *I* frighten you, Colonel?" asked Robbie kindly.

"Not as an individual, no. But once you get your stethoscope out, that's a different story."

"Well, you know where I am, if you need me, eh? My surgery's in Marlborough Street."

"I'll think about it. More tea?"

"No thanks," said Robbie, rising to go. Bernard shook the colonel by the hand. "Please think about what we've said. You should go to the police."

The colonel smiled ruefully. "I'll chew it over, but I'm not making any promises."

Once out in the street, Bernard turned to his friend and sighed. "He won't, you know."

"Won't what? Go to the police or consult me in my professional capacity?" Robbie said with a raised eyebrow.

"Neither, I shouldn't think."

Chapter Twenty-Six

"There's a young lady downstairs wants to see you, Vicar."

"Did she say what she wanted?" asked Bernard, already interested. Young lady visitors were few and far between at the vicarage.

"Nope," shrugged Mrs Harper. "I asked 'er but she didn't want to tell me. Skinny as a rake, she is. Like an ironing board."

"All right, Mrs Aitch, that will do," said Bernard. "Just send her up."

Bernard greeted his guest at the top of the stairs. "I don't think we've met before, have we?"

The young girl, who looked very pale, as well as skeletally thin, gave him a wary smile as he ushered her into his study.

"I hope you don't mind me coming to see you, as I'm not a churchgoer, and I know you're a busy man. But I didn't know who else to turn to. My name's Minnie, Minnie Knox, by the way."

"Hello, Miss Knox," said Bernard, smiling. "I never mind seeing anyone if they wish to see me, whether they're a member of my flock or not. It's what I'm here for."

"Thank you," she said meekly.

"Now, dear," said Bernard, showing her to the chair by the fireplace, the one usually occupied by Robbie most evenings. There was no fire, as the weather had turned markedly warmer. He sat down in the chair opposite and steepled his fingers under his chin.

"I don't know if you know this, Vicar," Minnie began, "but I'm – er, was – Helen's best friend." She stopped abruptly, and Bernard could see the tears standing in her eyes.

"You mean Helen Carstairs? The poor lass who was murdered last week?"

Minnie nodded her head, too choked to speak. Bernard waited patiently for her to regain her composure. "Take your time," he said quietly. "You must be very upset. I'm so sorry for you."

This made Minnie even more upset, and the tears started to flow. Bernard fished in his pocket for his handkerchief which, after a quick inspection, looked reasonably clean. He passed it to her without a word.

She scrunched it in her hands, as she gained control of herself and managed to speak again. "Sorry, Vicar," she said. "I can't help it. You see, we were inseparable most days. We always saw each other for at least a couple of hours every day, if we weren't going out with boys, that was. We were in the same class at school. I loved her."

Bernard felt inadequate to the occasion, as the girl dabbed the tears that had started to flow once more.

"Anyway," she continued after a little while, "I came to see you because of what she told me the last time we met."

"Before you go on," said Bernard quickly. "Is this something you should be telling the police?" He began to think his role as father confessor was leading him down alleys he didn't particularly want to go down.

Minnie looked at him sadly. "I just thought... You see I didn't want Helen's private business spread all over the papers ... You're the one person who will take what I say and not tell anyone else – aren't you? Like confession?"

Bernard smiled wryly. "I'm not a Catholic – I don't take confessions, you know."

"I know that," said Minnie. "But you're still not supposed to tell anyone's secrets, are you?"

"Of course not," said Bernard, a trifle huffily. "You can be assured I will treat what you say in the strictest confidence."

He felt slightly guilty, however, knowing he would probably tell Robbie at the earliest opportunity.

"It's such a dreadful thing to say," Minnie continued. "I don't know if the police know that Helen was going to have a baby?" She stopped after saying this, watching Bernard's face for signs of shock. Seeing none, she continued, "So, Vicar, you know about that?"

Bernard nodded his head sadly. "Don't worry, dear," he said kindly. "The police know already. It would have been discovered at the post mortem. I think they're keeping it out of the papers for as long as possible, though, for the family's sake."

"Family – huh!"

Bernard looked at her, puzzled. "Why do you say that? In that tone, I mean? Are you saying that Helen's family knew she was pregnant?"

"Well, let me put it this way – one of them wouldn't have been all that surprised," she said somewhat enigmatically.

Bernard knew now that what Minnie had come to tell him was something much darker than the mere fact her friend had been pregnant. He fervently hoped it wasn't what he was now beginning to suspect.

He had to tread carefully. "When you say one of them wouldn't have been surprised she was pregnant – was it her mother?"

"God, no!" said Minnie, shocked. "She'd have had a blue fit."

Bernard was having his worst fears confirmed and he really didn't like to think what he was thinking. "Then," he started slowly, "was it her father?"

Minnie nodded.

∝

Inspector Craddock stood up as a thin, dark-haired girl entered his office, escorted by a forbidding-looking policewoman.

Minnie Knox had, with some reluctance, been persuaded by Bernard to go to the police. The policewoman, who seemed all chest, introduced her and handed her over to Craddock. This done, she promptly left the office, her duty discharged.

Craddock could see she was nervous. "Take a seat, Miss Knox," he said gently. "No need to be afraid of me." He gave her a smile.

Minnie sat down gingerly and stared around the sparse office with curiosity.

"Right, dear, what can I do for you? You have something to tell us about poor Helen Carstairs, I understand."

Minnie looked down at her hands, which she was twiddling nervously, and then up into Craddock's kind eyes. "Yes. The vicar said I should come and see you about her."

"The vicar?"

"Yes – er, Reverend Palto – er – he's got a funny name."

"Oh yes, Paltoquet. No business having a name like that, in my opinion. If he's English, why have a French name?"

Ignoring this, Minnie continued, "Anyway, I went to see him and that's why I'm here now."

"I see," said Craddock, scratching away on his pad.

He was reminding himself in indelible blue-black ink to go and see that confounded interfering vicar of St Stephen's and tell him to mind his own sodding business. He waited for Minnie to continue.

"You see," she said after a moment, "he told me it could be a vital piece of information – about the murder."

"Yes, go on."

At this point, Brian Rathbone came into the office, having heard about the young girl's visit.

"Ah, there you are, Rathbone," said Craddock. "Miss Knox here is about to tell us something very interesting." He paused, looking pointedly at Minnie. "I hope."

Minnie gulped several times before continuing. "She told me that her father had got her – er – in the family way…" She flushed to the roots of her hair.

"I see," said Craddock, riffling through some papers, trying to keep a lid on what he was feeling. "Let me get this straight. Are you telling us that Henry Carstairs got your friend, Helen – his daughter – pregnant?"

"Yes, sir," Minnie almost whispered, looking down at her knees.

Rathbone spoke up while his superior got command of himself. "This is a very serious accusation, Miss Knox," he said. "Are you sure that is what Helen Carstairs told you?"

"'Course I am," said Minnie, impatient now. "Helen was at her wit's end. Didn't know where to turn. Couldn't face telling her mother she was *pregnant*, let alone telling her who the father was."

"It must have been an awful situation for the poor girl," said Rathbone, coming over to Minnie and patting her shoulder comfortingly. "Thank you for coming to tell us. This information throws new light on our investigations."

"Yes," said Craddock, "thank you for coming to us. You have been most helpful. Is there anything else you think we ought to know?"

"Well," Minnie began, then stopped.

"Yes?" Craddock's breath was well and truly bated now.

"I don't know whether it's of any importance, but as Helen was desperate to get rid of the baby, she told me she was going to see if the Rowan sisters could give her anything to help. You know, like. To get rid of it."

So that, thought Craddock, explains the visit to the Rowans on the evening of her murder. If there was one thing he hated to think about, it was abortion. He'd have a few words to say to those women if they were dispensing anything to cause miscarriages.

While Rathbone was showing Minnie out, Craddock sat on at his desk, deep in thought. It was all very well dealing with straightforward murder, but when it came to incest and illegal abortions, that was a whole new ball game. He wished, with all his heart, he wasn't on the case at all.

Suddenly he stood up, grabbed his coat and, as Rathbone was returning to the office, Craddock swung the younger man round, passing him his coat as he did so.

"Come on, Rathbone. You and I are in need of a stiff drink," he said.

Chapter Twenty-Seven

"That Rowan woman's 'ere again, Vicar," announced Mrs Harper, standing at the door of Bernard's study, hands on hips. She was out of breath. The stairs were getting a bit much for her these days, especially as it was the fourth time that morning she had had cause to climb them. "You know, she came 'about the cat' the other day." Nancy said this in a way that showed her scepticism in no uncertain terms.

Bernard was sitting by the unlit hearth, that very cat snoring happily on his lap. He gave it a stroke under its chin.

"Oh dear," he said, "I'm expecting Robbie any minute. We'd planned to take a picnic lunch to the park."

The sun was shining bravely outside the window, beckoning. It was a glorious spring day, a day not to be wasted sitting in a stuffy study writing sermons.

"Don't I know it, considering as 'ow I've been making the sandwiches all blessed morning." She sniffed ominously.

"Oh yes, of course. Thank you, Mrs Aitch. Did she say what she wanted this time?"

"Didn't ask 'er. Shall I send 'er packing?"

"No, of course not. All my parishioners are welcome if they need me."

It wasn't strictly true; like now, for instance. He hoped Elvira Rowan wouldn't keep him too long.

A few moments later, Elvira tapped softly on Bernard's study door.

"Hello, Miss Rowan," he greeted her. "Please do come in."

He ushered her over to a chair and sat down opposite her.

"Thank you …"

"Now, what can I do for you?"

"I'm sorry to bother you again so soon, Vicar," Elvira began. "But I didn't know who else I could tell."

"My dear, that's what I'm here for. You can tell me all your troubles, and I will certainly help if I can. And God will always be on your side, don't forget that."

"I'm not so sure about that," laughed Elvira mirthlessly. "According to the folks round here we're wicked heathens. Witches stirring their cauldron, throwing in the entrails of frogs and bats and things."

"I don't take any notice," smiled Bernard, "and neither should you. I've already told my congregation to do the same. So, don't worry, they'll soon get tired of it."

"No, well, it's easy for you to say," said Elvira.

"I know," said Bernard, "but people are suspicious of people who aren't quite like themselves, I suppose. One just has to try and ignore them and carry on. As long as *you* know you're doing no harm, that's the important thing."

Elvira took some comfort from this and even smiled a little. "The cat looks very well and contented," she observed.

Beelzebub looked up at his erstwhile mistress and yawned. There was a world of meaning in it. Bernard had removed the cat to open the door to his visitor, but it had leapt back on his lap directly when he had sat down again. He put the protesting feline down on the floor once more.

"Off you go, Beelzebub. Go and see what Mrs Harper's got for your dinner. A nice whiting head, I shouldn't wonder."

The cat stalked out of the room, flicking its tail offensively as he did so.

"I hope your sister isn't missing him too much," Bernard said.

"I don't think she's in a position to miss anything right now," said Elvira and, to Bernard's horror, suddenly broke down in tears.

He never got used to parishioners blubbing in front of him, but he usually had a hanky on hand for such

149

eventualities. This time was no exception, and he passed her a bright red spotted one from his inside jacket pocket.

"I'm sorry," she wept, blowing her nose vigorously. "I was determined not to cry, but everything's been such a trial lately."

"Please, take your time."

Elvira looked at the kindly young vicar through teary eyes and smiled again. "You're very kind," she said. After a moment, she continued, "You see, my sister's had some sort of breakdown recently. We – er – we've lived in Appleby Cottage for more than thirty years, and it's finally got to her."

"What? Living in the cottage? How do you mean?"

"I thought of coming to see you sooner, but I kept putting it off."

"I'm sorry that you felt you couldn't confide in me," offered Bernard, eaten up with curiosity.

"It's just that – er – ever since – well, I won't go into that…" She paused. "I hope you won't think me a stupid old woman for telling you this …"

Bernard could only reassure her that he would think nothing of the kind; in fact, he had rather warmed to her. Stiff and unbending though she seemed to be, there was a kind of old world courtesy and exactness about her that he admired and even liked. He knew she wasn't very popular with the locals, and he supposed he could understand why. She presented a forbidding front to the world but, as was so often the case, he felt sure it masked a softer, kinder interior.

"The thing is, our cottage has been haunted for many, many years."

"Haunted, you say?"

He was at once intrigued, as he knew Robbie would be, too. The good doctor was a firm believer in the supernatural and had a deep consuming interest in it. He was also psychic, something that Bernard wasn't, at least not in the same way as his friend. But he didn't dismiss such things out of hand, especially as Robbie had been able to contact and help the troubled spirits of two little Norwegian children several years ago. Also, their mutual friend, Dorothy Plunkett, was a well-respected professional medium. All in all, Bernard was inclined to believe Elvira's assertion and, he suddenly realized, it also backed up something the old colonel had recently told him.

"Yes. I know you'll think I'm mad, and that you'll tell me there's no such thing as ghosts. But there are..." Elvira started to weep again.

"My dear," said Bernard, reaching out and patting her knee gently. "I *do* believe in them. At least, I'm sure there are things we mere mortals don't fully understand. My friend, Dr MacTavish, is also a strong believer in the supernatural, you know."

Elvira looked pleased, as well as surprised. "Really? I like Dr MacTavish. He's very kind. I didn't know you two were friends."

"Oh yes. We are. In fact, he is due here any minute. We're planning on taking a picnic to the park as it's such a fine day."

"Oh, I'm sorry. And here's me keeping you. I could come back another time ..."

"I wouldn't hear of it. You stay right where you are."

Elvira looked almost beautiful to Bernard now. She had a beatific smile on her face as if some terrible burden had suddenly been lifted from her and it was lighting up her fine features. Her almond-shaped grey eyes were gentle and her pale, but flawless, skin was slightly flushed now. Maybe her lips were a little too thin and her nose a little too long, but otherwise she looked very charming to Bernard at that moment. She must be in her sixties, he reckoned, but she looked a good deal younger somehow.

"So," he continued, "are you telling me your sister's nerves have been affected by this haunting? It's quite understandable, if so. And I'm sure you must be affected, too."

Elvira nodded. "I've got used to it over the years, but I think it's been getting to Vessie much more lately. Especially now, with this awful murder …"

"But why should it make any difference to how she feels about your ghost?"

"Well, that's just the point. I really shouldn't be telling you this, but I know it won't go any further."

Bernard mentally crossed his fingers, knowing that he would break Elvira's trust the minute he met Robbie later on. "Go on," he said.

"You see … that poor girl came to see us on the night she died. Well, it was the afternoon, actually…"

"She came to see you? Did you know her, then?"

"Well, no, not really. She only lived around the corner to us in Cherry Lane, and we've spoken on occasions to her parents. But the poor thing was pregnant, and she'd come to see if we had anything we could give her to help her get rid of it."

"Ah." Bernard was beginning to understand, if not approve. "And did you give her anything?"

"I shouldn't be admitting this, really, but we only gave her one of our granny's herbal remedies. It doesn't really bring on a miscarriage, but it can do sometimes. We then told her to have a really hot bath and said she could use our bathroom if she wanted to. You see, she didn't want to raise any suspicions at home by having a bath at a time she never had one."

Bernard wasn't sure where this was going and wasn't sure he wanted to listen to any more. Then suddenly Elvira stopped talking and stood up, almost as if she had realized for the first time just what she was saying: to a man of the cloth, of all people.

"I – I must go…"

Bernard stood up too. He could tell she was regretting her visit. She had told him too much.

Just then, Robbie burst into the room.

"Hi, Bernie," he cried cheerily. "Mrs Aitch told me to come on up. Oh, I'm sorry…"

He stopped in his tracks as he saw the older Rowan sister standing in the middle of Bernard's study.

"I was just leaving," she said, handing Bernard his now sodden hanky. "I – I'm sorry to have taken up so much of your time."

With that, she swept out of the room. Bernard turned to Robbie, who looked puzzled.

"That's one troubled lady, if I'm any judge," he said. "What goes on?"

"Let's head for the park and make the most of this fine weather," said Bernard quickly. "I'll tell you when we get there."

વ

Bernard, after munching through his fifth fish paste sandwich, took out the thermos flask from the hamper that Mrs Harper had carefully packed for them, and poured out the tea. He and Robbie had grabbed the only vacant bench in the park that afternoon, as the spring sunshine had given everyone the same idea as themselves.

"Is there anything stronger in there?" asked Robbie.

"I shouldn't think so," smiled Bernard, rummaging through the goodies in the hamper. "You know what Mrs Aitch thinks about strong liquor."

"Of course," laughed Robbie. "I wasn't really expecting anything." Saying this, he fished in his jacket pocket and brought out a small silver flask. He tipped some of the contents into his tea. "Want some?" he asked, giving him a nudge.

"Not for me," said Bernard, quickly putting his hand over his cup. "You're turning into an alcoholic, Robbie." He wasn't entirely joking.

"Nonsense," said his friend, as he screwed the cap back on the flask. "Just a little nip to keep out the cold."

"But it's baking hot! It's like June today," Bernard pointed out, tucking into a wedge of angel cake.

Robbie didn't reply. Grinning, he put the flask back in his pocket.

They sat in companionable silence for several minutes, watching the antics of the ducks and geese as the people fed them tit bits. Bernard enticed a particularly scrawny looking duck with a piece of cake.

"Don't encourage them, old boy," pleaded Robbie. "We'll have all the pigeons here in a minute."

As if on cue, at least a dozen of them descended at their feet, scrabbling for the poor duck's morsel of angel cake.

"Shoo!" shouted Bernard, waving his arms at them.

This made them flap their wings in a fluster, but none of them flew away. Bernard tried to lure the poor duck with another piece of cake, but the bird knew when he was beaten and sadly waddled away.

"What did I tell you, man?" said Robbie, brushing crumbs off his jacket. "Hurry up and finish eating and put the food away, otherwise they'll never go. I can't stand pigeons!"

"They're all God's creatures," remonstrated his friend mildly, starting to stack the hamper with the remains of their lunch.

The sun continued to blaze down as the two men sat on, neither in any hurry to leave the park. Robbie's evening surgery didn't start till five, and Bernard's evening service was at six. It was still only ten to three.

"Come on, Bernie. Don't keep me in suspense," Robbie broke the silence at last. "What did Elvira Rowan want this morning? Don't tell me she was on about that blasted cat again."

"No. It was quite disturbing, actually," said Bernard thoughtfully. "She's very worried about her sister. I think she might be going a bit senile, from what she was saying."

"Really? I think Vesna Rowan is one of my patients. Perhaps I should look in on her."

"I think that would be a good idea, although there's another possible reason for her distress."

"Oh? And that is?"

"Elvira told me that their cottage is haunted, has been for many years, apparently. She said her sister is at the end of her tether with it."

"Haunted, eh? Well, well. What makes them think that? What form does this haunting take?"

"She didn't say. But that's not all she told me, and that was even more worrying."

Robbie was very intrigued now. "Do tell, Bernie."

"She said that Helen Carstairs came to see them the day she died."

"What? Do the police know?"

"I don't know. I was about to advise her to go to them when you barged in." He gave his friend an old-fashioned look.

"Sorry, I'm sure. But I wasn't to know, was I?"

Bernard shrugged. "No, of course not. Actually, I was quite glad you interrupted when you did. She was telling me stuff I didn't really want to hear."

Robbie's eyebrows shot up at this. "What sort of stuff?"

"I don't know whether I should tell even you, Robbie. What she told me was in the strictest confidence. I *am* a priest, remember?"

"That's never stopped you before. Anyway, you know it won't go any further. But don't tell me if you don't want to." Robbie seemed annoyed.

"Okay, okay. You know I'm going to tell you, it's just not very nice, that's all." He paused before continuing. "The poor girl went to them, hoping to get something to bring on a miscarriage."

"My God! I know the sisters are accused of being witches, but I didn't know they were back street abortionists into the bargain! This throws an entirely different light on the matter, Bernie. You do see that, don't you?"

"But what should we do? We can't go to the police. You know that."

"I always felt sorry for those sisters up to now. But if there's one thing I hate, it's abortion. Especially by people who don't know what the hell they're doing."

Bernard smiled weakly at Robbie who had got up from the bench and was pacing up and down the path, trying to control his anger.

"Those women have got to be stopped. They're dangerous!"

"I don't think so, Robbie. Elvira told me they just gave her something herbal and said that it didn't usually work anyway. She told Helen to have a hot bath as well."

"No doubt accompanied by a bottle of gin."

"She didn't mention any gin…"

"God, Bernie, these old wives' tales! You'll be telling me next they tried using a knitting needle!"

Robbie was beside himself now.

"Calm down, old chap," said Bernard quietly. "People are looking. Elvira certainly never mentioned anything about a knitting needle. I got the impression she felt sorry for the girl and only wanted to help her out of her predicament."

Robbie slumped down beside him, his anger spent. "Well, one thing's for certain, Bernie. We've got to persuade that woman to go to the police."

Bernard knew he had no alternative but to agree.

Chapter Twenty-Eight

So, Henry Carstairs was responsible for his murdered daughter's pregnancy, was he? Craddock mulled this over as he swung his wreck of a Ford round a particularly sharp bend. Rathbone, by his side, was too busy hoping to stay alive to think too much about what they were about to do.

They were on their way to arrest a man for incest and abuse of a minor. And that was just for starters. Craddock was sure he'd also got his man for Helen's murder. Carstairs' daughter's pregnancy gave him a very good motive, a very good motive, indeed. If he could bring himself to rape his daughter, he would surely also be capable of murdering her.

"I never liked or trusted that man, you know, Rathbone," he said, veering round an articulated lorry that was illegally parked. This was done with much aplomb combined with a disregard for human life that was positively frightening. Rathbone held onto his seat, closed his eyes and prayed.

It was with some relief that he stepped out of the car outside the Carstairs' front door a few minutes later, closely followed by his daredevil chauffeur.

The inspector tapped his size twelve boot impatiently on the polished red step, pressing the doorbell. The door opened almost immediately on his second ring and Mrs Carstairs stood before them, a shadow of her former self. The tragedy had taken its toll on her. Her hair seemed to have turned grey overnight, or maybe she hadn't bothered with her roots.

"Oh, hello, Inspector," she said wearily. "Sergeant," she acknowledged the younger man too. "Please come in."

"Is your husband at home?" asked Craddock as they followed her into the hall.

"Yes. We've just finished supper. Please come through."

The two men exchanged wary glances as they followed her down the passage. They entered the room to see their quarry sitting in a comfortable fireside chair, the evening paper, open at the crossword, his little Jack Russell asleep at his slippered feet.

"It's the police again, dear," she said.

"Ah, good evening, gentlemen," he said politely, standing up to greet them.

Rathbone wanted to punch him in the face, while what Craddock wanted to do to him was beyond description.

"Have you got any news for us?" he asked, giving them the briefest of smiles. His wife hovered eagerly in the background.

"Would you like some tea? I was just making some for Henry," she said.

"No, thank you," said Craddock quickly. "We won't be here that long, and I wouldn't bother about your husband's tea. He won't be here that long either," he added, rather brutally.

Rathbone gave his boss a disapproving look. Craddock would never win any prizes for tact.

"What do you mean?" Ivy Carstairs was taken aback at Craddock's rudeness.

"Henry Carstairs, I'm arresting you for the rape of your under-age daughter and for incest. You do not have to say anything, but anything you do say will be taken down and may be given in evidence."

Ivy screamed and fell to the floor in a dead faint. Henry Carstairs, who had stood up on the policemen's arrival, remained upright, his jaw practically hitting the floor with her. His Jack Russell began to yap piteously, and even Craddock felt a bit sorry for it.

"What's all this?" Henry Carstairs managed to say after a moment. His cold eyes blinked at them uncomprehendingly, and two red spots appeared on his sallow cheeks. Rathbone noticed that he didn't seem to have any eyelashes.

"I think you understand perfectly, Mr Carstairs," said Craddock. "Rathbone, can you attend to Mrs Carstairs?"

Ivy was now recovering consciousness and looking very disoriented as Rathbone helped her to the sofa and fetched her a glass of water from the kitchen.

"Just what cock and bull story have you been told?" demanded Carstairs.

"You needn't concern yourself with that. I must ask you to accompany us to the station. You may call your solicitor from there."

Craddock could see the man was about to argue, so he brought out the big guns. "If you wish to be handcuffed, I can certainly oblige," he said. That did the trick.

"No need for that, Inspector. I'm sure this can all be cleared up at the station."

అ

Craddock was feeling decidedly uncomfortable looking at Henry Carstairs as he sat on the opposite side of the table in the interview room. Beside him sat a sleazy solicitor who had, on more than one occasion, cramped his style. Rathbone was sitting beside Craddock, looking green.

Knowing what Henry Carstairs had done, Rathbone had never felt such revulsion for a human being in the whole of his life. In his line of business, he had met many criminals, rapists and perverts among them, but this man's crime beat everything. The rape of his own under-aged daughter, for God's sake! His eyes met Carstairs' and he quickly looked away.

He was also secretly worried about their witness, Minnie Knox. He feared she wouldn't be able to stand up well under cross examination in court. Even if she was telling the truth, which Rathbone had no doubt she was, a wily defence lawyer would run rings around her in five minutes.

The solicitor was already demanding they release their prisoner, as they had no proof of the charges. Carstairs remained silent throughout, his only words, on his solicitor's instructions, being 'no comment'.

Suddenly the door opened, and young PC Jenkins entered, a flushed look on his excited face.

"I hope you've got a good reason for this interruption, Jenkins," grumbled Craddock, not nearly as cross as he sounded. He was getting bored with hearing 'no comment' and could see he was getting nowhere with the interrogation of his prisoner.

"Sorry, sir, but I think you'll like to hear this."

Outside the interview room, Craddock folded his arms and stared up into the face of young Jenkins, who stood almost eight inches taller. Craddock only just managed to scrape into the police force at all, being only five foot seven and a half inches, although what he lacked in height he certainly made up for in width and bombast.

"Well, what is it?" he demanded.

"We checked Carstairs' finger prints against those that were on the knife," he said, smiling broadly, "and – guess what – it looks like we have a match!"

The knife! Of course! It had soon been discovered close to the body, hidden in undergrowth. Craddock had almost forgotten about it. It was all he could do to stop himself from jumping up and down on the spot and kissing the young constable on both cheeks.

"Are you sure?" he demanded.

"Definitely," smiled Jenkins. "There was enough detail on the knife to get a positive match. We've got him!"

"We've got him!" echoed the ecstatic Craddock. "And we'll make sure he swings!"

Chapter Twenty-Nine

Mrs Harper was very excited, a state she hardly ever allowed herself to get into. But this was an exception because, the following week, she and her friend Gladys were going on a Mediterranean cruise together. They would be gone for a fortnight, a point of information she had been taking great delight in reminding poor Bernard at regular intervals as the time for her departure drew ever nearer. Now, with only a week to go, the frequency with which she reminded him had increased proportionately until he was sick and tired of hearing it.

"A whole fortnight!" she cried, as she set down the vicar's breakfast. "Just one week to go and then *a whole fortnight* without 'aving to do a hand's turn. Just lie on the deck and bask in the sun. Gladys says I won't know myself."

Bernard tried to raise some enthusiasm on her behalf. "That's jolly nice, Mrs Aitch, I'm sure you'll have a lovely time."

He took the top off his egg with uncharacteristic vehemence as he listened to his housekeeper singing in the kitchen. "*See the pyramids along the Nile, See the sunrise on a tropic isle, Just remember darling all the while.... You belong to me.*" He thought that, if she started singing *Faraway Places*, he would strangle her. Because, while she was happily singing her untuneful head off, what was he supposed to do without her for 'a whole fortnight'?

She still hadn't found anybody to take her place, and there wasn't much time left. It looked as if he would have to rely on some part-time help from Lucy Carter, which he didn't really think a good idea. Apart from the fact that she would be overworked, looking after both Robbie and himself, her cooking wasn't a patch on Mrs Harper's.

"Did you hear the news, by the way, Vicar?" Mrs Harper was standing by his side again, pouring out his morning tea.

"News?" Bernard wasn't in the least interested in any 'news'. The only news he wanted to hear was that Mrs Harper had hired a Cordon Bleu chef to cook his meals in her absence. Nothing short of that would cheer him up today.

"Vesna Rowan's dead."

"Vesna Rowan? Oh, really?" Bernard was interested, despite himself. In fact, he was quite shocked.

"Yes, Vicar, I 'eard it from Gladys yesterday. She told me that the woman had been found dead in bed in the morning. 'Er sister's beside 'erself, she said."

"Then I must go and see Miss Rowan at once," said Bernard, finishing his boiled egg with undue haste.

"I don't think you should go and see 'er just yet, Vicar," said Mrs Harper knowingly.

"Why ever not? Remember, she came to see me and confided in me about her sister. She would welcome a visit from me. She would *expect* a visit from me."

"Well, I see it like this," said Mrs Harper, undeterred. She sat down at the table and poured herself a cup of tea. "If you leave it to me, you might just 'ave – might, I say – a replacement 'ousekeeper next week."

"What on earth are you talking about, Mrs Aitch?" he said, beginning to feel the faintest stirrings of hope.

"You see, the poor woman's on 'er own now, and I bet she could do with some company. Also, I bet she's the kind of woman who needs to be useful. After all, she's looked after Vesna all 'er life, did all the cooking and 'ousework. That silly sister of 'ers wasn't one to get 'er 'ands dirty with 'ard work, you know. A bit of a flibbertigibbet, if you ask me."

Bernard was one step ahead of her now. "You mean you think Miss Rowan could be persuaded to come and work here at the vicarage while you're away? Don't you think it would be an imposition, given the circumstances?"

"Nuh," said Mrs Harper dismissively. "It'd be just what the doctor ordered. Take 'er mind off it. I bet she'd jump at the chance. Anyway, between you and me and the gatepost, I bet she's relieved. 'Er sister was twopence short of a shilling and she must 'ave 'ad 'er 'ands full. Never 'ad a moment to 'erself."

"Well, if you think so," said Bernard, still unsure. "Will you go and see her, then?"

"I will," said Nancy. "Believe me, she'll be only too pleased. Especially if she's seen to be working for a vicar, any rumours of 'er being a witch will be knocked on the 'ead once and for all."

Bernard smiled for the first time that morning. It did seem an ideal solution to both his and Elvira's predicaments. He tried not to think about the last time she had visited him and what she had told him. He assumed she hadn't gone to the police as there had been nothing on the news or in the papers about the abortion attempt. Perhaps it was better to let sleeping dogs lie, after all.

"By the way, do you know what Vesna Rowan died of?" he asked.

"No idea. Probably 'eart failure. Dr MacTavish was called in so I'm sure 'e'll put you in the picture. Now, I must get on if I'm to go and see this woman today. I've got to go shopping for some clothes for the cruise later, and I've still got all my packing to do. And you'll want a meal on the table at one o'clock, I take it?"

"Yes, please, Mrs Aitch," said Bernard meekly, anxious not to upset his housekeeper now that she was on a mission to save him from two weeks of Lucy Carter's cooking.

⌇

So, shortly before eleven o'clock that fine, sunny June morning, Mrs Harper could be seen waddling up the path to Appleby Cottage. Having promised Bernard she would ask Elvira to stand in for her, she was now feeling slightly nervous of her reception. Maybe Bernard was right. It probably was an imposition.

She rang the bell and waited, but no one came to the door. She rang again, but still no response. She wandered over to the front window and peered through, but the curtains were, not unnaturally, closed. As she stood pondering, she saw a tall, gaunt figure turn into the crescent. Elvira Rowan was approaching the cottage, armed with a wicker basket of groceries.

Elvira eyed her suspiciously as she came to the front gate. "What do you want?" she asked bluntly. "Did the vicar send you?"

"In a manner of speaking," replied Mrs Harper. "Can I come in for a minute? I won't stay long. I was sorry to 'ear about your sister. I 'ope she never suffered."

Elvira ignored Mrs Harper's attempt at commiseration as she inserted the key in the lock and stalked down the passage, leaving her visitor to follow or not, as she pleased.

"Rude cow," said Mrs Harper to herself. "Serve her right if I just go. She won't know what she's missing then." She sniffed. But curiosity and a latent sense of pride forced her to follow Elvira into the cottage.

Nancy stood in the kitchen doorway, watching the remaining Rowan sister putting food away in the larder. "You're still here, then?" observed Elvira unnecessarily.

It was a warm day, but it could have been January instead of June in the cottage kitchen. The sun's rays were streaming in through the kitchen French windows, but they had no effect whatsoever on the chill in the air.

Mrs Harper shivered. "Why is it so cold in 'ere?"

"Is it? I hadn't noticed," was all Elvira said.

"Look, I've not got all day, and I don't want to catch pneumonia before I go on my 'oliday." Mrs Harper paused, pulling her cardigan tightly across her ample bosom, causing one of the buttons to pop off in the process. "I've come to do you a favour, actually."

Elvira finished emptying her groceries into the larder and turned to face her. "You must forgive my rudeness," she said. "I'm all over the place at the moment. As you can imagine …" Tears were standing in her eyes, threatening to burst like a dam.

"'Course, ducks," said Mrs Harper, looking away. "I've got a clean hanky in 'ere somewhere." She rummaged in her capacious handbag.

"It's all right," said Elvira, pulling a handkerchief from her sleeve. "I've got one here." She dabbed at her eyes and managed to regain her composure after a few moments.

"Don't you go upsetting yourself," said Mrs Harper, kindlier now. "Let me put the kettle on. A nice cup of tea will set you right. It'll warm us up a bit too."

Elvira gave a hollow laugh. "Will a 'nice cup of tea' bring Vessie back then?"

"Well if you're going to take that attitude…" Mrs Harper stopped filling the kettle and glared at her. You can't help some people, she thought crossly.

"Sorry," said Elvira. "I'm being rude and ungrateful. I'm no company for anyone at the moment."

Mrs Harper softened once more. "Sorry, love, I can see you're up against it. I'll make the tea. But don't you notice how cold it is in 'ere?"

Elvira smiled sadly. "Of course, but I'm used to it. This place is always cold – winter or summer."

"You should get your pipes lagged," advised Nancy, spooning three heaped spoonfuls of tea leaves into a big china teapot that was standing conveniently on the shelf beside the gas stove.

"Wouldn't do any good," replied Elvira, shrugging.

When the tea was poured, Mrs Harper asked Elvira if she had had a chance to think about her future now her sister was gone. "I know it's early days, but you should think about yourself now. For a change."

"I don't know what I'm going to do," said Elvira, sipping the hot tea gratefully. "I don't fancy living here on my own though. Not with …"

"Not with …?"

"Oh, no one, nothing. I just don't like being here on my own. I'm not used to it. Even though Vessie wasn't much company lately, what with her funny turns and all that, she was another person to have around. I don't even think she recognised me most of the time. I suppose it was a blessed relief for her when she died."

"Must have been for you too," observed Mrs Harper. "You can look after number one now."

"I don't know how to do that. I need to be useful. That's all I know is how to look after someone. Feed them, clothe them, even wash them. Vessie was like a child at the end."

"Well," said Mrs Harper, smiling, "I wonder how you'd feel about coming to look after the vicar for a couple of weeks? You won't have to dress and wash 'im, of course, just feed 'im and do the 'ousework."

Elvira's gloomy visage seemed to lighten slightly. "Why? Where will *you* be?"

"I'll be in the Mediterranean with my friend Gladys. I told you I was going on 'oliday, didn't I? We're going on a sea cruise."

"Lucky you," said Elvira, not without a hint of envy in her tone.

"Yes, it's exciting," grinned Mrs Harper. "The sunny Mediterranean! I've never been abroad before. Got my own passport and everything. Only fly in the ointment's the vicar. I need someone to look after 'im while I'm gone. Would you like to do that?"

"Well, I'd have to think about it," said Elvira slowly.

Mrs Harper stood up. "Well, don't be too long about it, otherwise I'll 'ave to make other arrangements."

"No, I won't. Thanks for thinking of me."

"You'll get paid for it, by the way. Not much, mind."

"I'm not bothered about the money. I can manage. Especially now there's only me."

"Not even the cat, eh?" Mrs Harper gave her a wink.

Elvira permitted herself a half smile at this. "All right," she said suddenly. "I'll do it."

Chapter Thirty

Robbie MacTavish was standing at the bar of the Feathers, ordering a whisky for himself and a sherry for Bernard, when his friend arrived. He was also giving Babs, the pretty barmaid, the benefit of his best chat up lines. Curtailing their conversation somewhat reluctantly, Robbie made his way over to him.

"So, old boy, how's the Mrs Aitch replacement situation?" he asked, setting down the drinks.

Bernard raised his glass to Robbie and smiled. "It's sorted, I think," he said.

"Yes, I heard on the grapevine that Elvira Rowan is doing the honours. Although you know that Lucy would have been only too happy to help out…"

"That's all right," said Bernard quickly. "Don't think I'm not grateful to her, but Elvira can live in while Mrs Aitch is away so it'd be better all round. Anyway, I think she'll welcome the change now that her sister's gone…"

Robbie's face clouded over. "Yes, I'm sure she will. Poor thing," he said. "She was beside herself when I was called in that morning. I'll never forget that visit. I couldn't get over how cold it was in the cottage despite the heat outside. I could see straightaway that there was nothing I could do for Vesna. She'd been dead for several hours, by my reckoning. I'm glad that Elvira's coming to you. That will give her something to take her mind off the tragedy. I really don't know what she'll do without her."

Bernard sighed. "Yes, it is a shame. But I think Vesna hadn't really been herself lately."

"Oh, the senile dementia, you mean? Yes, she was certainly suffering from that, even though she wasn't that old. Elvira must have had her work cut out looking after her. I don't suppose she'd ever admit it, though."

168

"No, I don't suppose she will," agreed Bernard, draining his sherry glass and looking at the clock behind the bar. It was showing five minutes to one and Mrs Harper's steak and kidney pie was calling to him. "Better get back, Robbie," he said, standing up.

The two friends left the pub together and sauntered up the sunny street. This June had turned out to be one of the hottest they could remember, with temperatures in the eighties and early nineties nearly every day. Bernard even had to remove his jacket, a thing he hardly ever did in a public street. Robbie was altogether more casual, with no jacket and even an open collar. His tie was stuffed in his trousers pocket, making a rather unsightly bulge. Bernard didn't approve of unsightly bulges but refrained from saying so. It was too hot to argue anyway.

"By the way, I understand Carstairs' trial is coming up soon," said Robbie as they reached the doctor's house. "They say it's an open and shut case."

Bernard shuddered despite the heat. "How can a parent murder a child? It's beyond human understanding."

"Tut, tut," said Robbie, opening the gate. "You of all people shouldn't jump to conclusions. A person is innocent until proved guilty, you know. I, for one, don't think he did it."

Bernard stared at him in disbelief. "You don't? Even after what Minnie Knox said – you know, about him being the father of his daughter's unborn child? A man capable of that is capable of anything."

"We mustn't assume that he's a murderer, old boy," said Robbie calmly. "He's a very unfortunate man, whatever he's done."

Bernard remembered his dog collar and ran his finger around it. His neck was sticky with sweat. He realized he wasn't being very Christian at the moment. Robbie was being much more sympathetic, but somehow, he couldn't feel any compassion for Henry Carstairs; the man was evil.

Bernard carried on to the vicarage deep in thought. Robbie was right, of course. One shouldn't condemn a man without incontrovertible proof. But the fact that he had defiled his daughter was something that he couldn't get past. There was no reason to think that Minnie Knox would lie about such a thing, so Bernard couldn't even think it might not be true. But if the man wasn't a murderer, he had done something that was nearly as bad. And Bernard knew that he wasn't alone in what he was thinking. The man wouldn't stand a chance with a jury if they found out he had made his only daughter pregnant.

Chapter Thirty-One

Elvira Rowan had seamlessly taken over from Nancy Harper and was up at the crack of dawn on her first day to see to Bernard's breakfast. She wanted to get off on the right foot and she prayed her cooking would be up to scratch. She needn't have worried. Bernard cleared his plate of bacon, eggs and tomatoes with relish.

She breathed an inward sigh of relief. Now she was ensconced in the vicarage in Nancy's room, she saw her ice-cold fridge of a cottage in unfavourable comparison. She dreaded going back to it when the fortnight was up. She'd heard of people being lost at sea, of boats capsizing. The Titanic, for instance. Still, she sighed, there wasn't much likelihood of an iceberg in the Mediterranean, and it was wicked to wish poor Mrs Harper under one. She scrubbed at an obstinate egg stain on the table cloth, putting her heart and soul into it as penance.

Later that morning, Bernard asked her to come to his study. Oh dear, she thought. He's not happy with me. He wants me to go.

"I – I hope I'll give you every satisfaction, sir," she mumbled, her heart beating nineteen to the dozen. Don't send me away. Don't send me away.

"Well, Elvira, if your breakfast is anything to go by, you'll suit me fine," smiled Bernard. "And don't call me 'sir'. Please – sit down a moment."

Faint with relief, Elvira flopped into the chair opposite. "I- I'm so glad. I know I can't hope to compete with your housekeeper's cooking, but I usually manage to turn out good, wholesome food when it's required."

"Your cooking is just as good as Mrs Aitch's," grinned Bernard. "But don't tell her I told you." He gave her a friendly wink.

Elvira relaxed now. Bernard was a nice man. She was generally suspicious of vicars and their ilk; doing good works supposedly, but just as prone to human frailty as the layman. But Bernard, she realized, was a genuinely good person.

"Anyway, er – Vicar, if that's all, I must get on. All the silver needs polishing and I've got the front room and the hall to clean."

"All that can wait, dear," said Bernard kindly. "I just wanted to talk to you about what you told me when you came to see me a while ago. You know – about the visit you had from Helen Carstairs on the day she was – er – the day she died."

Elvira tensed up immediately. She wished with all her heart that she hadn't confided in him. Apart from anything else, he now knew about her special receipt for bringing on a miscarriage, something that was strictly illegal.

"I don't really think there's much point in going over that again," she said, a little more abruptly than she intended. "I mean, nothing will bring her back, will it? And, anyway, they've got the man who did it, haven't they? The father, I mean. It was him, wasn't it?"

Bernard felt in his very bones that Henry Carstairs was the murderer of Helen Carstairs, but he remembered his conversation with Robbie only a couple of days ago and thought carefully before replying.

"They've charged him, certainly, but he hasn't been found guilty yet. I think we should wait for the outcome of the trial, don't you?"

Elvira nodded. "I suppose you're right. But, you see…"

"Yes?"

"I've already been interviewed by the police about Helen's visit…"

"You have? Well, why didn't you say?"

Bernard was relieved at hearing this news. He had been worrying about what he should do if Elvira didn't confide in the police. But what she said next wasn't at all what he needed to hear.

"...and I told them that she never came to see us."

"You mean – you lied? To the police?" Bernard was shocked.

"I'm afraid so. You see, they said that they'd been told by someone that they saw Helen at our door the day she was murdered. I just denied it – said that the witness must have been mistaken. It wasn't her. I said it could have been another young lady. They seemed to believe me."

"But why on earth did you lie to them?" Bernard was still shocked.

Elvira glared at him. She was on the point of packing up her rubber gloves and leaving him in the lurch. "Because if the police knew that I dispensed something that could bring on a miscarriage they'd have arrested me. And I couldn't leave Vessie on her own if I went to prison. Or they would probably have arrested both of us and she was in no fit state for all of that."

"But, don't you realize that you were obstructing the police? The fact that Helen came to you for help will have to come out at the trial. They'll call that witness and cross-examine whoever it was – as well as you. You'll be in a right pickle then, won't you?"

"I'll just have to cross that bridge when I come to it," said Elvira with more confidence than she felt.

"Look – it's not too late to put matters right, dear. You must go to the police and tell them the truth now."

"Oh dear," said Elvira.

Bernard was being so persistent. This nice, kind vicar was expecting her to give herself up to the police.

"I know it's hard for you," Bernard was saying. "But I'll come with you and speak for you. I'll tell the police that you lied to them because you were afraid they would arrest you for performing illegal abortions. You can then say that you rarely, if ever, give out these preparations and that you only gave Helen the powder because you felt so sorry for her. I'm sure they'll take that into consideration."

Elvira stood up suddenly. "I've got the silver to clean. You go to the police and tell them, if you must. But I won't. They'll put me in prison. If you want that on your conscience, go ahead."

With that, she left the room with a sweeping gesture that left Bernard in no doubt where he stood. If he went to the police and told them what he knew, she would never speak to him again and, far from never cooking him another meal, she'd probably poison it instead.

He sat there, wondering desperately what to do. In the end he decided to do nothing. For the time being, at least.

☙

It was in the second week of Elvira's stay at the vicarage when Minnie Knox paid another visit to Bernard. He felt immediately nervous, knowing what she knew and what he hadn't done about it.

"It's about Mr Carstairs' trial," she began.

"Ah, right. I see." He rather supposed it had to be, or why else was she here?

"I've been called as a witness for the prosecution," she explained. "And I'm dreading it."

"That's quite understandable. Courts can be daunting places, especially if someone is on trial for murder and, consequently, their life."

At that moment Elvira knocked and entered with a tray. Bernard took it from her. There was a steaming pot of tea and two cups.

He poured out the tea and handed her a cup. "So, Minnie, do you want me to come with you to the trial? Give you some support? I'll be happy to do so, if I'm free."

"Well, that would be kind," said Minnie. "But, really, I came to ask your advice."

"Go on," said Bernard, intrigued.

"It's just that what I'll be telling the court will be very damning to Mr Carstairs' case, won't it? After all, it doesn't necessarily mean that he's a killer, the fact that he had – er – relations with his daughter. That's a completely different crime."

Bernard steepled his fingers under his chin and frowned in concentration. "Well, Minnie," he said slowly. "All you can do is tell the truth. If it's damning to him, it's unfortunate, but you will be in no way to blame. Besides, the courts don't take kindly to people who commit perjury…"

"Perjury?" Minnie's complexion turned even paler than its usual hue.

"Yes – telling lies. You must only tell the truth to the court; otherwise, you could be looking at a prison sentence yourself, or a fine at the very least."

Bernard watched Minnie's sweet face carefully. "I see," she said, mulling over what he had just told her. "You see, Vicar," she said, "I used to like him. I would often go to tea with the Carstairs in the old days – after school. When Mr Carstairs came home from work, he seemed always pleased to see me. He used to tell me and Helen jokes. He was a lot of fun then."

Bernard was taken aback at this. The Henry Carstairs he knew had never struck him as 'a lot of fun'. He had always seemed so straitlaced and serious. He couldn't imagine the man having a joke with two schoolgirls. Or, given what he now knew about him, maybe he could.

"So, Henry Carstairs was quite a jolly chap in those days, was he? Well, he hasn't any cause to be jolly now, has he?" It was an unkind remark, he knew, and immediately regretted saying it.

"No. Not now," agreed Minnie sadly. "But he was always friendly towards me, although he seemed to be rather bitter lately. I think someone was promoted over him at work – that's what started it. And Mrs Carstairs told me that he suffers from bad headaches, although he won't see the doctor about them. I was so shocked when Helen told me what he had done to her. I would never have believed it of him."

"You don't think she was lying, do you? Covering up for somebody else? A boyfriend, perhaps?"

"Oh no!" Minnie was shocked at such a suggestion. "She would never do that. But I found it hard to believe it, all the same. D'you know…" She stopped suddenly.

"Go on – do I know what?"

"Oh nothing."

Bernard leaned towards her. "Come, my dear," he cajoled, rather like a music hall villain only minus the moustache twiddling. "Please tell me – you *do* want me to help you, don't you?"

Minnie sighed. "Yes, of course. It wasn't really important, but I think you might take it the wrong way."

"Why don't you try me?"

"Well, it was one afternoon. Helen was helping her mum with the washing up and Mr Carstairs and I were in the front room. I think he'd been drinking before he came home that day, because he was in a particularly jokey mood – not offensive or anything. He came up to me and took out a ten shilling note. He said he would give it to me if I gave him a kiss…"

"Oh, my dear," said Bernard, shocked. "You don't think that's important? It sheds even more light on the man's dubious character."

"Yes, I suppose you would see it that way. So would most people. But it was all very innocent. The thought of that ten shilling note was too much for me, and I pecked him on the cheek and grabbed the money. I was just as much in the wrong as he was. I found out much later that that ten shillings was the housekeeping money for the week. I felt terrible."

Bernard almost laughed. Poor Ivy Carstairs would have had to scrimp and save that week. But the story didn't do her husband any favours, that was for sure. The fact that he had been the worse for drink didn't excuse him either. It made it worse, if anything.

"I won't tell anyone," said Minnie adamantly. "It was a private moment. Nobody else will ever know about it and I hope you'll treat what I've told you in confidence."

"Of course," said Bernard. "Anyway, dear," he continued. "I will come with you when it's your turn to be a witness at the trial. Do you know the exact date?"

"Well, the trial itself starts on the fifth of September." Minnie got up to leave. "Thanks for listening to me, Vicar. I'm really grateful. As you advise, I can only tell the truth." She flushed again. "And it *is* the truth," she iterated firmly.

"That's all any of us can do, dear – tell the truth. Except not enough people do."

Bernard opened his study door for her and accompanied her down the stairs, showing her out the front door. Was it his imagination, or did she seem a little flustered? Was there something she wasn't telling him?

Chapter Thirty-Two

Henry Carstairs hadn't received many visits while being held in prison, pending his trial. Ivy came as often as she could, continuing to believe in his innocence. She didn't bring him any cheer on these visits, however, as all she did was sit on the other side of the grill, dabbing her tear-stained eyes and complaining about Charlie. Carstairs was extremely fond of his pet Jack Russell and couldn't bear to listen to her.

"He keeps on whining and looking for you, Henry," she told him. "I can't keep him under control, and I don't have the time to take him for walks."

"Why? What else do you have to do?" he demanded, worried that his poor little pet wasn't getting enough exercise. "You *must* find the time – until I get out of here."

"But …" It was all Ivy could do to get herself up in the morning, let alone go out of the house with a boisterous dog.

"But what?"

He wished she wouldn't bother to visit him if all she could do was complain. He'd rather she kept away. He would have much preferred a visit from his pet Charlie, but the prison didn't allow it.

"Well, Henry love, we have to face the possibility that you – you may be found guilty." She dabbed her streaming eyes again. "I can't look after Charlie indefinitely. He's started to mess around the house."

"That's because you don't take him out," said Henry crossly. "And don't you fret, Ivy, I'll get out of here. I'm innocent. I never murdered our lovely daughter. You know I didn't."

"Of course I do, love, but it's the jury that has to be convinced. And what about the other – other charge."

Ivy couldn't bear to think about this. She never, for one minute, believed her husband capable of such a heinous crime as incest. She had lived with him for long enough to know he couldn't be guilty of such a charge. And as for murder; she knew he worshipped the very ground Helen had walked on.

"I'm a respectable churchgoer, and I've been hard working all my life. Never put a foot wrong and look where it's got me."

"Oh, Henry!"

Seeing Ivy burst into tears, a prison warder took pity on her and brought her a cup of tea.

*

Later that day, Henry received another visit. Two visits in one day was something he hadn't experienced in a long while. The only visitor he really wanted to see had only come once; he'd told her not to come again in case questions were asked. However, he was comforted when she told him she believed in him completely. He couldn't have murdered his only daughter; it was unthinkable.

But this visitor was someone he'd never seen before. He was accompanied by the friendly prison warder who sometimes brought him cigarettes or pills for his headaches. A middle-aged, greying-round-the-temples individual sporting a pink bow tie and a carnation in his buttonhole introduced himself to Henry as Ernest Pickles, his barrister.

When the warder had left the visiting room, Ernest Pickles coughed, took out a large handkerchief and wiped his mouth.

"I will be conducting your defence, Mr Carstairs."

Pickles sat down at the table in Henry's cell and opened a large file. He wiped his mouth again, this time more thoroughly. As he riffled through the pages, the prisoner stared at the man's well-manicured hands in

179

fascination. He could almost see his reflection in the polished nails.

"Mr Carstairs, you have been accused of murdering your seventeen-year-old daughter. Did you do it?"

Henry was shocked at the man's bluntness.

"No, I did not."

Ernest Pickles studied Henry's haggard features thoughtfully. He took in the watery grey eyes under which were heavy dark rings, his hollow cheeks and unshaven chin. He searched for a sign of some humanity in the man, but he looked so miserable, almost other worldly, that he could see no trace of natural emotion. He looked down at his file.

"Right. I need to believe you, Carstairs. I need to have your assurance that you are speaking the truth when you say you didn't kill your daughter. Do I have it?"

"You have it." Henry continued to be monosyllabic.

He was uncomfortable having to talk to someone he couldn't relate to. All his life he had avoided men like the kind this Pickles seemed to be. They were an abomination in his eyes. He firmly believed that, as a Christian, he should revile such unnatural doings.

Ernest Pickles was an astute and able barrister and an extremely intelligent man. He could see revulsion in his defendant's eyes, but he was used to the suspicion his appearance and mannerisms provoked in so-called 'normal' men.

"You need to open up to me. I need to have your side of the story. While you think about what you are going to tell me, I have to ring my wife. I'll be back in a few minutes."

In the barrister's absence, Henry visibly relaxed. Ring his wife! Well, he could have knocked him down with a feather. A family man, after all. Appearances can be so deceptive, he thought. On Pickles' return, he even managed a weak smile which in no way endeared him to his defending counsel.

He had deliberately misled Carstairs. He had simply left the man alone to gather his thoughts and get his temper under control. Telling the bigot he had a wife had taken the wind out of the prisoner's sails, he could tell. He smiled inwardly with satisfaction. He didn't like the man he was to defend, but that was nothing new. He never let his own personal feelings get in the way of justice, even though he was almost prepared to make an exception in Henry Carstairs' case.

"Right," he said, studying his file again. "I am defending you on the count of murder. This trial is one of murder. We are not concerned with the – er," he coughed and wiped his mouth with his handkerchief again. "We will not be going into the incest charge at this trial."

"But won't it come up in the course of it?" asked Henry.

"It will inevitably be touched upon. One of the witnesses for the prosecution was a close friend of your daughter's. I believe it is she who told the police about the incest. This was according to your own daughter's allegation. Even though it can be treated as hearsay, the prosecution counsel will no doubt make a meal of it. We have to minimise this as much as possible and stress to the court that the only charge is one of murder. I think we may be able to throw out this Minnie Knox altogether. After all, she has nothing to contribute as regards the murder charge. We must keep it simple. If you are acquitted – and with me defending you, you will be – then there will be a further trial on the incest charge. If you want me to defend you on that, I need to ask you again – are you guilty?"

Henry looked down at the table, covered as it was with coffee and tea stains. He stared at a cigarette burn in the grain of the wood but remained silent. He seemed to be fighting some demon deep inside him.

Ernest Pickles flicked through the file and waited patiently for him to answer. "Well?" he said finally as Henry didn't speak.

"I'm not guilty," spat Henry Carstairs. "I find it an abomination in the eyes of God. I have never broken any of the Commandments…." He paused. Except one, he thought. "I could never bring myself to do anything so vile. I say again, I'm not guilty. I didn't rape my daughter; I did not make her pregnant; and I didn't murder her."

Ernest Pickles wrote something in the file. "I see. Well that's categorical enough."

He narrowed his eyes and looked closely at his client. "Good. I believe you. I will defend you on both counts. Once you have been cleared of the murder charge, we will mount your defence on the incest charge. This Minnie Knox shouldn't be that difficult to discredit."

Henry Carstairs, if he had been a different sort of man, might have been tempted to hug Ernest Pickles. Here was a ray of hope, at last. For days he had sat in his cell, wondering how on earth he could be accused of such evil. Why had Minnie told such a barefaced lie about him? He knew of only one reason, but he didn't think she would lie so outrageously just because of that… But, then again, you never really knew people, what went on in their heads.

"Now," said Ernest, coughing into his voluminous hanky. Wiping his nose several times, more than seemed strictly necessary, he began again. "Back to the murder trial. We have one most important factor to deal with, Henry."

Henry was surprised at the sudden use of his Christian name and was fully prepared to resent it but found he really didn't mind. "What's that?"

"The knife. The murder weapon that has your prints on it. I understand there are other prints on it, which is good. But, on the other hand, we need to know how *your* prints got on there in the first place. Do you have any explanation for that?"

182

Henry Carstairs racked his brains. He couldn't, for the life of him, think how it could be possible. "I have absolutely no idea."

"Very well, that is a difficulty, but not the end of the world. I think that, for now, I have everything I need. I'll be back in a few days and, in the meantime, I want you to think long and hard about the knife. Also think about Minnie Knox and why you think she may be out to discredit you. You mustn't, and I stress this, mustn't leave anything out. You must tell me everything. If you lie or duck the issue, I will be unable to help you. Do you understand?"

Henry nodded. He knew only too well that he had to be frank with this man but knew that he couldn't – not in every detail. Other people – well, one other person, was involved. He couldn't speak the whole truth – not to Ernest Pickles – not to anyone.

The barrister stood up and closed the file. "Well, I think we understand each other, Henry. Rest assured that I will do everything in my power to get you acquitted."

Pickles shook Henry's hand without looking him in the eye and left.

After his lawyer's departure, he felt more alone than ever. It seemed ironic now, especially as the fussy little barrister was on his side and was going to help him get off. But would he succeed? Without knowing all the facts, would it be possible?

Chapter Thirty-Three

Robbie had been to dinner at the vicarage during Elvira's reign a couple of times, telling Bernard that he thought her cooking well up to the standard of Nancy Harper's. In fact, he would go so far as to say her steak and kidney pie was even better! Bernard had to agree. He began to wish that Elvira was there to stay, and that his faithful and long-standing housekeeper was being wafted out to a remote desert island right at that moment. Although, on the other hand, he couldn't imagine his life without her wise maxims, curmudgeonly temper or drop scones. It was unthinkable.

The day after Minnie Knox's second visit, Robbie was at the vicarage again, enjoying another meal courtesy of Elvira Rowan.

"Oh dear," said Bernard when the dinner things had been cleared away and he and his friend were seated in the vicarage study smoking their pipes. "I feel so disloyal to Mrs Aitch, but I wish she wasn't coming back quite so soon. I never thought anyone could cook as good as her, let alone surpass her."

Robbie laughed. "No, dear boy, it's a bit of a facer, isn't it? I wish I could take Elvira on myself, but I'm sure Lucy would have something to say about that."

Then Bernard had an idea. "Why don't you just take her on as a cook? You can tell Lucy that it will lift the burden off her as she has so much else to do."

Robbie sucked on his pipe thoughtfully. "By Jove, Bernie, that's an idea. Do you think she'll wear it?"

"Who? Elvira or Lucy?"

"Well – both, I suppose."

"Well, my betting is that Elvira will jump at it. And I'm sure if you put it to Lucy properly, she will be fine about it. From what you tell me, she doesn't enjoy cooking that much anyway."

"True, true," laughed Robbie. "I'll see what she says. I'll clear it with Lucy first before I say anything to Elvira, though."

"Quite right. Changing the subject, I had another visit from Minnie Knox yesterday."

Robbie became serious at once. "Ah, poor Helen's young friend. What did she want this time?"

"Oh, she was worried about the trial. It's quite soon now. In September. She wants me to go with her and hold her hand. She dreads giving evidence against Mr Carstairs."

"I don't see why. She only has to answer questions and tell the truth. Shouldn't be nervous about that."

"Well, I think she doesn't want to be the one to put him on the end of a rope. And she is rather young. Must be daunting for her."

"I don't think she should be called at all," said Robbie thoughtfully. "Not to the murder trial. It will prejudice the case. I bet they don't call Minnie in the end."

"You think so?" Bernard felt relieved. "Yes, you're probably right. If Carstairs didn't kill his daughter, then he doesn't deserve to hang. Having sex with her is one thing, murdering her is quite another."

"Absolutely. Any whisky going, old boy?"

"Well, the sun's over the yard arm, I suppose," laughed Bernard, and he went to the cupboard where he kept his secret bottle of Glenfiddich away from the disapproving eyes of Mrs Harper.

When it was poured out, with a small sherry for himself, Bernard became thoughtful again. "You know, Robbie, I got the impression that Minnie was holding out on me. There was something she wasn't saying. She seemed very nervous when I told her that all she could do was tell the truth."

"Well, I suppose that's only natural," observed Robbie. "As you said yourself, she's very young to be put through this sort of thing. And poor Minnie would hardly want to be the one to sway the jury to find him guilty. Not on her evidence alone, and certainly not if he's innocent."

"But do you think he is? Innocent, I mean. If he's been fiddling with his daughter, he's more than likely the one who killed her. To keep her quiet."

"There is that, but I really can't see him as a murderer. Not of his own flesh and blood, anyway."

"It's hard for you and me to understand, I suppose. But we don't know what the provocation was. Maybe Helen taunted him – threatened to tell her mother – or the police…That would be grounds enough for murder, surely?"

"Yes. Could be. But I don't think so. Another theory of mine concerns his state of health."

"State of health?"

"That's right. When Mrs Carstairs came to see me recently, she mentioned her husband was getting these awful headaches. Now these could be caused by all sorts of things, but one could be a brain tumour. If a mass is pressing on a part of the brain this could cause the person concerned to undergo a change of personality."

"Ah!" Bernard took in this new piece of information. "He could be suffering from a brain tumour, you say? Make him act abnormally?"

"It's possible – yes."

"Well, you may have something there, but it would depend when these headaches began as to whether they have been making him act differently. You see, Minnie told me something else about him that shows that he could well be a pervert."

Bernard told his friend what she had told him about the ten shilling note. As he expected, Robbie was appalled.

"If he did that, then that clinches it for me. The man must be an absolute cad and a bounder," declared Robbie. "Hanging's too good for him."

"Well, you've changed your tune," observed Bernard wryly. "You were the one who told me not to jump the gun – a man's innocent until proved guilty and all that."

"Oh well, there's a limit to what you can believe about people. If what Minnie says is true, there is no excuse for him. How could he rob his wife of the week's housekeeping just to get a kiss from a schoolgirl! The man's capable of anything."

Robbie fumed while Bernard just smiled to himself and sipped his dry sherry.

Chapter Thirty-Four

Elvira Rowan watched as Mrs Harper bustled about her bedroom unpacking her suitcase. "I 'ear you did a great job while I was away," she said with a sniff. Elvira didn't know the vicar's housekeeper well enough to realize that sniff meant she wasn't entirely pleased by that.

"How was your holiday?" Elvira asked politely. "You look very brown. Was the weather good?"

"Good? It was wonderful," sighed Mrs Harper, remembering the warm Mediterranean sun and how it had eased her arthritis, which had been getting worse before her holiday. Now she was back in England, she dreaded its return. It was almost as hot as Greece at the moment but, come the autumn and the damp weather, she knew she would suffer again.

"I'm so glad. It looks like it's done you the world of good, anyhow."

"You can say that again," grinned Nancy. She was holding a Spanish doll in a crimson frilled dress and mantilla. "Do you like it?" she asked.

"It's beautiful," said Elvira, reaching out and touching the lace of the doll's frock.

"It's for you," said Mrs Harper.

Elvira's features lit up with pleasure. "For me? You can't possibly give me this. It must have cost a fortune."

"No dear," said Mrs Harper graciously. "They are quite common in Spain. All the tourists buy them. Don't give it another thought."

Elvira took the doll in her arms and started to cradle it like a baby. "Thank you so much," she said, tears starting in her eyes. She wasn't used to such kindness.

Nancy sat down on the bed and patted the eiderdown beside her. "Come and sit down a minute, ducks," she said kindly. Elvira did as she was bid, still cradling the precious doll.

"Have you thought what you're going to do – now I'm back, I mean?"

Elvira's face fell. "Go back to the cottage, I suppose." She shuddered at the thought of returning to that cold, uninviting place she called home. "This will have pride of place on the mantelpiece," she said softly, smoothing the doll's dress.

"I suppose you're not looking forward to living there on your own?"

"Not really. I shall miss Vessie."

Just then, they heard Bernard call up to them. "Elvira! Mrs Aitch!"

Mrs Harper stepped out onto the landing and looked down at Bernard who was standing in the hall with Robbie beside him.

"What d'you want?" she yelled. "Me and Elvira are 'aving a chat."

"Robbie is here to speak to Elvira. Can you send her down?"

"Oh, all right," said Mrs Harper grudgingly.

It hadn't taken the vicar long to start ordering her about. She had got used to being her own boss these last two weeks on the high seas. Gladys had admonished her on more than one occasion to 'keep that pesky vicar in his place'. She had as much right to a life as he had, she told her. Let him fend for himself sometimes and put your feet up occasionally, she advised.

Elvira was puzzled as to why Robbie wanted to see her. She only hoped he wasn't going to try to persuade her to go to the police like Bernard.

"Hello, Elvira," smiled Robbie, shaking her warmly by the hand. "Please come into the front room for a minute. I would like a word with you."

Elvira was pleased at his politeness. He was very handsome, too. No one had ever bothered to treat her so kindly before. First there was the vicar. He had been kindness itself. Then Mrs Harper had given her that lovely doll. Now this. Dr Robbie MacTavish wanted to talk to her. To her! Not to Vesna. Although she missed her sister terribly, she had played second fiddle to her all her life. Maybe it was time she came out from her shadow.

"Thank you, Doctor," she said meekly, following Robbie into the room. Bernard closed the door after them. She turned to look at the closed door. The vicar had left them alone to talk in private. It must be something important. Again, she feared she was going to be advised to go to the police. This was a telling off, she suspected. A polite one, but a telling-off, nevertheless. She felt deflated all of a sudden.

"Bernard and I are very pleased with your work – especially your cooking," he began, once they were seated in the cool parlour.

Evidence of Elvira's housekeeping skills was all around them. The windows and table surfaces sparkled in the sunlight. There was a vase of roses on display, their scent filling the air.

"I'm glad I gave satisfaction," she said. He couldn't have asked to see her privately just to compliment her on her housekeeping skills, surely?

"I was wondering, Elvira dear," said Robbie, clearing his throat. "Whether you would consider coming to work for me – as cook only. I have Lucy to do all the other chores."

"Be your cook?" said Elvira in wonderment. She hadn't expected that. "But doesn't Lucy do the cooking?"

"She does … but, er – between you and me, she's not up to your standards. I'd pay you well."

"It's – er, it's very good of you, Doctor, but I don't think I can," she said.

Robbie's eyebrows shot up. "But why ever not? You mustn't worry about Lucy, dear. She's quite happy to let you do the cooking – she doesn't enjoy it at all."

"It's not that," said Elvira, feeling close to tears. In any other circumstances she would have loved to work for him. "It's the cottage. I'm thinking of moving away. Now that Vessie's gone, I don't think I can live there anymore."

"Oh, that's a shame. I wish I could put you up, but I don't have a spare room."

"I'm so sorry," said Elvira. "Please don't think I'm not grateful for the offer."

"Please don't worry about it," said Robbie. "But, tell me, is it just because of Vesna that you don't want to stay at the cottage? Or is there another reason?"

Elvira remained silent for a moment. Should she tell him? Should she tell him about Private Rodney Purbright? Should she tell him all about what happened all those years ago? Not about the murder itself. She could never tell anyone about that. But she needed to explain about the curse. The curse that was Rodney Purbright's legacy for what they had done to him.

Robbie broke the silence. "Is it – is it anything to do with the cold? I noticed how cold it was when I came to see your sister."

"To tell the truth, yes," said Elvira with a long sigh. She didn't quite know why, but she had a feeling that Robbie would be sympathetic, even if he didn't believe her. "It's – it's being haunted, you see. When Vessie was alive, she said she felt a *presence* the whole time. I never did – I only felt the cold."

"A presence, you say? Do you know who or what that presence could be?"

"You – you believe me, Doctor? You don't think I'm mad?"

"No, I don't. I have had experience of psychic phenomena before. I'm a bit psychic, too. I could maybe

191

come and try and contact this 'presence'. Do you know who it is? Some dead relative that hasn't been able to pass over? Something like that?"

Here was the crux of the matter. If she told him who it was, the whole thing would come out. She would have to tell Robbie the whole truth. Could she tell him about the murder? No, that was a step too far. Telling him the cottage was haunted was one thing; telling him *why* was quite another.

"I've no idea," she said ruefully. "But thank you for believing me anyway. It's my problem, and I'm the one who has to live with it."

She knew that if Robbie was able to contact Rodney Purbright, the truth would come out and she couldn't let that happen.

Robbie looked at her with sympathy. "You have friends, you know, dear," he said. "I would like to help you, if I can."

She felt like crying. Everyone was being so kind to her and she didn't deserve it. It was almost better when they all believed she was a witch.

"Thank you, Doctor. I'll – I'll bear it in mind," she said.

Chapter Thirty-Five

"You've got to tell them, Henry. You'll hang otherwise."

Henry Carstairs had received another visitor, not his wife this time, and not Ernest Pickles either. This was a rather attractive, plump, middle-aged woman who had visited him just once before, shortly after he had been charged.

"What makes you think they'll find me guilty?"

Henry pressed his fingers to his aching head and coughed. He wasn't sure how much longer he could stand these headaches; they were making him thoroughly miserable. And now, if it wasn't enough, he had such constant pain and was about to stand trial for his very life, the one woman whom he thought he knew and who he thought understood him was adding to his problems.

"Have you got any aspirins?" he asked crossly.

Sylvia Knox rummaged in her capacious handbag. "Here," she said, pushing a packet of Anadin under the grill. A warder rushed over.

"What's that you're giving him?" he asked gruffly.

"Just some headache pills," said Sylvia meekly.

"Oh, right," said the warder. "No funny stuff – okay?"

Henry Carstairs gave a hollow laugh. All he wanted was this pain in his head to go away. He was in no fit state for any 'funny stuff', whatever that meant.

"Could you get me a glass of water to wash these down, do you think?"

"Okay." The warder grudgingly rose to his feet and tapped on the iron door. Another, much younger, warder appeared. "Glass of water for 'is nibs," demanded the first warder.

When Henry had swallowed his pills, Sylvia Knox gave him a puzzled look. "Didn't the stuff that Rowan woman gave you do any good?" she asked.

"A damn sight more good than these blessed Anadins. But I haven't been able to get another supply – stuck in here."

"You should have said, Henry. I'm sure I can get you some more. Did you know that Vesna Rowan was dead, by the way?"

"No, I didn't." As if he cared, he thought bitterly. He'd be joining her soon, he suspected.

"Henry," Sylvia began again.

"I know what you're going to say and I'm not going to tell."

"Then you're a fool," said Sylvia sharply. "Stop being so chivalrous. I'm going to tell the police where you were on the night your daughter was killed. I'll not see you hang. Even if *you* don't care, I do!"

"Look, Sylv," Henry leaned forward so that the tip of his nose was touching the grill. "I don't want you getting involved. And, anyway, I've got my reputation to consider too, you know."

Sylvia Knox stared at him crossly. "Your reputation! How can you think about that at a time like this? You haven't got a reputation anymore, unless it's as a pervert and a murderer."

Henry shrugged. "I've got a good brief. He says he can get me off. Prove to the world how wrong they all are."

"Hmmph! And you really think he can get you off without my help?"

"As a matter of fact, I do," smiled Henry Carstairs wearily. "So, let's have no more talk of going to the police, eh?"

She wasn't convinced. "I don't think you should rely on your barrister to get you off, Henry. What about the

194

fingerprints on the knife? How do you explain that to a jury?"

"There are ways to twist things – lawyers know all the tricks."

He had to admit his heart had skipped a beat when he had been shown the knife. It was identical to the one he used to carve the roast meat every Sunday. But it was an ordinary, common-or-garden carving knife that could be found in every kitchen the length and breadth of Britain. It didn't belong to him, not that one. Not the one that had murdered his precious daughter.

Sylvia Knox realized Henry meant what he said. He would, on no account, let her tell the police he had been with her on the night his daughter died, even though it would probably save his neck.

His wife had been away that night, visiting her sister in Stoke Newington. And it hadn't been the first time he had shared Sylvia's bed, although it was the first time he had stayed all night. He usually only visited her when he left work early, keeping Ivy Carstairs in blissful ignorance.

He had wrestled with his conscience about his adultery, something that had happened so easily and naturally. When Sylvia Knox's husband had died of cancer several years before, he had taken to looking in on her to make sure she and Minnie were all right. It wasn't long before he had slipped into the role of 'man of the house', seeing to various odd jobs that needed doing with Ted Knox no longer there to do them. When he had first slept with Sylvia it had started as a comforting hug. He hadn't intended it to happen, but nature had a way of taking over free will, as he had found out. Once the irrevocable step had been taken, it was easy to make a habit of it.

"Look, Sylv, if you want to help me, you can do two things for me…"

"Of course, Henry."

"First, go to that Elvira woman and get her to make up a supply of those headache powders she gave me. These Anadins don't touch it." His hand shot to his head again as a violent pain jolted all other thoughts out of it.

"Okay. What's the second thing?"

"Will you look after Charlie for me?"

"Charlie? Oh, your dog, you mean?"

"Yes. Ivy's not keen and I don't think she's looking after him properly. He needs regular exercise. Can you do that for me – just until I get out, that is?"

"Well – I – I suppose so. But what if you don't get out? What shall I do with Charlie then?"

Henry's nose scraped the grill and the warder watched suspiciously, as if he expected him to transfer something to his visitor via his nostrils.

"Don't let's think about that, Sylv. Just look after him. I'll think of something."

"If you say so, Henry. But what will Ivy think when I ask her for the dog?"

"She'll be relieved, that's what."

"But won't she wonder why you've asked me to look after it? Me of all people?"

"You can just say that Minnie asked about the dog. She used to play with Charlie when she and Helen were younger."

"All right. Minnie's not talking to me, by the way," she told him, getting up to leave. "She hasn't spoken to me for months – not properly, like. She always used to be such a loving daughter, especially after Ted died. But I suppose she's at a difficult age. I remember I wasn't the nicest person in the world when I was seventeen."

"Yes – Helen…" he began, a sob stuck somewhere in his throat as he uttered her name. " Er – she could be difficult too. Minnie'll come round, you'll see."

Mrs Knox walked out of the prison into the bright afternoon sun which was blazing down as usual. June had

196

turned into July and still there was no break in the fine weather. She had never known such a summer. Why hadn't it been as fine as this last year when the young Queen was crowned? It had been raining all day, she recalled. So unfair. She was such a pretty thing. Sylvia had a scrapbook full of pictures of the Royal Family: handsome Prince Philip, as well as the cute children, Prince Charles and lovely, golden-curled Princess Anne. The perfect family. Not like her own, or poor Henry's either.

She walked down the street, making a mental note to visit Elvira Rowan first thing in the morning. The sooner she got Henry those headache cures the better.

∾

Henry's worries would have been eased a little that afternoon if he had known that Ernest Pickles had been as good as his word. He had managed to get Minnie Knox's testimony thrown out, much to the chagrin of Inspector Craddock.

"Would you Adam-and-Eve it, Rathbone?" he muttered. "That slimy git Pickles has managed to prevent that girl giving evidence. Said it was inadmissible, hearsay, whatever. Bastard!"

"Well, guv, strictly, he's right." Rathbone had meant this to be placatory, but it only served to rile his boss even further. "Er – I mean, didn't you know that?" This remark didn't help either.

"I'm not a bleedin' lawyer, am I?" he screamed at him.

"Don't worry, guv. If he gets off the murder charge, we'll have him on incest. Minnie Knox will be called to testify then."

"It won't wash," said Craddock, calming down a little. "It's still bloody hearsay, isn't it?"

Rathbone couldn't argue with that, of course.

"Make yourself useful," said the inspector after a moment. "Go and get me a bacon butty from the canteen."

Looking on the bright side, there wasn't much in life that couldn't be improved by a bacon butty, he thought.

Chapter Thirty-Six

Elvira stared around her at all the things that reminded her of her beloved sister. She had never felt so alone. What was she going to do? She couldn't stay there, not anymore. She shivered as the first blast of cold air wrapped around her.

"All right, Rodney Purbright," she said out loud, "you win."

She would pack a bag tonight and go and stay in a B&B until she could think of something else. Right now, she would make a cup of tea and try and warm herself up. As she was about to put the kettle on, the doorbell rang.

Who could that be, she wondered. No one ever called on her, callers only ever wanted her sister. Well, she thought, if someone wanted to see Vesna today they were out of luck. She opened the door and stared at the beautiful woman standing there. She had chestnut hair tied up in a fashionable chignon and wore a floral print dress that accentuated her shape in the all the right places.

"Hello?" she said enquiringly. Obviously, this vision of loveliness had come to the wrong address.

"Bonjour," replied the woman. "Are you Mrs Purbright?"

Mrs Purbright? What was she talking about? And *bonjour*? What kind of a word was that? French, of course. She knew that. Just like the woman's hairstyle.

"Mrs Vesna Purbright?" The young woman was looking at a crumpled postcard.

"Er – no. I'm not. She is – was my sister."

Elvira was taken aback. Somehow, this young woman with a rather attractive accent thought that Rodney Purbright had married Vesna. Why should she think that? And, more to the point, who was she?

"You – you'd better come in," said Elvira.

As she ushered her visitor into the parlour, she noticed the woman shiver. "I was just about to make some tea. Would you like some?"

"Zank you," said the woman. "Why is it so cold in here?"

"It's a long story. Do sit down."

When the tea had been poured, the woman introduced herself. "My name is Jeanne Dupont and I've come here to – " She broke off.

"Yes?"

"Well, it is another long story, but the short one is I believe this man is my father." She reached into her handbag and pulled out a battered, sepia photograph. She passed it to Elvira.

There was no doubt who it was. Private Rodney Purbright in his soldier's uniform, looking as arrogant as she always remembered him.

"This man is – is your father?" Elvira handed it back to her.

"Yes. You see, my mother died recently, but before she died, she told me all about him. How they'd met in the War – the first one, I mean – and, well you know how it is in wartime. I was the result. She never told him, and he left her after the War ended and went back to England. Maman gave me his photograph and this letter. Here."

Jeanne showed Elvira the letter, still in its envelope. "Ma mère – mother – she found it in the jacket of his uniform and kept it. It is a letter to his fiancée, the one my mother thought he must have gone back to. Ze address led me to a place in Bottle – er, no Boo-ootle."

Elvira smiled. "Yes, Bootle was where my sister and I were born."

"Well, I found an old woman there. A Mrs Rowan."

"So, she's still alive, is she?" Her stepmother must be a hundred if she was a day.

"Yes, although she looked rather vieux – er, frail. She told me Vesna was no longer living there."

"No, we moved from there many years ago," said Elvira, pouring her another cup of tea. "Go on."

"Well, to – how you say? – cut a long story short, she found an old postcard – I have it here – from Vesna to her father, asking him to send her some money and giving zis address. So here I am."

Here she was, thought Elvira, but to what purpose? "I see," was all she could think of to say.

"Yes, you see, I just wanted to meet my father. I was brought up by my mère and grandmère, and I was very lucky to have them. But I always wondered about my père. He was zo handsome, no?"

Elvira sniffed. "Handsome is as handsome does," she commented.

"*Comment?*"

"It's a saying. Means he might look like an angel, but what he *does* is the important thing."

Jeanne Dupont looked sad for a moment. Elvira watched her face, which was the most charming she had ever seen outside of the cinema screen. The only thing that spoiled it was the resemblance she could see to Rodney Purbright. However, as his looks were the only good thing she could say about him, Jeanne was lucky to have inherited just them and, hopefully, not his nature. Her mother and grandmother must have been good people, Elvira reckoned, judging by the woman's polite and friendly demeanour.

"Do you mean to imply zat he wasn't very nice?"

Elvira thought for a moment. She didn't know this woman from Adam, but she instinctively liked her and didn't want to hurt her. On the other hand, she didn't want to give her the false impression that Rodney Purbright was some kind of a saint.

"Well, let me put it this way," she said, "he left your mother in the lurch, didn't he? With a baby. What kind of a man does that?"

"Oh, but he never knew! My mother only found out she was pregnant after he had gone. Back to his fiancée, she expected. She said it was only right he should go back to her. She had told him he should."

"What, even after they'd – they'd – " Elvira couldn't bring herself to say the words. Still a virgin at sixty-two and likely to remain so, she couldn't think of how to say it, let alone how to do it.

"Even after that," smiled Jeanne, sensing the older woman's discomfiture. "People were drawn together in wartime. They found comfort in each other. Zey did not know if they would still be alive tomorrow. They took happiness where they could find it."

Elvira hadn't managed to grab any happiness, either in wartime or in peacetime. She wondered now what she had missed. She could have had a beautiful daughter like this if she had been luckier. So could poor Vesna.

"Anyway, from what you tell me, Vesna is dead?"

"Yes, dear. She passed on a few weeks ago." Elvira waited for the obvious next question.

"And – my père?"

"I'm sorry, he's dead, too." There didn't seem to be any other way to say it.

The woman was shivering violently now. "Zut alors! It is so cold!" she cried.

Elvira immediately apologized. "I'll fetch you a shawl."

"Zank you," said Jeanne. "I haven't brought any warm clothing with me because it is so warm. I don't understand why it is so cold in here."

Elvira ran up the stairs to her bedroom and rummaged in the ottoman for the warmest shawl she could find.

"Here we are," she said, draping it around Jeanne's shoulders. She saw that she had been crying a little. "I'm sorry I had to tell you this bad news, dear. After you have come all this way, too. From France, I take it?"

"Yes. From Fécamp."

Elvira had never heard of the place. "He – he, well, I can't say I liked him very much. I think you were better off not knowing him." Was she being heartless, she wondered.

"Maybe you are right," said Jeanne, hugging the shawl about her. "But you must get something done about the cold in here."

"It's not that simple," said Elvira.

"*Pour quoi*?"

"Eh? Oh, why, you mean?"

"Sorry, yes. Why is it not that simple?"

"I don't know where to start…"

"It is always best to start at the beginning," smiled Jeanne, still shivering.

But where was the beginning, wondered Elvira. When Rodney Purbright came back to stay or when her sister murdered him? Or even before that, when Vesna had first become engaged to him? From the moment Purbright had entered their lives, everything had started to go wrong.

"It is something that I have to deal with, my dear," she said at last. "It isn't your problem."

"Well, if it's a question of money – I will be happy to pay for someone to come and take a look. This cold must be coming from somewhere…"

"I've already told you it's not that easy," Elvira snapped, then stopped herself. "Please don't think I'm not grateful – but I couldn't accept anything from you. After all, you're a complete stranger."

"I'd like to think we could be friends."

So would I, thought Elvira, beginning to feel like crying at the suggestion that this lovely young woman wanted to be her friend. *Her* friend!

Jeanne smiled. "Why won't you let me help you?"

"Because, well, I don't think you can." All the money in the world won't rid this place of Rodney Purbright, she thought. "Anyway, you came to me for help in finding your father. You came to meet Vesna, too. Only all you found was me, her sister, Elvira."

"Elvira is a pretty name," said Jeanne, touching her hand.

Elvira withdrew it at once. This strange intimacy was unnerving her.

"Th-thank you," she said. Pretty it may be, but it didn't really suit her. It never had.

"I am sorry that your sister is dead, and that you didn't like my father," said Jeanne. "But I'm glad I've met you."

Elvira felt like crying again. All this interest in her was overwhelming. Everyone was being much too kind to her. She didn't deserve it.

"Can you tell me what happened to my father?" she heard Jeanne say.

My sister shot him, and we buried him in the garden. How could she tell her that? Now was the time for Elvira to decide. She still could tell her the truth. If she did, her life would be over. On the plus side, a prison cell would be warmer than Appleby Cottage, but, on the minus, she'd lose the good opinion of this beautiful French woman who seemed to have taken a liking to her.

"He died of a heart attack," she said. "Over thirty years ago."

Chapter Thirty-Seven

Elvira sat in the stone-cold cottage, watching the minutes tick by on the mantelpiece clock, beside which stood her beloved Spanish doll. It was half past seven in the evening, and her thoughts turned to Bernard.

She had got to know the vicar's habits during the two weeks she had acted as his housekeeper, and every evening at this time he had retired to his study to smoke his pipe. She resolved to go and see him, to try and explain what had happened when Helen Carstairs had come to her for help that night, and why she couldn't go to the police about it. She had to make him understand somehow. Without betraying her sister, of course. That was the most important thing.

&

"Well, dear, I hope you're settled back home. I'm so sorry you didn't see your way to accepting Dr MacTavish's offer. He's very upset, you know."

"I need to explain something to you, Vicar," Elvira began, ignoring Robbie's disappointment. "You need to know –"

Bernard was intrigued straightaway. He was also a little worried. He remembered the last time she had confided in him which hadn't been entirely resolved to his satisfaction. Did he really want to hear this next revelation? he wondered. He offered her a sherry and he joined her. It was about the time he usually had a glass, and he found he needed it at that moment.

Elvira cleared her throat nervously. "You know I told you that Helen came to see us that evening – shortly before she was murdered?" She lifted her sherry glass to her mouth with a shaking hand.

"Go on."

"Well, she came because she wanted something to help her get rid of her unborn child. And I gave her a powder and suggested she had a hot bath."

"Yes, yes, you told me all that, and I told you to go to the police."

"And I refused."

"And you refused."

"Well, what happened a bit later makes it very difficult. Difficult to go to the police, I mean. Also, I'd be betraying my sister's trust. She made me promise – well, I won't go into that."

Bernard finished his sherry and found he needed another. He resisted the temptation, however, suspecting he would need a clear head for what was to follow.

"Helen went upstairs to take a bath like I told you," Elvira continued after a few moments. "She didn't want to draw attention to herself by bathing at home as they only bathed on Sundays. They would want to know what she was up to."

"The Carstairs only have baths on Sundays?" Bernard raised his eyebrows.

"It's not all that unusual, Vicar," said Elvira, somewhat testily. "Many families can't afford to bathe more than once a week. A good wash down does the trick most days. I do that myself."

Bernard, who wallowed in gallons of hot soapy water every morning, was suitably chastened. "Of course. I understand. Do go on."

"Well, she hadn't been up there very long when I heard a clatter in the kitchen. I went to see what it was, but all I saw was one of the drawers had been opened. I couldn't remember opening it, but I suppose I must have done.

Vessie, you see, hardly ever went into the kitchen. Not in those last few months."

She paused again. "I – I'm not sure whether to tell you more but, you see, that was when I felt this overpowering presence in the room."

"Presence?"

"Yes, up until then only Vessie had felt it. The presence. Now I did. And I knew who it was."

"I – I'm not sure where this is all leading, Elvira," said Bernard quietly. "Are you telling me that some sort of psychic event caused Helen's death? I mean, there's no refuting the actual *cause*, is there? A knife attack?"

"Oh, no, that's right. She was stabbed. But, well, I'm sorry to have to confess that the spirit of Vessie's former fiancé was instrumental in what happened."

"How come?"

"That's all I have to say," she finished. "That's all."

"That's very interesting," said Bernard, clearly disappointed.

He was in two minds whether to tell her about what the colonel had told him but decided against it.

"It's not easy to explain, Vicar. I'm sorry. I suppose I shouldn't have come."

"I'm glad you did, but are you sure that's all you can tell me?" he asked her.

"That's all I'm *prepared* to tell you at this stage," she replied firmly. "Now, I mustn't take up any more of your time." She started to get up. "Oh, there's just one other thing…"

"Yes?"

"I remember thinking at the time that Helen looked a lot like Vessie when she was young. I'd seen her around, of course, as she was growing up, as she only lived around the corner. The likeness wasn't so apparent when she was a schoolgirl, but that night I could see how like the young Vessie she was."

"Your sister must have been very pretty, then," Bernard observed, not sure why Elvira thought Helen's likeness to Vesna was significant.

"Oh, she was – very. It was horrible what happened to her – at the end. Vessie had always been so full of life, it was pitiful to see her decline like that."

Bernard nodded in sympathy as he accompanied her to the door.

Elvira got back from visiting Bernard at around nine o'clock and went into the kitchen. Filling a saucepan with milk, she turned on the hob underneath it and sat and waited for it to boil. Her nightly ritual of cocoa and a good book in bed were calling to her. Bed was the only place in that Godforsaken cottage where she could get warm.

While she waited, she thought over the events of the day. Who would have thought that pretty French woman would turn up like that? After years of no visitors, the most exotic person imaginable had arrived on her doorstep. She realized, of course, Jeanne Dupont hadn't come to see her, but that didn't detract from the pleasure of her visit. She still wasn't quite sure if it had been a dream. But no, she had been real enough. She was, in fact, Rodney Purbright's daughter. Suddenly, she stood up.

"Are you listening to me, Purbright?" she said out loud to the four walls. She took the precaution of turning down the gas under the milk. "Can't you be pleased about seeing the daughter you never knew you had? And you've taken your revenge on Vessie and me. Isn't that enough? Can't you leave me in peace, now?"

There was no reply. She hadn't expected any. But she noticed the kitchen wasn't quite so cold now.

Chapter Thirty-Eight

Sylvia Knox was feeling nervous as she rang Elvira's doorbell. She had promised Henry she would get him some more headache powders and she was as good as her word. She thought about him languishing in that prison cell and sighed. It was too cruel. He wouldn't harm a fly, that man. Many people found his manner off-putting. Those people would probably like to believe he was capable of such cruel acts, she knew, mainly because he wasn't particularly prepossessing. But *she* knew he was innocent, only she couldn't tell anyone because he wouldn't let her.

She rammed the doorbell again, this time with some anger. "Stupid man!" she thought. What a hypocrite. Quite happy to share her bed as long as no one found out. Went to church on Sunday and asked for forgiveness. 'Forgive me Father for I have sinned.' Isn't that what the Catholics said to their priests, usually after committing some heinous act? She wouldn't be surprised if Henry went over to Rome one of these fine days. If he lived that long.

Elvira opened the door to her visitor with a scowl on her face. "Give me a chance, can't you? I've only got one pair of legs, and I'm not as young as I used to be."

"Oh, sorry, love," said Sylvia, contrite. She realized she shouldn't be taking out her anger on this woman or, more accurately, on her doorbell. "I was thinking about something, and I got angry. I didn't mean to ring again."

"Well, all right." Elvira's features softened slightly. "Do you want to come in? I'll put the kettle on."

Mrs Knox followed Elvira into the kitchen. It was cool, but certainly not as cold as it had been. Elvira had even managed to shed one layer of clothing that morning. However, Sylvia shivered, as the temperature inside didn't match the warmth of the day outside.

"Sorry it's so chilly in here," said Elvira. "It's rising damp."

She set out the cups and a plate of homemade biscuits on the kitchen table. Sylvia sat down and arranged the biscuits absent-mindedly.

"Rising damp? But can't you get something done about it? You shouldn't have to put up with it. You'll catch your death."

"It's not as cold as it was," Elvira told her. She poured out the tea.

"What was it you wanted to see me about, Mrs Knox?" she asked.

"Er, I need some headache powders."

"Do you suffer badly with them?"

"Oh, no, it's not for me – it's for…" She hesitated. "Well, actually, it's for Henry Carstairs. You supplied them to him before but, well, he can't actually come and get them himself, as you probably know."

Elvira stared at her. "For him? But why are you coming for them and not Mrs Carstairs?"

Sylvia Knox stirred her tea more times than strictly necessary while she thought rapidly.

"He asked me yesterday when I went to visit him. I think his wife wasn't due to see him until today, and he needed them as soon as possible." She stopped. "So, I said I'd get them for him."

"I see. I didn't know you were friendly with Mr Carstairs," said Elvira, trying to hide her prurient curiosity as best she could.

"Oh, we got to know each other quite well because Minnie and poor Helen were best friends at school."

"I see. Of course. I'll go and make up the powders right away."

While she was gone, Sylvia stepped out through the French windows into the back garden. She felt the welcome sun on her as she walked slowly around, admiring the flowers and listening to the hum of bees. Why didn't Elvira get something done about the damp in her cottage, she wondered. This place could be a little paradise, if it wasn't so cold in there.

❧

As Elvira slowly mixed the powders for Henry Carstairs, she remembered the occasion when he had come to see her himself. She had seen, just by looking at him, that he was suffering badly. She remembered he had been rather severe in both looks and manner, as well as stiffly formal, but she had put all that down to the headaches. She remembered, too, how he had been of help to her that day.

She smiled at the memory. It was one Sunday morning, about a year ago. Vesna was in the kitchen while Elvira was talking to him. She recalled thinking she must check on her as her sister wasn't safe anywhere near gas or sharp kitchen implements. Suddenly, she had heard a scream. Rushing to the kitchen, she had seen her poor sister holding the carving knife with blood pouring from her hand.

"What on Earth are you doing, Vessie?" she had cried. "I told you to leave the carving of the joint to me. I told you I'd only be a moment or two with Mr Carstairs."

"I'm not daft," Vesna had yelled back at her. "I can carve a joint of beef. I'm not incapacitated."

"Well, you are now," Elvira had declared, taking the knife from her injured hand. "Let's run that cut under the cold tap. I don't think it's gone that deep."

While she had been pouring water over her sister's wound, Henry had come into the kitchen. "Is there anything I can do? Is she all right?"

"Who's she? The cat's mother?" Vesna had screamed at him. "Don't talk as if I'm not here!"

"I'm sorry, Miss Rowan," Henry had been politeness itself. "Are you all right?"

211

"'Course I'm not all right! I've stabbed myself."

Elvira had apologized to Henry out of the side of her mouth. There had been no excuse for her sister's rudeness, and she felt embarrassed as the man had only been trying to help. "Could you possibly carve the meat up for us?" she asked.

"Of course," Henry had replied, without a moment's hesitation.

Elvira finished preparing the powders and wrapped them up carefully. She was glad that her remedy was obviously doing him good. Henry wasn't one of nature's charmers, but neither was she. She sensed a kindred spirit when she thought of him.

Sylvia was still in the back garden when she returned to the kitchen.

"Here you are," said Elvira, handing her a small packet. "I hope they help him. It must be awful being in prison. Especially suffering with headaches like he does."

Sylvia put the powders in her handbag and thanked her. "You are kind," she said. "I mean, not just about the powders, but by not condemning Henry like most people have done."

"I believe in a person being innocent until proved not to be," Elvira smiled.

"Yes, that's what I believe, too. Henry's always been a good friend to me and Minnie, especially after Ted died. Anyway, dear, what do I owe you for the powders?"

"Nothing. Just give them to him and wish him better from me. It's the least I can do."

Sylvia had never really cared for Elvira Rowan, or her sister either. Like most people in the neighbourhood, she had always tended to steer clear of them. But, today, she came away from the cottage feeling more kindly disposed towards her. There had been something almost like kindness in Elvira's eyes when she gave her the powders. No wicked witch would look at you like that, she thought.

Chapter Thirty-Nine

Inspector Craddock wasn't in a good mood. That wasn't unusual, but today he seemed even more irascible than ever.

"What's up?" asked Rathbone resignedly. "Lost your pen again?"

"My pen? No, no. It's here – I think." Craddock tapped the top pocket of his tweed jacket. "No, it's my wife. She's taken to leaving my meals in the oven until they burn. Even when I tell her I'll be late and not to keep my dinner hot, she doesn't listen. She says if I can't get home at a reasonable hour at least once a week, why should she bother to make sure my food's eatable. This morning she asked for a divorce, blast her. And Terry's been playing truant again, and the school is going to expel him. But, other than that, everything's fine."

"Oh dear, sorry to hear, guv. But maybe this'll cheer you up, or probably it won't, but there's a Reverend Palt – toe – something downstairs waiting to see you. And he's brought that Rowan woman with him."

"So, I wonder…" Craddock seemed calmer now. "Is she going to change her story? She told us Helen Carstairs never visited her on the night she died."

"That's right. It's quite possible she's here to retract her statement, guv. I mean, I believe Percy Banks saw what he saw. He struck me as an honest young man."

"Hmm, we'll see," said Craddock. "Better wheel 'em in, then." He stood up. "No, better use the interview room. All official. If the woman has been lying to us, I'll make sure she feels the full force of the law. I'm in that sort of a mood today."

Rathbone didn't need telling that, but he only smiled, following his boss out of the office. Craddock's bad temper was legendary at the station, usually brought on by his domestic troubles. Like today. Mrs Craddock threatened to divorce him at least once a week. One day, he supposed, she'd go through with it.

ے

Elvira had finally been persuaded by Bernard to tell the police the truth. She couldn't live with the guilt anymore. She had told Bernard as much as she could, taking into account Vesna's last wishes, but that hadn't helped her conscience at all. Her only hope was to take full responsibility for giving Helen the powder that was supposed to bring on a miscarriage, even though it was her sister who had insisted on giving it to her. She had told Elvira to make it up for the young girl, despite knowing it was against the law. Whatever Vesna had done or not done, she was dead now and somewhere where she couldn't be hurt anymore. But Elvira didn't want people to think badly of her, not if she could help it. They had done worse things and got away with them, but this was something she could take responsibility for by herself.

Seated in front of the bulky frame that was Inspector Craddock, she felt immediately intimidated. Bernard, seated beside her, cast her a reassuring glance, but it didn't help. Her insides had turned to water, knowing what she was about to confess.

"Well, Miss Rowan, we meet again." Craddock's steely glint bore right through her. "Hello, Vicar." There were no handshakes or friendly smiles.

"Miss Rowan has something to say, Inspector," Bernard began. "She wishes to – er, amend her earlier statement about the visit of Helen Carstairs to Appleby Cottage on the evening of her murder."

"Visit? What visit? According to Miss Rowan…" Craddock glared at her. "We understood there *was* no visit. Do I take it that there was, after all?"

Oh God, thought Elvira, this was even worse than she had expected. It looked like she'd be spending the rest of her days behind bars.

"Well, er, I may have – er – said something that wasn't – altogether – er – correct," she stuttered.

"You mean you lied?" Craddock looked like he was about to spontaneously combust.

"Well, I didn't mean to – that is, I didn't want to …."

"Just tell us what you came to tell us, Miss Rowan," interrupted Rathbone. "The sooner you tell us, the sooner you can leave."

"Helen came to see us that evening to – er – to get some advice."

"Advice? What sort of advice?" Craddock's manner wasn't improving much, but his face had lost the violent beetroot colour of a few moments before.

"Er, I – er dispense herbal remedies," she explained. "People often come to me for something to help them when other, more orthodox, methods have failed."

"So, you're some sort of a quack?"

"I – I wouldn't put it quite like that," said Elvira quietly. This man wasn't making it easy for her. "Herbal remedies often work when patent medicines don't."

"Very well. Let's leave that aside for the moment. So, Helen wanted you to give her something to help her. In what way?"

This was the crunch. Bernard looked at Elvira encouragingly.

"To help her – get rid of the baby," she said resignedly. Bring on the handcuffs.

"Miss Rowan, are you aware that unauthorized abortion is a crime in this country?"

"It's not abortion, what I do. I hardly ever give anyone this powder. When I do, it's because people are in severe straits and have no other options open to them." She was determined to go down fighting.

Craddock scribbled violently on his pad. "We will need to remove this 'remedy' from your house, Miss Rowan. You are never to dispense it again, do you hear?"

Elvira nodded. She knew she never would, anyway. She had learnt her lesson, well and truly. She closed her eyes as she remembered the awful time she had helped her sister abort her baby. The powder had worked that time only too well. She remembered the blood and Vesna crying in pain all night. And the little blob that ended up down the privy.

She realized she didn't care anymore. There was so much more she could tell the irascible inspector, but she knew he wouldn't believe her, and it would be betraying Vesna's trust. She had nearly told Bernard but had stopped herself in time. This large, red-faced representative of the 'long arm' invited no confidences, and he therefore didn't get any.

"I'm fully prepared to take the consequences of my actions," she told him. "I know it was wrong, even though it was only because I felt so sorry for the girl."

Bernard came to her rescue. "I can vouch for that," he said. "She meant no harm. On the contrary, she has done much good for many people over the years."

Craddock sighed and looked up at the unlikely pair. "Oh, go away. I can't be bothered. We'll send someone round to your place to make sure you haven't got any offending stuff on the premises. Don't do it again!" He shouted at their retreating backs.

Elvira looked at Bernard as they stood outside the door. "I never want to go through anything like that again," she said, relief flooding through her.

Bernard put his arm around her quivering shoulders. "Well, look on the bright side," he grinned. "You've got away with it!"

"Got away with it? What do you mean?" It didn't feel like it to her at that moment.

"By rights, Elvira, they should have arrested you – on two counts, actually."

"Two counts?"

"Well – the abortion thing, of course. But also, you lied to the police. They can be very tough on that, you know. You should get down on your knees and kiss the inspector's feet whom, I strongly suspect, has a bark much worse than his bite."

Elvira smiled for the first time that morning, although she didn't agree with him about Craddock. His bite, she was convinced, was just as scary as his bark.

Chapter Forty

Bernard sat with Elvira outside Court Number One, his stomach churning with nerves. He could only guess how his companion was feeling. It was the first day of Henry Carstairs' trial, and Elvira was there as a witness for the defence, although, as she pointed out to Bernard, she couldn't see how her testimony would help the defence, or the prosecution for that matter. As they sat waiting, Inspector Craddock appeared through the door, glanced across at them and nodded briefly.

"Morning," he said as he walked past them into the court.

They watched as various bewigged and black gowned men bustled their way into the various courts. Court officials were also in abundance, carrying important-looking document files. Elvira found the whole place intimidating. She looked up at the high, ornate ceiling and shivered.

"Don't worry," said Bernard. "All you have to do is tell the court the truth."

"I don't see how my evidence will help, though," said Elvira.

"Whether it helps or not, is not for you to worry about," he said.

Just then, old Colonel Powell strode through the door. "Hello," he greeted them. "You two here then? Come to give evidence, eh?"

"That's right," said Elvira primly. "Why are you here?"

The colonel heaved his bulk down beside her. His right foot was heavily bandaged, and he leaned on a stick. "The old gout playing me up as usual," he grimaced. "I've been called to give evidence too. Darned if I know why, though. They all think I'm a sandwich short of a picnic. I don't suppose anyone'll believe me."

"Why should you think that?" asked Elvira, puzzled. "And if you think that, why would they call you as a witness?"

"Blowed if I know. Anyway, this chap here," he said, nodding at Bernard, "persuaded me to tell the police what I knew, so here I am."

"What you knew?" Elvira was still puzzled, but also a little worried now. Bernard looked down at his feet.

"Yes. Or, rather, what I *saw*. What I saw on the night of the murder."

Elvira looked positively scared now. "What *did* you see?" she managed to ask.

"Dear lady," he said in his most ingratiating tone, "it is nothing for you to worry about." He looked at Bernard as he said this.

Bernard, knowing full well what the colonel supposedly saw that night, looked quickly away. Then he turned back and cleared his throat.

"Er, Colonel, could I have a private word with you?"

Elvira looked from one to the other of them. Just what had the colonel seen and why did Bernard seem to know?

The two men excused themselves and moved along the corridor out of Elvira's earshot.

"Just what exactly did you tell the police?" asked Bernard.

"Oh, don't worry," said the Colonel airily. "Not what I told you. Not the full bit, anyway."

"Who's calling you? The defence or prosecution?"

"Defence, old boy."

"Are you going to drop Miss Rowan in it?"

The colonel shrugged. "I suppose I am. But I haven't got any choice. It's the truth and, if it prevents an innocent man being hanged, then I have to tell it."

"But don't you see what it means to Miss Rowan? Suspicion will fall on her when you say what you're going to say."

"Can't help that. Sorry for the woman and all that. But, if she's in any way implicated, then she'll have to take the consequences."

The colonel was right, of course. Bernard, however, had grown very fond of Elvira and he was sure she wasn't capable of murder. Besides, what possible motive could she have?

Elvira's mind was racing. What were they saying that they didn't want her to hear?

As the trial progressed, things began to look very black indeed for Henry Carstairs. As luck would have it, the prosecution barrister turned out to be Sir Malcolm Pym, QC, a man whom Ernest Pickles had clashed with in court on many occasions, and whom he had cause to fear. If anybody had a better reputation than Pickles, it was Pym. In private, the two men got on splendidly, but in court you would think they were deadly enemies.

But when it all came down to it, it was the fingerprints on the knife that was the most damning. It was obvious to Pickles the jury would find Carstairs guilty on that evidence alone. He couldn't foresee any other outcome.

And, as Elvira sat outside the court, waiting to be called, she continued to wonder what good confessing her part in the tragedy would do. It wouldn't save Carstairs' neck, that was for sure. And now there was Colonel Powell to contend with. Once he told the court what he saw that night, all would be up with her.

All this while, Bernard watched over her, fetching her coffee and making sure she was prepared for the ordeal to come. If he hadn't been there, she didn't know what she would have done. She would probably have run out of the building by now. She wished they would call her and get it over with.

Suddenly, Inspector Craddock shot out of the court and stormed past them, muttering under his breath. Things didn't look as if they were going well for him, which meant, she dared to hope, that Henry Carstairs' luck was turning at last.

&

It wasn't until the second day of the proceedings that she was called, which was earlier than she had expected. But you never knew with trials. The prosecution's case was open and shut according to Pym, and he had got through his witnesses like a dose of salts. Despite her fears, she did remarkably well under his cross-examination, and told her story to the court, leaving nothing out. There was an audible gasp as she explained about the abortion powder, but somehow, she rode the brief storm her evidence had produced. Pym, himself, didn't seem that interested in what she had to say, either, obviously certain of Carstairs' guilt. She even caught him looking at his watch while she was speaking.

She looked over at Henry Carstairs sitting between two prison warders. She felt sorry for him and almost wanted to catch his eye to convey as much. He had been so helpful that time, carving the joint. Come to think of it, she had looked for that carving knife only the other day because she had treated herself to a piece of beef, but she hadn't been able to find it.

Funny that.

Chapter Forty-One

Although Elvira was relieved after giving evidence, she couldn't settle to anything when she got back to Appleby Cottage at six o'clock that evening. Bernard had suggested they go for a drink at the Feathers before returning home, but she had refused, wanting only to be on her own to think. There was something nagging at the back of her mind, and she couldn't shake it off.

After she had lit the fire and put on a cardigan, she sat looking at the flames, trying to put her thoughts in order. She was so preoccupied, she didn't notice it wasn't nearly as cold as usual. She had been dreading her court appearance, but it hadn't been nearly as bad as she had feared. Pickles hadn't asked her more than a couple of minor questions after she had given her evidence, and Malcolm Pym had been almost kind to her.

At least her part in Henry Carstairs' trial was over, and she hoped and prayed her evidence wouldn't adversely affect the verdict. She continued to sit in front of the fire, deep in thought. What was it she was not getting? What was the uneasy feeling she had? What was causing it?

After a while, she got up and went into the kitchen. Pouring some milk into a saucepan to make her nightly cocoa, her eyes fell upon one of the kitchen drawers. Even though it hadn't shut properly for years, she now remembered it had been more open that night. Someone had opened it, and it hadn't been her. Or Vesna. At least, she was pretty sure it wasn't. But her sister had been prone to do things out of character recently, so she supposed it could have been.

She went over to it and tried forcing it shut, like she had tried many times before. It was no use. It needed easing somehow. It was difficult to open properly as well, which was annoying because it contained all the cutlery. Then she remembered the missing carving knife. Now where on earth had it got to? She couldn't remember the last time she had seen it.

Leaving the milk to nearly boil over, she rummaged among the knives in the drawer in vain. There was no sign of it. She scratched her head and tried to think. Yes, of course! She suddenly remembered. The last time it had been used was when Henry Carstairs had carved the joint for them after Vesna had cut her hand. She searched her mind. Had she used the knife since then? No, she was pretty sure she hadn't. She hadn't had a joint of beef for many a day. Oh, except on her last birthday, not long before Vesna died. But the knife had been there then. So where was it now?

She stood looking in the drawer, not seeing anything. The cutlery was a jumble before her eyes. Why was it so important that she find the knife, or at least know where it had gone?

As she stood there, trying to puzzle out the conundrum, she heard a man's voice. It came from behind her back. She leapt round in horror, but no one was there. However, she knew that voice; it was one she would never forget. It belonged to Rodney Purbright.

"Hello, Elvira," he said. "I can see you at last. You look a lot older than when I last saw you. You don't look any prettier though."

Elvira glared in the direction of his voice. Suddenly, she didn't know why, she wasn't in the least bit afraid. "What do you want, Rodney? Can't you go and leave me in peace? It wasn't me who killed you. Vesna did and she's dead herself now."

"I know."

"So, you've got your revenge," she said. "Now, please just go to wherever you should be." Wherever it was, she was pretty sure it wasn't heaven.

"You needn't worry. I intend to go soon. I am being released at last," he replied.

Was it her imagination, or could she see a man's vague shape forming? Please God, she hoped not. She had seen enough of Rodney Purbright to last her a lifetime. His image was seared on her brain. Fortunately, the shape did not develop further, but hovered there, giving out ectoplasm but nothing more.

"Well, good. I won't be sorry."

"Don't you want to know everything?"

"Everything? What else is there to know? You've been haunting this place ever since – ever since we – got rid of you. You hounded poor Vesna all through those years. I'm glad she's dead, so she's no longer tortured by your presence."

"Yes, well. We may meet again soon." Purbright's voice dripped pure evil into the room.

"Please say what you've got to say and go," insisted Elvira.

"You're shielding the wrong person, you know," came his voice steadily.

"What – what do you mean?"

"Didn't Vesna tell you? I heard her with my own two ears."

Elvira wondered, somewhat irrelevantly, if ghosts had ears or any other body parts, come to that.

"She told me, yes. And, yes, I know. I know only too well. I suppose you're glad I can't tell anyone."

"Well, they would certify you if you did." His horrible laugh sent a shiver down her spine. "You'll just have to let justice take its course, won't you? She was such a pretty girl, too. Just like Vesna. That's why she had to die, of course."

"It was cruel! How could you involve an innocent human being? Someone with her whole life before her?"

"It had to be done," was the only reply.

"And would you have been so content if the victim had been your own daughter?"

There was silence. "Did you hear me?" Elvira had hit home with that. Now he knew he had a daughter of his own, maybe there was a shred of decency in him somewhere. For Jeanne, at least. But the silence continued.

"You know that a man is on trial for the murder, don't you?" Elvira prompted.

He spoke at last, but his voice had a quiver in it now. "How would I know that? I've been trapped here in limbo all this time."

"You know. I know you know."

"Maybe I do and maybe I don't. Even so, there's nothing you or I can do about it, is there?"

Elvira sank down on a chair by the kitchen table. The cocoa she had poured had gone cold now. "No, there isn't."

"Right. And why are you so puzzled about the carving knife?"

"What – what do you mean?"

"Didn't you know?"

Elvira hadn't known, but suddenly now she did. It all made sense. The knife that killed Helen Carstairs had once been in her kitchen drawer. It was the murder weapon, now labelled 'Exhibit A' at the Old Bailey.

Chapter Forty-Two

Craddock clapped Rathbone on the back. "Hooray! They've seen sense at last."

He loomed out of court number one to find his sergeant seated outside, awaiting his turn to give evidence.

"Sense, sir?"

Rathbone was glad to see his boss was in a good mood for once. In fact, he was positively ebullient.

"Yes, Rathbone, sense! You should see Pickles' face."

"What are you talking about, guv?"

"Oh, sorry, getting ahead of myself there. The prosecution's managed to persuade the judge to call Minnie Knox. That'll scupper that bastard for sure."

"Which bastard? Carstairs or Pickles?"

"Both, Rathbone, both."

"But I thought Pickles had managed to get Minnie's evidence thrown out. How come they've changed their minds?"

"It's that Pym. He's an even more devious bastard than Pickles. Said the fact Carstairs got his daughter pregnant meant that he had a motive for killing her. So, Minnie's evidence is admissible after all."

"But it's only her word. Not enough, I would have thought…"

"Of course, it's not enough. Whether it's true or not doesn't matter to the prosecution. The doubt will be put into the minds of the jury who will now hate Carstairs so much that, even if they brought in a man who confessed to the killing at the eleventh hour, they would still bay for Carstairs' blood."

Rathbone was uneasy in his mind. "It's wrong, you know, sir," he said quietly. "If Carstairs is innocent, he'll never be believed now."

"No, he won't, will he?"

≈

Minnie Knox looked nervously around the court from her vantage point in the witness box. She cleared her throat and shuffled her feet as the clerk asked her to take the Bible in her right hand and repeat the words on the card he was holding up for her.

"I sw-swear by almighty G-God," she stumbled.

"Take your time, dear," said the judge kindly. "And speak up."

Minnie looked across at him, taking in his wizened features, piggy blue eyes and ridiculous wig. He looked like something out of the Dark Ages to her and, far from being intimidated by him, found she wanted to laugh.

"Th-that the evidence I shall give will b-be the truth, the wh-whole tr-truth and n-nothing but the t-truth."

Pym stood up and tucked his thumbs into the lapels of his gown in the time-honoured manner. "Is your name Minnie Knox?" he asked.

"Y-yes," she replied.

"Now, don't be nervous," he said. "We only need to ask you a few questions, then you can leave. All right?"

Minnie nodded her head.

"For the benefit of the jury, you must speak up," interjected the judge, who was a trifle deaf himself.

"She hasn't said anything yet," Pym pointed out.

"Well, when she does – tell her to speak up."

"Right, Your Honour. So, Miss Knox, you told the police, did you not, that Helen Carstairs was your best friend?"

Minnie nodded again.

"Answer the question with a 'yes' or 'no'."

"Er- sorry – y-yes."

Bernard and Elvira were sitting at the back of the court following the proceedings with nervous interest. Elvira was still trying to digest what had happened the previous evening at the cottage. They had no need to attend today, but both felt they needed to see it through to the end. It was more interesting to sit in the public gallery and watch the drama below them than it was to sit outside the court, unaware of what was going on.

Elvira felt sorry for young Minnie Knox, standing up there in the witness box, with all eyes on her. She was too young to be going through such an ordeal. She had found the experience bad enough, but the girl looked ready to faint with fright. Which is what she did.

An official rushed over to her with a glass of water. The judge banged his gavel. "Order!" he demanded. "As we – er – have come to a natural break, as it were, we will adjourn for the day," he said. "It's almost half-past three. Let us give this young lady time to recover. We will reconvene tomorrow morning at ten."

Minnie was slowly coming round as the judge addressed her kindly. "Miss Knox, you will be in attendance to give your testimony at that time." He looked meaningfully at the young girl as she sat in the witness box sipping her water.

"Court will rise," ordered the usher.

The order of witnesses changed the next day, giving Minnie more time to calm herself. Her mother was sitting beside her outside the court, holding her hand.

"I still don't know why they've called you, dear," said Sylvia Knox. "Why didn't you tell me?"

Minnie, who didn't want her mother to know what lie she was about to tell to the court, took her hand away. "You

228

don't have to hold my hand, Mum," she grumbled. "I'm not a child."

"But why have you been called? And why didn't you tell me before so I could have come with you yesterday? You shouldn't have to go through this on your own. Whatever it is."

"Look, Mum, it's all a misunderstanding. Don't worry. I suppose they just want to talk to me about Helen, as I was her best friend."

Sylvia wasn't satisfied but could see she wasn't going to get anything more out of her daughter.

As they sat there, they looked up to see Colonel Powell who had just come out of court number one. He was muttering to himself.

"Hello, Colonel," Sylvia called out to him. She liked the old duffer and often passed the time of day with him. "Have you been called as a witness, too?"

He turned at her voice. "Oh, hello, dear lady. Er, dear ladies, I should say. I didn't see you sitting there. Are you here to give evidence at the Carstairs trial?" he asked, coming to sit beside them.

"Not me. My daughter," answered Sylvia. "Although I'm not sure why and she won't tell me."

"Oh, Mum. Don't keep on."

"Anyway, what is your part in all this, Colonel?" Sylvia asked, ignoring her daughter's rudeness. She was used to it.

"I had to tell them what I saw on the night of the murder. I got a right telling off for my pains, as well."

"Why was that?" She glanced nervously at Minnie, hoping her daughter wasn't about to suffer the same fate.

The old man shrugged. "I told them what I saw, but that prosecution bod gave me such a hard time. It was dark, I told him, and I'd had a few." He coughed nervously. His drinking was legendary throughout the neighbourhood, and he could see Sylvia smiling slightly. "I told them I saw two people, I thought they looked like women, but I couldn't be sure. Anyway, I saw two people that night, about midnight, carrying what looked like a rolled up carpet between them."

"Oh? Why was that significant?"

"Because, dear lady, it could have concealed a body. And they were carrying it towards the Common where that poor girl's body was found."

"Oh, I see. But why was the barrister cross with you?"

He looked down at his feet, one of which was still bandaged up. He could feel it throbbing through the layers. He gave a derisory snort.

"Just because I couldn't tell him that one of them was Henry Carstairs. He pushed and pushed, but I wasn't going to say I'd seen him when I hadn't. I wasn't going to perjure myself."

"Quite right," said Mrs Knox. The prosecution couldn't prove Henry was somewhere where he definitely wasn't.

"Hmmph!"

Although Colonel Powell was inarticulate, Sylvia understood him completely. To her, he was a harmless old duffer who drank too much, but his heart was in the right place. No court of law could intimidate the likes of him. He'd seen too much on the battlefields of the Somme and Ypres.

"Well, if you're not sure who it was you saw, then you can't say, can you? You can only tell the truth."

They watched the colonel hobble off along the corridor, and mother and daughter exchanged a grin, united for once in their amusement at the poor colonel's affliction. He looked a comical figure to them as he disappeared from view.

"Poor old soul," observed Sylvia. "He doesn't know the time of day, does he?"

Minnie giggled in agreement.

Chapter Forty-Three

Minnie Knox lay on her bed, listening to the noise of the radio in the room below. It was a comedy, she could tell by the bursts of laughter every so often. She wished she could laugh along with them. Once or twice she heard her mother laugh too, something she hadn't heard her do for a while.

Sylvia Knox had ordered her daughter to bed on their return from the court. They hadn't spoken a word to each other on the journey back. "I don't want to see you or hear you, is that clear? I'll come and talk to you when I'm ready."

Minnie had known what she was in for when she had stood in the witness box that afternoon. Her mother, despite Minnie's protests, had insisted on coming into the court with her. If only she had remained outside waiting for her, all would have been well. She would have been sitting with her mother now, enjoying Tommy Trinder too.

She must have dozed off, fully clothed, for the next thing she knew her mother was in the room, holding a cup of tea.

"What's the time?" she asked groggily, rubbing her eyes.

"Nine o'clock," replied Sylvia. "I've made you a cup of tea."

Minnie sat up and took it from her. "Thanks, Mum," she said, realizing she was very thirsty. After taking one sip, however, she pulled a face. "You've put too much sugar in it," she complained.

"Sugar's supposed to be good for shock," said her mother. "You've had a shock today. At least one of us has."

Minnie put the cup down on her bedside table. "I – I'm sorry, Mum."

Sylvia Knox glared at her daughter. "Sorry? Sorry for what? Sorry for not drinking the tea I kindly made for you or for lying in court? If it's that, then 'sorry' doesn't begin to cover it. What were you thinking? I still can't believe I heard you say those words. About Henry of all people. He's always been so kind to you."

Minnie started to sob uncontrollably.

"Oh, yes, you can cry, missy." Sylvia's face was stern, but her heart was already melting. "Just tell me why. You know what you told them isn't true. Why did you lie?"

"I ... I don't know ... I wish ..." Minnie continued to sob.

Sylvia put her arms around her daughter, unsure what to say or do. Although she loved the very bones of her, she had never been a demonstrative woman and had rarely given Minnie hugs, even when she was small. So why now? she wondered. Now, when she should be chastising her instead?

Minnie gulped back her tears and tried to regain her composure. "I – I need to tell you something...."

"Okay. You can tell me anything, you know that. And, well, if it explains what you said in court today, I think you'd better."

Minnie climbed off the bed and retrieved her slippers from under it. "You like Mr Carstairs, don't you, Mum?"

"That's an odd question," said Sylvia nervously. "You know I do. He's been a tower of strength since your dad died."

"You like him more than a bit, don't you?" Minnie stood in front of her.

Sylvia, still sitting on the bed, stared up at her. "What are you getting at?"

"He's been coming round here more and more often, even when we don't need anything. Well, not anything like fixing a leaky tap, at least."

Sylvia was beginning to realize her daughter knew more about her relationship with Henry than she had ever suspected. "Well, of course. He's been a good friend to us," said Sylvia. "He – he sometimes came for a cup of tea and a chat. What's wrong with that?"

"Nothing, if that's all it was. But, all right, Mum, I know. I've known for a long time."

"Known what?"

Sylvia Knox stood up and went over to her daughter, a wild look on her face. She grabbed her by the shoulders and shook her violently. "Known what?" she repeated.

"He's been sharing your bed." It was out at last.

"Wash your mouth out, my girl," Sylvia screamed. "That's a wicked thing to say."

Minnie stood her ground. "It's true, though, isn't it?"

"Of course it's not true! Who's been telling you such lies? Helen again?"

"I wasn't *told* anything. I saw with my own eyes."

Sylvia Knox stepped back and fell onto the bed, her limbs too weak to hold her up. "How – how could you h-have seen us? We were always so careful."

"You never knew," said Minnie. Her mother was at her mercy now. "I came home from school earlier than usual one day – they'd sent me home because I had a headache. I came home expecting you to comfort me and give me one of your endless cups of tea, but instead there was no sign of you. I thought you were at the shops, and then I heard voices coming from your bedroom."

Her mother gulped. "You – you h-heard voices? Coming from the bedroom?"

"Yes," said Minnie. "Need I go on?"

"I – I – er – you m-must understand – a woman has needs…"

"I *saw* you in bed with him. You never saw me…"

"Oh God," said Sylvia. "I never knew. Why didn't you say anything? We never meant for it to happen, but one thing led to another…"

"How many times did – 'one thing lead to another'?"

"Oh, dear, you don't need to know. Just that Henry's a kind man. He was a rock after your dad died. I couldn't have managed without him."

"I bet you couldn't."

"Look, Minnie, I'm not proud of myself. But you must never tell Ivy. It'd break her heart."

"What's the betting she already knows? She's not a fool. She must have noticed something."

"Why would she? Henry always came in the afternoon – except that time when Ivy was away visiting her sister. It was the night of the murder – so I know for a fact that he couldn't have done it. He was here with me – *all night*!" She spat the last two words at her daughter.

"Then why don't you tell the police?"

"Because he won't let me. He wants to protect me."

"Or his own rotten reputation, more like."

"Whatever the reason, he won't let me tell them. But I'm going to if they find him guilty."

"Don't forget the other charge." Minnie smiled snidely. "The jury believed every word I said, I could tell."

"You can't let people believe that of him. You have to tell the truth."

"Do I?"

Sylvia wondered when her daughter had become so hard. It seemed her secret liaison with Henry had turned her into a lying little bitch.

"Helen's baby isn't Henry's. Whatever you say about her, and I know she was your best friend, she wasn't a saint. You know she'd got in with a bad crowd, don't you?"

Minnie shrugged. "So?"

Sylvia couldn't control herself any longer. She slapped her daughter across the face. "You bitch! You told the police that he was the father as some kind of sick revenge on him? You wanted him to be put in prison for something he didn't do – just because – just because I slept with him?"

234

Minnie put her hand to her cheek. Her mother hadn't hit her hard, but she pretended it hurt more than it did. "Mum! That hurt!" she protested.

"Serve you right. Anyway, I didn't hit you that hard."

Still rubbing her cheek, Minnie looked contrite now. "I – I didn't mean to let it get this far. But I can't retract now, can I? Won't I be done for perjury?"

Sylvia Knox stood up again. "You should have thought of that before. Anyway, you have to put the record straight. Hopefully, they'll let you off with a caution when I explain to the police why you said it in the first place." She wasn't convinced it would be that easy, but Minnie was young, younger even than her age. And as long as she was genuinely sorry, all would surely be well. "Did – did Helen tell you who the father was? Was it that Tyrone?"

"No – no it wasn't him. She said it was just some boy she met at an all-night party. I don't think she even knew his name. I didn't approve, of course."

"You don't really approve of anything, do you, Minnie? You just can't accept that people are human with human failings – even your own mother."

Minnie burst out crying again. "Please, Mum, you've got to help me."

"The only way I'll help you, my girl, is to march you straight down to the police station so you can make another statement. A true one, this time."

Chapter Forty-Four

After Elvira had finished her third port and lemon, courtesy of Bernard, she felt on top of the world, as if she could do anything she set her mind to. Her state of near euphoria wasn't just down to the port and lemons, either. Colonel Powell's evidence had been inconclusive at best, leaving the prosecution case no further forward. She was happy about that. But she was even happier that the old colonel hadn't given her away. He must have a sneaking liking for her, she thought. It was becoming clearer to her, by the day, that she had more friends than she had once thought.

Robbie had joined them in the Feathers that evening and, after Bernard and Elvira had brought him up to date with the day's court proceedings, he bought another round.

"I really can't believe Carstairs would rape his own daughter," said Robbie rather graphically, setting the tray of drinks down. "I've no liking for the man, but I don't see him as that kind of a monster."

Both Bernard and Elvira agreed. "He's a bit of a stuffed shirt," observed Bernard, "but I'm sure he's a decent enough man."

"Is that because he comes to church every Sunday?" Robbie raised an eyebrow at him.

"Not just because of that, no," said Bernard huffily. "He has given quite a lot to St Stephen's one way or another. Only last month he gave me a cheque towards some repairs. He loves the church."

"So, you can't see him writing that cheque with one hand and fiddling with his daughter with the other?" Robbie continued to be uncomfortably graphic.

Elvira gave a startled half laugh. "Dr MacTavish!" she remonstrated.

"Please call me Robbie, dear," he grinned. "Sorry. Just my way."

"I suggest you moderate your language in front of a lady," said Bernard primly.

He felt very protective of Elvira at the moment. What Colonel Powell had told him and what he had told the police and the court didn't tally, but he needed to be sure. She was a respectable citizen, just like Henry Carstairs, of that he was certain, but there only needed to be a hint of controversy about her and the locals would be baying for her blood. And no doubt the general population too, if the news ever got out.

"Anyway, as I said, I don't believe Carstairs molested his daughter and I certainly don't believe he killed her," Robbie was saying.

"But how do you explain the fingerprints?" Bernard sipped his fourth sherry of the evening. He was beginning to feel a little tipsy.

"I can't," sighed Robbie. "But there must be an explanation."

Elvira was sure she knew what that explanation was, but she was enjoying her port and lemon and the company too much to even hint at it. She would never tell a living soul, unless Carstairs was convicted. Then, she supposed, she would have to say something.

Her thoughts returned to Colonel Powell, while the two men entered into a discussion about the fingerprints. When the old boy had entered the witness box that morning, she had wondered why he had been called. But it had soon become clear. Completely sober for a change, he told the court he had seen two people carry a roll of what looked like carpet past his home in Hallows Mead Crescent towards the Common. It had been, he had estimated, about a quarter past midnight on the night (or morning, rather) of Helen Carstairs' murder. A ripple of excitement had spread around the court as he told his tale.

237

As she listened to it, her stomach had plummeted. She'd had no idea he had seen them that night. He must have been nosing out of the window as usual. And there was no chance he could have been mistaken because there was a lamp post directly outside his cottage and he would have seen them both clearly.

She had noticed Bernard look at her while Powell was giving his evidence. He had known! Colonel Powell had told him what he had seen, and Bernard had advised him to go to the police. Just like he had tried to persuade her to tell the police when she had confided in him about Helen's visit and the abortion powder. She knew how persuasive he could be. As she sat there, listening to Powell's words, she waited for her name to be mentioned. But what came next was both a surprise and a blessed relief.

He hadn't seen who they were! He had gone so far as to say he thought they were women, but it was too dark to be sure. But then the prosecuting counsel had pointed out the street lamp. He had done his homework, all right. How could the colonel, he had suggested, be mistaken when the light would have been shining directly on them? The colonel had a ready answer, however. That street lamp was notorious for going on the blink every so often. He had written to the council about it on more than one occasion. He blithely told the prosecution barrister that it had been out at the crucial time he had looked out of his bedroom window and seen the vague shapes below in the street. You could ask anyone in the Crescent, he had challenged. Elvira smiled to herself. That lamp post had been blazing away as she and Vesna passed under it that night.

Pym had persisted, despite the colonel's evidence, suggesting that one of the people the colonel had seen could have been Henry Carstairs. Possibly his wife could have been the other person. Powell had laughed at this. There was no possibility, he said, that one of them was Carstairs. Carstairs was a big man, over six feet. The two people he saw were well under that, that's why he thought they were women.

Bernard was looking at her now just as he had looked at her in the court. Robbie, swigging down his whiskey, looked bemused. He had wanted to come to the court himself, but his list of patients, now that the colder weather was upon them, was too long to allow him time off for such pleasures.

"You know, don't you? Colonel Powell told you it was me and Vesna, didn't he?"

"Yes, dear, he did. I was surprised he didn't tell the police the whole truth. He must have a soft spot for you."

A smile played around his lips as he said this. Robbie still looked bemused.

"For Vesna, more like," she sniffed, but she was secretly pleased. "I will have to thank the colonel, I suppose, even though he's a nosey old so-and-so."

"But you do realize that you have to come clean, Elvira," said Bernard, looking sideways at Robbie.

At this point, his friend intervened. "I don't think so, Bernie," he said, giving him a meaningful look. "Whatever happened, I'm certain no blame can be attributed to either you, Elvira, or your sister."

Elvira felt like crying now. He understood. But no policeman on earth, no matter how enlightened in psychic matters, would wear it. Certainly not that awful Inspector Craddock.

"Thank you, Robbie," she said. A look passed between them.

Now it was Bernard's turn to look bemused.

☙

Elvira was feeling an unaccustomed elation, not entirely due to the four port and lemons she had drunk earlier that evening with Bernard and Robbie. For the first time in years she felt positive about life and decided to push the boat out by holding a little dinner party. She would get a nice leg of lamb from Percy Banks and some decent wine. And candles, too. She grew excited at the prospect.

When Vesna was alive, they had led a very quiet life, used to the suspicion they aroused wherever they went, and only interacted with those people who needed one of their herbal remedies. But all that was behind her now. She would give up the trade altogether. The police were onto her, anyway, so she would have to be careful who she supplied and, more especially, *what* she supplied. She didn't think she had anything more dangerous than the abortion stuff, but there were certain substances she used in her remedies that could be regarded as suspicious by the police.

Jeanne Dupont's visit had opened her eyes to new possibilities. Elvira had been sure, if not a little surprised, that the woman had taken a liking to her. Then there was the evening in the pub she had spent with Bernard and Robbie. They seemed to like her too. She was beginning to realize she wasn't as alone as she had believed. She had expected her life to be one long, lonely path to the grave now that Vesna had gone, but it seemed she had been wrong. Even Colonel Powell hadn't given her away in court.

Yes, she thought, she would give a little dinner party. She would invite Bernard, Robbie, Jeanne and Colonel Powell. Her eyes strayed to the Spanish doll on the mantelpiece as she made a list. And Mrs Harper as well. She added Nancy's name at the bottom. Elvira didn't know how to take her, but there was no doubt about the gift. So, she was yet another person who seemed to like her. Things were definitely looking up.

She thought about Jeanne, Rodney Purbright's natural daughter. She had wanted to know more about him, but Elvira hadn't had the heart to tell her just what sort of a man he really was. The woman had persisted for a while but had finally realized Elvira wasn't prepared to tell her. But she hadn't quite given up. She had left the phone number of her B&B with her, saying she would be in London for a while, seeing the sights. Well, thought Elvira, maybe she would tell her a bit more when she came to the dinner party. Wrongs needed to be righted, and telling Rodney Purbright's daughter what had really happened to him would be a good place to start.

While she was thinking these thoughts, she hadn't been aware that the habitual below-zero temperature in the cottage had given way to a more normal one. In fact, she suddenly realized she was actually sweating, and she removed several layers of clothing. Had Rodney Purbright finally gone? Was he satisfied now? He had made Vesna pay for his murder, so there wasn't any need for him to remain. She wondered what he really thought about his daughter. He couldn't be anything but proud of her: a beautiful woman in her mid-thirties, with none of the arrogance or other negative characteristics of her father.

Then her thoughts turned to Henry Carstairs and her heart sank. It seemed he was some sort of vile pervert. But she couldn't believe it of him. That Minnie Knox was a sly little piece, in her opinion, not above lying her head off if it suited her book. But why had she lied? Especially about something so awful. She supposed it must be true. Perhaps he deserved to die, even though he wasn't guilty of murder. She sighed as she put the milk on for her bedtime cocoa.

Chapter Forty-Five

Sylvia Knox stood on the Carstairs' doorstep, reluctantly accompanied by her daughter. Following Minnie's confession the previous evening, it was Sylvia's first resolve to go straight to the police station. However, she realized it would come as very much of a shock to Ivy when she learned the reason why Minnie had lied in the first place. And heaven only knew what the poor woman was thinking about her husband now. There was no help for it. It would all have to come out. She had been sleeping with Ivy's husband. She hoped it wouldn't be one shock too many for the poor woman.

From her own point of view, it would be a relief to tell her, even if it meant that Ivy would never speak to her again. Still, they were hardly bosom friends, so she wasn't so bothered about that. The most important person was Henry and, once the police and the prosecution knew the truth, he would be a free man. She could provide him with a cast-iron alibi and no court in the land could convict him once they knew that. Henry might be angry with her for telling Ivy, but it couldn't be helped. There was no point in hoping for a not guilty verdict without her testimony. She had to save his stupid neck at all costs.

As for Minnie, she would have to come clean and risk the consequences. Sylvia hoped she could persuade the police not to prosecute, but that was the least of her worries. Now she had to face Ivy.

Ivy opened the door to them, wiping her wet hands on a tea towel. She brushed a stray lock of hair back under her turban as she eyed her two visitors.

"Oh, hello," she said. "I – I'm rather busy at the moment. Get down, Charlie!"

The little dog was running excitedly around Minnie's feet, yapping furiously. Sylvia remembered her promise to Henry about looking after it, but she had broken that promise. Getting him his headache powders from that Rowan woman had been one thing but taking on a yapping canine was quite another. She was a cat person herself, but she felt a little guilty all the same.

"It's okay," said Minnie, giving Ivy a nervous smile. "He's sweet."

"Can we come in for a minute?" asked Sylvia, as Ivy made no move to invite them in. "You see, I need to tell you something. That is, we both do."

"I don't think I need to hear anything from young madam here," she said coldly, staring at Minnie. "I heard all I wanted to hear in court yesterday."

"Look, we can't talk on the doorstep," insisted Sylvia. "Please, it's important."

Ivy sighed and turned on her heel, leaving Sylvia and Minnie to follow in her wake. The dog continued to yap around Minnie's feet as they entered.

"You'd better come through to the kitchen," said Ivy, "I'm still doing the washing up. Well, what is it you have to tell me?" She didn't ask them to sit down.

Sylvia began her story, clearing her throat several times and stopping frequently to gauge Ivy's reaction. Throughout her speech, Ivy stood by the sink rigid, her face expressionless, her eyes watery with grief.

Sylvia took out a lace handkerchief from her handbag to wipe her mouth as she finished. "Please...," she said, looking appealingly at her, "say something. I know what we did was wrong, but at least Henry has an alibi for the night of your poor daughter's murder. And you know, too, that he's not capable of molesting her. You should take some comfort from that, at least."

"Do you think I didn't know?" asked Ivy finally.

"Well, I'd assumed you'd thought him innocent of both charges – but it's good to have it confirmed, isn't it?"

"I didn't mean that," said Ivy, almost spitting the words out at her. "Although I knew he was innocent, of course I did. You don't live with someone for as long as I have without knowing that much about them."

"Then – er – what did you mean?"

"I'm not a fool, you know," she said. She carried on with the washing up, as if they weren't there.

"I – I never thought you were," said Sylvia, not knowing what was coming, but having a good idea. She looked at her daughter for moral support, but Minnie's eyes were firmly on the dog.

"Then you shouldn't assume that I didn't know what you and Henry were up to," said Ivy, scrubbing away at a plate that was already thoroughly clean.

"You mean you knew all this time and you never said anything?"

"What could I say? It was best left. Let sleeping dogs lie, that's my motto." Ivy turned round from the sink and looked Sylvia Knox straight in the eyes. Suddenly she sighed, sagged and sat down. It was as if all the stuffing had gone out of her.

"Minnie," said Ivy, "would you mind taking Charlie for a walk? He hasn't had any exercise today."

Minnie was only too glad to leave the two women alone. She grabbed Charlie's lead and the dog jumped up and down in ecstasy. It was probably his first proper walk for weeks.

When they were alone, Ivy offered her visitor a cup of tea. Sylvia accepted gratefully, taking it as a sign that things could somehow be mended between them. She had never been very fond of Ivy, whom she thought of as a 'dry old stick', but at least they could be civilized together.

"I turned a blind eye," said Ivy, filling the kettle. "I sent Minnie away because I didn't think this conversation was suitable for her young ears."

"I quite understand," said Sylvia. "Thank you. I'm really sorry for what she said about Henry. She was upset – you see, she came home early from school and – well, she caught us…"

"At it, like?"

Sylvia blushed. "Well, y-yes. Of course, we didn't see her. She must have just looked into the bedroom and seen us and then run off. I wish she'd said something at the time, then all this might have been avoided."

"Well, I didn't mind Henry coming to see you – when your Ted died. You needed help to sort everything out after. And Henry's always been good at little jobs around the house, but I suppose I knew, deep down, they included sleeping with you. I mean, there's only so many shelves one house needs, isn't there?"

She poured out the tea and passed a cup to Sylvia. "I wasn't all that keen on the bed department, myself. Lie back and think of England, that's my motto."

Sylvia sipped her tea, thinking Ivy was fond of mottos.

"But I knew Henry had *needs*. So, I suppose I couldn't really blame him. He was always discreet, though. Never one to wash his dirty linen in public, that's my Henry."

"I wish we'd been better friends – like our daughters," said Sylvia. "I always thought you were a bit – well, stuck up. And I suppose sleeping with your husband wasn't the best way to treat a friend." She smiled nervously, and Ivy laughed.

"I think we understand each other," she said.

They drank their tea in silence for several moments before Ivy spoke again. "I wonder, though, how Henry's fingerprints ended up on the knife."

"It's very strange," Sylvia replied. "I don't know what to make of it, I really don't. There must be an explanation."

Ivy shrugged. "I wish I knew what it was."

"Whatever it turns out to be," said Sylvia, "he won't be found guilty now. Not with the alibi I'm about to give him. I'm so glad you understand, Ivy."

She didn't reply, but the look in her eyes was softer now.

Chapter Forty-Six

On the morning of her dinner party, Elvira received an official-looking letter in the post. She was looking forward to that evening, although she was a little nervous. Everyone had accepted her invitation, including Jeanne Dupont, who was due to return to France the following Monday.

Before the post arrived, she was sitting at the kitchen table with her toast and marmalade, the newspaper open in front of her. The headline jumped out at her. "WITNESS LIES IN COURT. THE CARSTAIRS MURDER TRIAL COLLAPSES". She read, with growing anger, that Minnie Knox had purposely deceived the court. How could she have done such a thing? And to her best friend's father, of all people. She must really hate him, she thought. But it was a blessed relief that poor Henry was now a free man. That was all that really mattered.

As she finished her breakfast, she heard the clatter of the letter box and saw the envelope lying on the mat. She got few letters unless they were bills, but this one didn't look like a bill. Curious, she picked it up, wondering who it could be from. Turning over the envelope, she saw it was from a firm of solicitors based in Liverpool. She recognised it at once. It was the firm her father had always used.

She opened the letter warily, fearing anything legal these days. As she read the contents, however, a smile slowly played around her lips. She folded it up and put it back in the envelope. Well, she thought, that's a turn up for the books and no mistake. She put it behind the clock on the mantelpiece, next to the Spanish doll.

ᥢ

Her guests all arrived in good time. She was relieved that the cottage was now warm enough and, although there was no real need, she had lit a fire in the parlour where she had set out the dining table. With the glow of the fire and the candles, the room looked very inviting, and everyone commented on this with pleasure. Even Nancy Harper permitted herself a nod of approval.

The meal couldn't have gone down better. The lamb was succulent and tender, the fruit fool to follow equally delicious. Elvira eyed Nancy across the table several times and saw, with satisfaction, that she was obviously enjoying the food as much as everyone else.

"Well, Mrs Aitch," said Bernard, as the cheese and biscuits were passed around, "even you must admit this meal is worthy of you." He didn't say it was actually better, although he thought it.

Nancy, in unaccustomed party mood, even managed to smile at this. She didn't often get invited to dinner parties. "Well, I like a night off sometimes," she said. "I think I wouldn't 'ave put so much mint sauce on the lamb, though."

Bernard laughed. "Maybe you're right."

Elvira was basking in the praise heaped on her culinary skills. The colonel, especially, was eyeing her with more interest than he had ever shown before. Vesna had always been his favourite, but he was obviously thinking how good it would be to have this kind of meal every day. Elvira avoided his gaze, blushing. If she suspected he was going to propose to her, she didn't allow the thought to linger.

"I'm so glad you all enjoyed the meal," she said. "But I – I have to admit that I had an ulterior motive in gathering you all here tonight."

The assembled company looked at her expectantly. Elvira wasn't used to such attention, and she grew nervous. It was time, she knew, to tell everything, but now the moment was here, she found herself wavering. After all, what purpose would it serve now? Henry was free, so she didn't need to say anything. But then there was Jeanne Dupont. She had the right to know what happened to her father. Her conscience had borne her guilt and shame for too long. Once they all knew the truth, they could go to the police. Do what they like. She wouldn't stop them. She *couldn't* stop them.

"Yes," she continued, looking now at Jeanne. "You came to find your father, dear, the father you never knew, and you wanted me to tell you about him."

Jeanne smiled, but said nothing.

"I'm sorry I wasn't able to tell you when I met you," Elvira continued. She looked around at everyone. Nancy looked quite relaxed, the wine obviously doing her good; Colonel Powell looked puzzled, while both Bernard and Robbie sent her warning looks.

"Please bear with me, everyone. I don't want to spoil the party atmosphere. I've enjoyed it so much, and I look on each of you as my friends. And that is why I must tell you what I'm about to tell you. Then you can decide what must be done." She paused before adding, "If anything."

Jeanne spoke. "I would rather you told me in private, Elvira," she said, "if it is about mon père, do zese peoples need to know?"

Elvira nodded slowly. "I think they do, yes. You see your father, Rodney Purbright, is the key to everything."

"Everything?" Colonel Powell spoke up. He was looking remarkably sober for a change, despite the excellent wine on offer.

"Yes. He is the key to the murder of Helen Carstairs."

There was a collective intake of breath. Only Jeanne didn't understand the significance of what Elvira said.

"But, let me start at the beginning." Elvira held up her hand. "And please don't interrupt until I've finished. It's taken me a long time to get up the courage to do this."

Bernard looked worried. "Is this something we should all hear, Elvira? Robbie and I know certain things, as does Colonel Powell. Mrs Aitch doesn't know what we know – "

Nancy sniffed, "I know more'n you think," she piped up.

Elvira smiled at her. "I'm sure you do, dear," she said. "And I'm happy for you all to hear what I have to say. I wouldn't have asked you all here if I wasn't."

"Might I suggest you get on with it, then?" urged the colonel.

"Yes. I intend to. Now, Jeanne, you asked me what your father was like and I wasn't very forthcoming. I'm sorry, but that was because I couldn't think of one good thing to say about him. He was manipulative, overbearing and he frightened me and Vesna very much. When he came back from the War, we were shocked as we had been told by the War Office that he was dead. We don't know how the mistake occurred, but we believed he'd done something pretty awful to get out of active duty. Anyway, as Vesna believed her fiancé was dead, she had got engaged to another young man. Purbright wasn't having that, so he saw to it that he was frightened off for good. He pushed him in the canal and, to this day, he has suffered with his chest."

Jeanne's eyes filled with tears as Elvira went on to tell her the depths to which Purbright had sunk, and what Vesna was finally forced to do.

"I had to help her cover up the murder. She was my sister."

"But zis is terrible!" Jeanne screamed. "What – what happened to his body?"

There was a deathly hush as Elvira cleared her throat.

"Colonel, do you remember asking me how I got my roses to bloom so well?"

"Er – yes, I do. I was very envious at the time. But – but what's that got to do with the murder?"

"Because that's where we buried his body. Under the rose bushes in the front garden. They've not done so well in recent years, as I'm sure you know."

The evening had started off so well, but suddenly the assembled company felt like they were in an Agatha Christie novel with Elvira as Miss Marple, naming the murderer and the modus operandi.

Jeanne stood at this point, ready to leave. "No matter how bad a person my father was – or you thought he was – zat is no excuse for murder. Now where did you put my coat?"

Bernard got up and came round the dining table to join her. "I don't think you're being entirely fair," he said quietly to Jeanne. "I understand how you feel, but Elvira was only protecting her sister. She had no part in your father's actual murder."

Jeanne seemed to calm down a little. "No, but she helped her – how you say? – dispose of ze body. Zat is punishable in law, yes?"

Bernard nodded. "Yes, but surely you can understand her wanting to protect her sister?"

"I suppose so," she said grudgingly, looking at Elvira with hurt in her eyes. "I liked you," she said to her. "How could you do such a thing to another human being?"

"I'm sorry, Jeanne," was all Elvira could say. "Please don't go."

Everyone in the room echoed this sentiment. The men, especially, as she was so pretty, and the smell of her French perfume was intoxicating them. Nancy Harper, not in the least impressed with the woman's beauty or smell, piped up again now.

"Get off your high 'orse, ducks. Worse things 'appen at sea. Sounds to me like this Purbright bloke got off lightly. You never knew 'im so don't make out you're so upset. Give Elvira a break. This must be 'ard for 'er, telling us all this."

There was a tangible gathering of bated breath while they waited for Jeanne's reaction to this piece of Harper homespun philosophy. To their collective relief, she laughed.

"You are right," she said. "I am on – how you say? – ze high horse. I will get off *immediatement*. But it is still murder, even if he was no good."

"But the *murderer* is dead." Robbie, who had been unusually quiet during these exchanges spoke. "And Elvira is still alive and deserves a chance of happiness for all she's been through."

He gave Elvira the benefit of one of his devastating smiles. She felt herself blushing again as a warm feeling spread throughout her body to her very toes.

"Anyway," said Colonel Powell, "what has this murder to do with the Carstairs case? Am I missing something?"

"I'm coming to that," said Elvira, still flushed with pleasure at Robbie's championing of her. "It has a bearing, I can assure you. But, the only problem is, I don't think you will believe me."

It was Bernard's turn to speak. "I will, for one," he said.

Robbie grinned and echoed this sentiment.

The other three just looked puzzled.

"Don't know 'ow you know you'll believe 'er without 'earing what she 'as to say," Nancy pointed out, not unreasonably. She was enjoying herself immensely.

"It depends whether you believe in the supernatural," said Elvira. "I take it that Bernard and Robbie do, because they have experienced the intense cold that I have lived with for over thirty years. This cottage was colder than an igloo up until just a few days ago."

"I thought it was rising damp," said Jeanne, now reseated, her search for her outdoor coat abandoned for the moment.

"Rising damp doesn't cause it to be that cold," said Elvira, "but the presence of a restless spirit does."

"But it's warm in 'ere," Nancy pointed out. "Too Pygmalion warm if you ask me."

"It's fine now, but it wasn't up until a few days ago." In fact, Elvira was feeling much too hot at that moment, she had got so used to the cold.

"So, are you saying your cottage is haunted?" Colonel Powell seemed excited at the idea.

"Yes, Colonel, at least, it was. By Rodney Purbright. But he has gone now. He's had his revenge on Vesna."

"Then, that makes sense of what I saw," he said.

"Yes, Colonel, you saw me and Vesna carry Helen Carstairs' body in a roll of carpet past your cottage."

"And that wasn't all I saw," he said.

Chapter Forty-Seven

Elvira was thrown for a minute. Just what had the colonel seen? He'd already said he'd seen Vesna and herself that night carrying the rolled-up carpet past his cottage. What else was there to see? Did he follow them and see them dump the body? Well, if he did, it didn't matter anymore.

She looked around the room at the expectant faces. What was going through their minds? she wondered. Did they believe her capable of murder? Did they think she had murdered Purbright and just put the blame on her sister now that she wasn't there to defend herself? No, she thought. Bernard believed her, she was sure. And so did the handsome doctor. The only ones who viewed her with suspicion were the colonel, Mrs Harper and Jeanne. Jeanne, being French (half, anyway), probably viewed all English people with suspicion, so that didn't count.

"What happened to Helen? That's what you're all wondering," she stated. "And I am about to tell you."

Her audience glanced at each other before returning their full attention to her. This evening was turning out to be one of the strangest in their lives.

"She came to us that evening in a very distressed state, telling us she was going to have a baby and she needed help to get rid of it. Her father would kill her if he found out, she said."

That, so far, was easy for her audience to believe. They nodded in sympathy at the plight of the poor girl.

"So, what could I do? Turn her away to face the wrath of her father? Carstairs isn't an easy man, although he is a fair one. But when it came to his daughter, I don't know how he would have reacted, and I wasn't prepared to find out. Nor was Vesna. She was already making up the powder."

She paused. "Yes, *she* made it up, not me. But I would have done, if she hadn't."

The gathering was with her so far. But, she feared, the parting of the ways would be coming soon.

"When she had taken the powder, we advised her to go home immediately and have a hot bath, as hot as she could bear it. But she said she would be unable to do that, as they only had baths at set times, and they would suspect something at once. So, we said she could have a bath here."

"Reasonable enough," mumbled Robbie, "although, as a medical man, I would say that hot baths, accompanied by gin, hardly ever work."

"The powder was more potent than gin," Elvira pointed out. "It had worked in the past, although not always. I told the police, and you, too, Bernard, that it hardly ever worked. That was untrue, I'm sorry."

She now felt the room begin to turn against her. Never mind, she thought, casting a glance at the envelope tucked behind the mantel clock.

"Anyway, Helen went upstairs and ran the bath as I told her. It was then I heard a noise in the kitchen." It was at that moment, as she was telling her story, she remembered exactly when she had heard the noise of the cutlery drawer being rattled. "Although I didn't realize it at the time, I now know it must have been Vesna."

"What was she doing and why is it important?" asked the colonel.

"I'm coming to that. Let me tell it in my own way, please."

The colonel harrumphed but let her carry on.

"I was sitting here in the parlour, looking through a magazine, I remember, feeling nervous and worried about the poor girl, when I heard a scream from upstairs. I thought Helen had probably just cried out because the water was too hot, but I ran up the stairs to make sure she was all right.

When I reached the landing, Vesna was standing there, holding a blood-soaked bundle.

"Bundle?" Nancy Harper looked puzzled. "Bundle of what?"

"I will tell you, dear, if you'll let me," said Elvira, impatient now to get to the end of her narrative.

"Well, I only asked," sniffed Nancy, looking around for back-up.

"Quite right, quite right," obliged the colonel.

"The bundle was the murder weapon wrapped in a towel. Vesna said it was dripping all over the bathroom, so she had wrapped it up. I pushed past her and saw Helen sinking into the bath water. I'll never forget it. It was pink and foamy. And she was dead. I could tell. Her eyes were glassy, and her mouth was open, still in mid-scream, the pink water dripping down her chin. It was – horrible!"

Bernard resisted the temptation to get up and go over to her. He could see she was about to collapse with the strain of her confession.

"So, there you have it," she continued after she had taken a few moments to compose herself. No one spoke in the meantime. "The rest you can probably work out for yourselves."

"So, you took zat poor girl's body to the Common, wrapped in a roll of carpet?" Jeanne was incredulous.

"Yes, I – we did. Vesna told me she hadn't been aware of what she was doing. I couldn't – wouldn't – believe it. Why would she have stabbed her like that? What possible reason? She had just helped her, for God's sake."

"What was ze reason, then?" asked Jeanne.

"She told me only later that night. This is where you won't believe me."

Elvira eyed them one by one. Bernard and Robbie would believe her, she knew. But no one else. She wouldn't herself, if someone told her what she was about to tell them.

"She told me Rodney Purbright told her to kill Helen. He said she had to, to even the score. She had killed him and now she had to pay. He said the girl was herself when younger. She had to kill *herself*!"

There was a collective intake of breath. Even Bernard gasped at this. He hadn't expected that. Robbie was the only one who seemed unfazed.

"Was Helen so like your sister as a young woman?" he asked.

"Almost identical. She could have been her daughter."

The colonel spoke into the silence that followed this comment. "I believe you," he said.

Elvira turned to him in surprise. "You do?"

"I do." He smiled, looking around him at the amazed faces. "You see, I saw him that night, following you."

"Saw him? Saw who?" Elvira's hand went to her mouth in astonishment.

"That Purbright feller. I wasn't sure until now, but that's who it must have been."

"It couldn't have been him, Colonel," said Elvira, trying to be patient but not quite succeeding. "He's been dead for over thirty years!"

"I know that. It was him, though. I thought I must have had the DT's when I saw what I saw. You all know my reputation – well, apart from you, Jeanne – no, don't try to deny it…"

He paused. No one did.

"I'm fond of a drop, I admit, but now I know I wasn't seeing things."

"But you must have been, Colonel." Elvira was insistent.

"It was his *ghost*, of course. You see, he disappeared as I was watching him. He was laughing. I couldn't hear him, but I could see the smile on his smug face. It was the last thing to disappear. Like the Cheshire cat."

"You are wrong!" cried Jeanne suddenly. "You are all wrong. My father was a handsome young man. He wasn't a monster, like you all want to believe. Look."

She fumbled in her handbag and brought out the old sepia photograph of Purbright in his solder's uniform. "See! How could a man as handsome as that be so wicked?"

The colonel stared at the photo, ignoring the woman's assertion. "Yes, there's no doubt about it. That's him! That's who I saw following you, Elvira."

Chapter Forty-Eight

"Well," sighed Elvira. "There you are. It's not very believable, is it? But, just ask yourselves this: would I be telling you such a story if it wasn't true? Would I even be telling you anything at all? What possible motive could I have for making this up?"

"You're quite right," said the colonel. He turned to the others. "I can vouch for what Elvira's told you, at least about what I saw." He turned back to her. "I take it you didn't know you were being followed?"

"No, of course not." She gave an involuntary shiver.

Jeanne stood up, this time seemingly determined to find her coat and leave. "I find zis all very strange," she said. "I do not believe one word of what you have said. I think we should tell the police that you are mad and have killed two people. You may have killed others, no?"

"Come off it," said Nancy, getting up on her fat little legs with an effort. "You ain't got no proof of that. Elvira's always been straight with me and with the vicar, too. And the doc. We all stand by 'er. You can protest all you like, Miss Fancy Pants, but we know Elvira and she ain't no mass murderer."

Jeanne couldn't help but smile. Nancy Harper was the sort of Englishwoman she had heard about but never met. Until now. A no-nonsense Cockney with a heart of gold.

"You are right," she said at last. She could feel everyone in the room willing her to agree with Nancy. "I am ze outsider here, and I will not interfere." And, to prove she meant it, she tore the photograph of her father in two. Everyone clapped.

She sat down for the second time and smiled at everyone. Despite her innate wariness of the eccentric English, she found herself responding warmly to the

259

assembled company. The half of her that was English seemed to relate to the Nancy Harpers and Colonel Powells of this world. She wasn't quite sure, however, how to take the vicar or the doctor, nice enough gentleman though they appeared to be.

"I have some decent port tucked away," announced Elvira. Now that the atmosphere had returned to its former conviviality, she became the generous host once again.

"Now that sounds like a plan," said Colonel Powell, rubbing his hands. "Let's forget all about murders for a while, shall we?"

"Er, there's just one thing I don't understand," said Robbie, "just before we pass the port."

Elvira's look of bonhomie and relief vanished. "What's that, Robbie?"

"What about the fingerprints on the knife?"

"Oh, yes. That's easily explained." Her face brightened.

"Yes?"

Everyone leaned forward.

"It was our carving knife, of course, as I finally realized. I never saw it at the time. I made Vesna sort that out herself. She said she buried it near the body, and I told her I didn't want to know. Maybe if I'd known it was our carving knife all along – "

"Yes, yes, Elvira. Carstairs' prints? How would they have got on the knife?" Robbie's eyebrows beetled.

"Because he helped carve our Sunday joint once," said Elvira. "About a year ago, I think it was."

"'Ang on a minute," squeaked Nancy, "you mean to say you ain't never washed it?"

"That's a point," muttered the Colonel.

"You don't wash your dirty cutlery?" Jeanne was disgusted.

Elvira smiled. "I rinse the blade under the hot tap, that's all it needs. And I don't often have roast meat these days. I've only used it a couple of times since."

That seemed to clear up the mystery. Both Jeanne and Nancy were satisfied with Elvira's explanation (as well as her sense of hygiene), and everyone was looking forward to the port.

"Cheers!" they said in unison, when it was poured.

∾

Elvira awoke the next morning with a headache. It was the port that had finished her off. Rising slowly, she drew her dressing gown around her and went to the window. It was a blustery Sunday morning in late September and, for the first time in over thirty years, she felt at peace with herself and the world around her. One of her headache remedies would soon take care of the pain, and she would be ready for anything.

Later that morning, she received a visitor. Jeanne Dupont stood on the doorstep, smiling, with a large bunch of flowers.

"Zank you so much for a very *interesting* evening," she said.

Elvira, her headache now dispatched thanks to her grandmother's old receipt, smiled back at her as she took the bouquet.

"Th-thank you, Jeanne," she said. "I'm so glad you enjoyed yourself."

"It was *formidable*," said her visitor, who looked prettier than ever in a stylish two-piece. Elvira particularly admired the black stockings. She supposed they were what men would call sexy. There was no doubt about it, only the French could look this chic.

"Would you like a coffee?"

261

"No zank you, I won't stop. I have much to do as I am returning to France tomorrow. I just wanted to say goodbye and to say that, if you ever plan a trip to France, I would be happy to see you."

"That's very kind," said Elvira, touched. Everyone was being so kind to her. She should have told the truth a long time ago.

"I came to England to find my father, but I have found a friend instead," said Jeanne. "Friends, I should say. You were all so kind to me last night, Robbie especially. He is – how you say – a ladies' man?"

Elvira laughed. "Yes, you could say that, I suppose."

"*D'accord!* I hope that the man who was wrongly accused of the murder will not be punished now?"

"Oh no, Jeanne. Our law doesn't allow people to be retried for the same offence."

"And you will not tell the police about the finger prints?"

Elvira looked down at her feet. "No, Jeanne. I don't think so. If he were still on trial, then I would. But it would be the end for me if I told them now. Do you see?"

"I zink so," smiled Jeanne. "And I know you are not a murderer. I am sorry about your sister. And about my father and how you both suffered because of him."

"It's all right, Jeanne. I feel free at last. He is no longer here, and everyone knows the truth now."

"You are very brave."

Elvira didn't feel very brave at that moment. She wanted to break down and cry in Jeanne's arms. She could have had a daughter like Jeanne if life had been kinder to her and dealt her better cards.

అ

Jeanne Dupont wasn't Elvira's only visitor that day, as it turned out. Not long after she had left, Colonel Powell turned up with a bunch of flowers too. Unlike Jeanne, however, he accepted a coffee and sat himself down on the sagging sofa, rubbing his aching foot.

"Thank you, Colonel," said Elvira, putting the flowers in a vase. Jeanne's superior blooms in the best vase were moved to make room. She would have to buy more vases at this rate, she thought. "You didn't have to do this. In fact, it is I who owe *you*."

"But why, dear lady?" The Colonel's faded blue eyes were twinkling.

"For not giving me away in court."

"Oh, that was nothing. I would have done anything to make sure your sister's reputation wasn't ruined."

Not mine? Elvira suddenly felt angry. Why was it always Vesna? Even when she was dead!

"Well, that was good of you," she said through gritted teeth.

"The meal was superb," Colonel Powell said, unaware he had hurt her feelings. "And you make excellent coffee too." He raised his bone china cup to her, as if in salute.

"I aim to please." Her teeth were still gritted. "So, if that's all, Colonel, I've got some things to be getting on with."

"Er, well, there was one more thing," he said. "The real purpose of my visit, actually." He looked shifty as he cleared his throat. His eyes were darting everywhere.

"Yes?" Get on with it, you silly old goat, she thought.

"It's just that, well, what I'm trying to say is we're both lonely. Since my wife died, I've felt the loss, as I'm sure you can imagine. Without your dear sister, you must feel very lonely yourself."

"Life hasn't been easy," agreed Elvira, not sure of what was coming, but beginning to get a good idea.

"So, why don't we – why don't we get hitched?"

"Get hitched?"

All her life, she had prayed for some man to get down on his bended knee and propose to her, and at last she had her wish. But, far from getting down on bended knee, the old duffer couldn't even walk properly on that gouty foot. And 'why don't we get hitched' was a far cry from 'would you do me the honour'.

"Yes. We would be company for each other," he encouraged.

"And I could look after you. Help you in and out of your armchair." And anywhere else, she could imagine. "And cook your meals."

"Yes, yes. What d'you say?"

"I say, Colonel, what's in it for me?"

"For you?" He said this as if surprised she should want anything apart from the benefit of his company.

"Yes. For me. You'll be getting good, solid meals and a housekeeper and a nurse and anything else you'd care to mention." She hoped he wouldn't mention *that*, of course. "But what about me?"

"Well, you wouldn't be lonely, would you?"

"With you knocking around the place all day, d'you mean?"

The colonel wasn't the most sensitive of men, but he could detect an icy note in her voice. "Well, yes."

"Thank you, Colonel, for your offer, but I have to decline it, I'm afraid."

The old man blustered and muttered his way out of the cottage a few minutes later, after remonstrating with her for as long as she could put up with it. She closed the door on him and leaned against it, grinning.

Silly old fool, she thought. If he hadn't said that about looking after Vesna's reputation, she might seriously have considered his proposal. There were positive aspects of his offer, she couldn't deny it, but she wasn't prepared to play second fiddle anymore.

She had other fish to fry.

AFTERMATH

Even though Henry Carstairs had been released from prison and was free to continue his life as before, his troubles were far from over. Things for him would never be the same again.

Ivy had welcomed him back and he had been grateful for that, especially knowing that she knew all about his dalliance with Sylvia Knox. His little Jack Russell had been ecstatic to see him again and was once more enjoying two vigorous walks a day. But, he noticed, even as he took Charlie across the Common, that people were staring at him with suspicion and dislike. Although he had been discharged, he hadn't been completely exonerated. There was still the problem of the fingerprints, as Elvira was holding onto her secret, at least for the time being.

Then, of course, there was the alibi. This had damned him in most people's eyes even more than the murder charge. Carstairs realized that, whichever way he looked at it, he couldn't win. They all knew he hadn't interfered with his daughter in any way, but people still crossed the street to avoid him. He couldn't face going to church either, where the congregation would no doubt stare at him with revulsion. It was true what they said: mud stuck.

Sylvia Knox kept a low profile after he was released. So did Minnie. They both, for different reasons, felt it wise to avoid him, so even that avenue was closed off to him. Maybe it was just as well, he supposed, although he was missing the comfort of Sylvia's soft flesh beneath the bedclothes.

He had gone back to work as soon as he felt up to it after his ordeal. His boss was a decent man, and he had kept his job as bookkeeper open for him. A man was innocent until proved guilty, he had said. But Carstairs' workmates were of a different opinion. They shunned him whenever possible, only addressing him when it was necessary in the course of business. Lunch in the canteen was another trial. If he came to sit at a table occupied by any of his colleagues, they immediately gathered up their trays and sought another table.

Henry Carstairs' life in Wandsworth was, in a word, untenable, and it wasn't very long before he, Ivy and Charlie had removed themselves from the borough altogether. Nobody, he thought sadly, would miss him. He threw a stick for his happy dog as he walked him across Ilkley Moor. He still hadn't had time to grieve for his daughter. Up until then, he had only been able to grieve for himself.

No one knew him here, the Wandsworth murder having made little impact in Yorkshire. He watched his excited little dog frolic with joy and smiled. It would be hard to start all over again, but he was determined to try and make a go of it now he had been given a second chance.

Inspector Craddock was still seething, having been robbed of his triumph in bringing the Wandsworth murderer to book, only to let him slip through his grasp in the end. The whole case had been a disaster, and the tired old copper felt like turning in his badge.

"Never mind, guv," Rathbone had tried to comfort him. "You did your best. That Minnie Knox didn't do us any favours, lying like that."

"I'd like to wring the little minx's bloody neck," said Craddock, biting into his bacon sandwich with vehemence.

"I don't think Carstairs did it, though, despite the prints," said Rathbone, watching his boss devour his breakfast with distaste. A buttered croissant was all he could manage in the mornings.

"Why not? How do *you* think the prints got on the knife, then?"

"Well, guv, I've a theory about that. He could have borrowed it from someone."

"Is that it? Is that your theory?" Craddock was incredulous. "That he could have borrowed the knife? And then given it back, I suppose, so that some unknown person could stick it into that poor girl's stomach."

"I know it sounds feeble, but, yes. I believe that's what happened."

Craddock laughed, spattering bacon and bread over his jacket and onto the table, narrowly missing his oppo by inches. "You're a comedian, Rathbone."

The inspector continued to laugh, and Rathbone reluctantly joined in. It was an unwritten rule at the station that, if Craddock found something amusing, then everyone else had to, as well.

"Silly me!" said the Sergeant.

&

"That blessed cat's up the tree again."

Bernard was seated in his warm study one December morning when Mrs Harper imparted this piece of news to him.

"Oh dear!"

"I ain't going to call the fire brigade again," asserted his housekeeper defiantly. "I got a mouthful from them the last time."

"But how are we going to get him down? Poor Beelzebub. Why do you think he keeps going up there?"

Bernard followed Mrs Harper out into the back garden where he saw his precious cat mewing on the topmost branch of the oak tree that overlooked the next garden.

"He's after that robin," said Mrs Harper. "I've been watching the blighter from the kitchen window."

"I'll go and fetch a ladder," said Bernard. "It won't reach up that far, but maybe he'll be able to reach the top of it."

As he struggled with the ladder, a young man, armed with a large bunch of white lilies, came sauntering along the alley which backed onto the vicarage garden.

"Hello, Vicar," Tyrone Larkin called to him. "Do you need any help?"

Bernard looked gratefully at the pleasant young man. He wasn't a regular attendee at his services, but he was always there for the big ones – Christmas, Easter, Harvest Festival.

"Well, if you wouldn't mind," he said. "You see, my cat's got himself stuck up that oak tree and I don't think I can reach him, not even from the top of this ladder."

Tyrone smiled. "No problem," he said, leaping with agility over the fence.

Taking the ladder from Bernard, he placed it up against the tree and began to climb. As he did so, the cat leapt from the branch onto the neighbouring tree and climbed down it with facile ease.

"Oh dear," said Bernard as he grabbed his precious feline. "I'm so sorry to have troubled you."

Tyrone laughed. "Cats are always doing that. Make you feel sorry for them and, when you try to help, they make you look a fool and snub you."

"Do you have a cat, then?"

"Yes. We've got two, actually. Regular comedians, they are."

"We called the fire brigade last time he got stuck up there," smiled Bernard. "They weren't amused."

Tyrone laughed again. "No, they wouldn't be. Anyway, I'd better get on. I'm on my way to take these to Helen's grave."

The young man looked serious now, and Bernard's heart went out to him. In all this trouble, the young victim's boyfriend had been more or less overlooked, but he must have suffered just as much as her parents, losing her like that.

"I hate graveyards, but I must say my goodbyes," he said, holding the lilies close to his chest.

Bernard watched him go, a tear poised in his eye. It wasn't fair that such awful things should happen to the young, he thought. He looked heavenwards, but he saw no enlightenment from that quarter. God, it seemed, was on another tea break.

Sighing, he returned to the vicarage study, holding Beelzebub firmly by the scruff of the neck, supporting his nether region with his other hand. "Naughty boy!" he admonished him.

Moments later, Mrs Harper brought him his mid-morning coffee and biscuits. She set the tray down on the table by his armchair and turned to leave the room. As she reached the door, she turned round.

"Oh, by the way, Vicar, I've just been to the shops and guess who I met coming back?"

"No idea, Mrs Aitch. Do tell," he said, tickling Beelzebub behind the ear.

"Elvira."

"Oh, how is she? I must go and see her again soon."

"She's fine, Vicar," said Mrs Harper, hoisting up her ample bosom. "She was carrying a suitcase."

"Oh? Going on holiday?"

"She didn't say." Mrs Harper sniffed. "She was very cagey about it."

"We haven't seen much of her recently, have we? I hope she's all right."

"She looked more than all right to me. Grinning like a Cheshire cat, she was."

Bernard smiled. Elvira Rowan was no fool. He recalled with pleasure her splendid dinner party with that excellent off-the-ration leg of lamb, and her confession, if that was what it was, after they had all eaten. Everything she had told them had been believed. They had all been taken in, even Robbie. But, when he came to think about it, her story was a little far-fetched.

"But we believed her because we believe in the supernatural," he had argued with Robbie the day after. "But should we have swallowed it all?"

"Well, there was the colonel's story which seemed to back her up," Robbie had pointed out. But he had looked doubtful as well.

"You know, Robbie," Bernard had said, "I'm not so sure. Now that she isn't here, talking to us, I don't know. She could have killed Helen. Maybe it was an accident. Maybe the powder they gave her had been too strong or something."

"But what about the colonel? He said he saw Purbright's ghost following them. What about that?"

"He could have been lying. Or drunk. Maybe he wanted to get on her good side, probably with an eye to marriage. With cooking like that, wouldn't you? Men have killed for less."

Robbie had laughed. "You know, Bernie, maybe we all fell for a pack of lies. Maybe Elvira Rowan is a witch after all."

Elvira Rowan smiled to herself as she sat in the first-class compartment of a steam train bound for Bootle. She was leaving Wandsworth and Appleby Cottage behind forever. The solicitors had informed her that the second Mrs Rowan had moved out of the family home to be with her ailing sister and, under the terms of her father's will, it was now all hers.

She would sell it, of course. Move right away. To France. Her schoolgirl French had been brushed up considerably at night classes during the past few months and now she was ready.

When she had received the letter from Jeanne Dupont telling her she was expecting a baby, she had been delighted. The mother-to-be was very happy, but the father had been killed in a motorcycle accident the day after she had shared the good news with him. It had been a shattering blow. The future would be tough for a single mother without any grandparents near at hand.

It was time for Elvira Rowan to make herself useful again.

Printed in Great Britain
by Amazon